THE
DAY
SHE
DIED

SHANNON HOLLINGER

THE
DAY
SHE
DIED

bookouture

Published by Bookouture in 2025

An imprint of Storyfire Ltd.
Carmelite House
50 Victoria Embankment
London EC4Y 0DZ

www.bookouture.com

The authorised representative in the EEA is Hachette Ireland
8 Castlecourt Centre
Dublin 15 D15 XTP3
Ireland
(email: info@hbgi.ie)

ISBN: 978-1-83525-489-9
eBook ISBN: 978-1-83525-488-2

In loving memory of my sweet Sully.

1

MAGGIE

I don't trust the peace. Not the balmy warmth that's finally arrived, chasing away the chills of what seemed like an everlasting winter, finally allowing me to leave my jacket at home. Not the puffy white clouds drifting lazily across the bright blue sky. Not even the colorful spring flowers that have emerged to paint the landscape, pastel heads nodding softly in the gentle breeze.

It feels like a trick. A trap designed to get me to let my guard down, to make me forget where I am. And who.

Because if there's one thing I've learned about Coyote Cove over the last five and a half years, it's that evil lurks beneath the surface. This tiny mountain town deep in the belly of the vast Northwoods has more than its fair share of shadows. I know this better than most. As the chief of police, it's my job to shine a light into the dark places. I've seen what hides there.

While this might seem like a gorgeous Maine day to everyone else, to me it's the calm before the storm. Of course, that might have something to do with the reason why I'm out here right now.

I coast around a bend on Old Mill Road and scan my

surroundings for signs of humanity. This area is beyond remote. There are miles between some of the ramshackle houses and trailers sheltering among the trees. Those who choose to live this far from the rest of humanity usually have a reason. So when I received a call reporting the strong smell of rotten eggs, I needed only one guess. Meth.

Unfortunately, the production of methamphetamine has become a real problem in the more rural areas of the valley. Given that use of the drug is on the rise in the entire state, I suppose it has to be cooked somewhere. But it was a mistake for whoever was foolish enough to decide to do it in my jurisdiction.

I slow as I spot a mailbox up ahead, the post sticking out of a faded orange five-gallon bucket. This has to be it. I look down for only a second as I press the button to lower my window. Glance up just in time to slam on the brakes.

The tires screech as I come to a sudden halt. There, standing in the middle of the road before me is a large black dog. Adrenaline makes my heart hammer. Guilt tightens my chest as I imagine what would have happened if I'd failed to react in time, thoughts of my own two pups at home adding to my distress.

The canine turns its head slowly in my direction and stares at me with golden eyes, shaggy fur bristled in layers around its neck. Maybe not a dog after all. At least, not one that's domesticated.

And it's much larger than the coyotes that the valley is named after. Not to mention that I've never seen a black one. Are black coyotes even a thing? I think they might be. But I don't think they look like this.

It can't be a wolf.

As if it can hear my thoughts, it takes a step closer to my vehicle. Its nose twitches, scenting the air as it regards me calmly. I hold my breath, transfixed, in utter awe of the moment. Suddenly, it swings its head in the opposite direction. Its ears pin and tail tucks before it runs off into the woods.

I gape after it, feeling stunned, mind racing with questions as I replay the encounter over and over. Wait for a couple of minutes, hoping it will return. When it doesn't, I lift my foot off the brake and ease down the road again, feeling disappointed, yes, but also a little excited as I turn into the pitted dirt driveway, gravel crunching loudly under my tires, because how cool was that? I feel fortunate to have had the experience.

The smell of rotten eggs assaults my nose, reminding me why I'm out here in the first place as I pull up in front of a trailer. Turning off the engine, I thumb the latch free on my holster and grab the handle to exit the vehicle as the door to the mobile home opens.

My ears ring, assaulted by a wave of sound and pressure. The Jeep bucks beneath me. It jolts again, my teeth gnashing together, neck snapping as something large crashes onto my hood.

I stare in horror through my cracked windshield at where the trailer had been only seconds ago, now replaced by a raging fire. Already, the heat is overwhelming. If I had arrived any sooner, been any closer... I might not have survived.

And as my focus shifts from the wreckage to the hood of my car, where a steaming black mass sizzles, it becomes clear. At least one person wasn't as fortunate as I was.

My hand shakes as I reach for the radio, unable to tear my gaze from the charred face pressed against my windshield. I watch the milky glazed eyes for signs of life, but there are none.

"Yeah, Chief?" My lieutenant, Kal Kishore, sounds distant through the shock wrapping me in its icy embrace and I find myself suddenly missing the jacket I'd been so relieved to leave at home.

My legs feel weak as I exit the vehicle. My voice cracks as I say, "I need fire and emergency response at 1077 Old Mill Road ASAP."

"You okay?"

I ignore the question, glancing around at the beat-up cars strewn around the yard like a toddler's abandoned toys, wondering how many of them work as I move unsteadily toward the wreckage. More importantly, how many of them belonged to people who were inside the trailer that's now engulfed in flames?

The front door, blown off its hinges, smolders to my left. A twisted mass of what I think was a window frame on my right. There's a rumble as part of the building's frame collapses.

The smell I'd noticed before—the one that brought me out here—grows stronger the closer I get. I pull my shirt up, covering my mouth and nose. The chemicals used to produce meth are extremely hazardous, especially when inhaled, which makes what I'm doing now even more reckless. And the Coyote Cove Fire Department is all volunteer. I'm not sure they have the proper equipment to respond.

"Chief?"

"Call over to Lincoln. See if they can send over a hazmat response for a probable meth lab explosion."

Kal curses, then asks, "Where are you now?"

"I'm at the scene."

"You know what I mean."

I do. Which is why I purposely don't answer.

"We have at least one fatality."

"Which means it's too late to help. I'm serious, Chief. You need to stay in your car."

"Okay."

"It would be better if you drove down the road. You don't want to breathe any of those fumes in."

"Sure."

"Maggie—"

"Get me backup out here, Kal. Now."

I end the transmission and continue toward the burning building and any survivors who may be trapped inside. The entire front of the trailer is a solid mass of licking orange tongues, but perhaps the back has fared better. Despite the burning in my lungs, the throbbing in my head, I have to see. I have to try.

Ash rains down from the sky as I skirt around the side of the building. Flames crackle like a piece of sheet metal waved like a flag. The structure groans as it's consumed.

My sweat-slicked skin reacts to the extreme heat, tightening uncomfortably, and yet there's still a chill in my limbs as I raise an arm to protect my blistering forehead. The hairs singe, withering into nubs like the Wicked Witch's legs once her ruby slippers have been removed. Still I continue onward. And then I stop.

I sink to my knees as my legs buckle. Stare at the ruins before me with a heavy heart.

There is no backside to the trailer, not anymore. Anyone who was inside never stood a chance.

Scraps of their life, whoever they were, lie scattered around me, blown from the trailer by the blast. A coffee mug that hates Mondays in perfect condition, besides a smudge on the handle. A scrap of fabric, the pattern and weave suggesting it was once part of a couch. A photograph, one edge glowing orange, curling as the embers destroy it.

Without thinking, I press my palm against it to smother the glow before more damage can be done. I jerk back, hissing. Stare at the pale backside as I rub my thumb over the burn, reluctant to turn it over, afraid of what I'll see—a happy couple? A baby? A family snapshot, a bunch of children smiling out at me?

What if they were in the trailer? How many people was I

too late to save? I'm not sure I can handle the answer. I flip it over anyway.

My stomach clenches. I feel off balance, dizzy. Raising a hand, I cover my open mouth as I stare at the photograph. After what feels like eons, I manage to tear my eyes from it and fumble for my phone, intending to check with Sue to find out who had reported the odor, only to remember that I'd received the call directly on my cell.

Checking my call log, I find that the most recent entry reads PRIVATE. Whoever it was, they blocked the number before they contacted me. I recall that the voice had been low, garbled. The speaker could have been young or old, male or female. At the time, I'd thought the connection had been bad, but now?

I look at the wreckage before me with renewed horror. If I'm correct about who the person in the picture is, they weren't in the trailer. I know that because they were already dead. And now I can't help fearing that's why I was called out here—so that I could join them.

2

MAGGIE

The sun is high overhead by the time the members of the Lincoln HMRT, or Hazardous Materials Response Team, have defeated the flames. What now remains is a blackened mass of twisted metal, charred wood, and ash. A thick haze of smoke lingers in the clearing. The acrid stench of melted plastic makes my sinuses ache.

I sit in the passenger seat of Kal's patrol vehicle, watching as a pair of amorphous figures in white hazmat suits bag the body sprawled across the hood of my Jeep, wondering if I know who it is. Coyote Cove is a small town. I'd guess the size of the rubber boot soles melted to the feet to be a men's size twelve, but there's nothing more identifying than that.

The corpse is unrecognizable. The clothes have mostly burned away, revealing skin that's blacked and blistered. How close had I come to being in the same condition?

I think about the photograph I found. I'd only met Wesley Banks once. I can't be sure it's him in the picture, not based on that single brief memory. And yet, I'm concerned enough that I might be right that instead of turning the picture over to forensics, like I should have once they got here, the evidence bag I'd put it in is in my back pocket instead.

Because if my suspicions are confirmed? No one can know what I've found until I figure out what connection the man who was terrorizing my fiancé could possibly have to this case, especially considering the anonymous call that brought me out here.

It might not be a coincidence that I was present when the trailer exploded—somebody may have intended to kill me. I shudder at the thought, wrapping my arms tight around myself, trying to stop the trembling still coursing through me as my lieutenant approaches.

Kal runs a hand through his dark hair, leaving it standing in unruly tufts as he stares down at me. Soot streaks his face, and I make a note to order him another shirt as I notice a large rip in the sleeve of the one he's wearing.

"You sure you're okay?" he asks.

"I'm fine," I answer, perhaps a touch too fast.

"We've got everything under control here."

I shake my head, knowing what he's thinking: that I should go home. I know because I keep thinking it, too. But I can't, not yet.

"You Chief Riley?"

Kal turns to face the man in protective fire gear behind him. I open my mouth to respond, but it's not me he's addressing. It's my lieutenant.

I stand before considering if it's a good idea or not to trust my legs to support me. The steel rod inside me that I use to keep myself upright at times like these was forged by anger. But mild indignation works, too.

"That would be me," I say, straightening my spine.

The man shifts his attention to me, his eyes widening at my appearance. I resist the urge to try tidying myself up, instead lifting my chin a little higher.

"You?"

"Yes."

He fumbles his glove off, wiping his palm repeatedly against the side of his leg before offering his hand. Flashes a lopsided grin, and says, "I apologize for the confusion. Dean Larson, fire investigator."

"Maggie Riley, Coyote Cove chief of police."

A bang sounds behind me. I flinch, breath catching in my chest.

"Car door," he says gently, placing a steadying grip on my arm.

My skin heats. I look away from his gaze, nodding. I feel like such a mess right now, skittish and on edge.

Clearing my throat, I shift sideways, breaking the physical connection between us as I say, "This is my lieutenant, Kal Kishore."

He gives Kal a friendly smile as they shake, but his eyes keep drifting to me. They're full of concern and curiosity and something else. Something that makes my pulse race. Something I'm not prepared to deal with right now. I need to put some distance between myself and... all this. Before I have the chance to think twice, I add, "Kal will be your CCPD liaison for this investigation."

I pretend not to notice the way Kal's mouth drops open at this uncharacteristic announcement, turning before either of them has a chance to respond, which I realize is a mistake two seconds too late. But I can feel their eyes on me or, at least, I think I can, so even though I have no idea where I'm heading, I continue to walk away.

Luckily, I get only several steps before there's the sound of crunching gravel and Sue's ancient Pinto chugs into the drive, the faded green vehicle seemingly held together by the thick cloud of black exhaust that surrounds it. It's barely come to a stop before she jumps out and stalks across the clearing toward me.

"What are you still doing here?"

Bristling, I glance over my shoulder. Feel my skin heat several more degrees as I find Fire Investigator Larson still looking at me.

"Take care, Red," he says, giving me that lopsided smile. "I'll catch you later."

I can't help feeling humiliated, like a teen whose mom has tracked her down after she snuck out. I spin back to face Sue and find that the petite woman has already crossed the yard and is now standing before me, hands fisted on hips clad in a pair of Curious George pajama pants. The stern expression on her face buckles as she takes me in. Her gaze bounces to my damaged Jeep, then the fire-ravaged trailer.

Her voice is barely more than a whisper as she says, "Oh, honey."

In all the years we've worked together, she's never called me that. Sue's always been more of the tough love type. Until now, I imagined that she was the kind of mother to tell you to dry your tears rather than to let it all out, but maybe I was wrong. Or maybe she just sees what I need right now.

"Let's get you out of here."

I nod and swallow down the lump that keeps rising in my throat as she wraps an arm around my back and ushers me toward her car. I pause for a second as she holds the door open for me.

This vehicle is a death trap. I climb into the passenger seat anyway. Why not? I already survived one close call today.

3

MAGGIE

Sue keeps sneaking glances over at me. I avoid her gaze, instead looking down at my hands, fingers curled tight around the edges of the seat to either side of my legs, the whites of my knuckles clearly visible despite the soot that streaks my skin.

I try to relax. I fail. Every part of me is in knots right now.

Pressing the back of my skull firmly against the headrest, I squeeze my eyes shut. My throat struggles to stretch enough to accommodate the hard swallow I push down.

"Are you sure you're okay?" she asks.

"I'm fine."

"Maybe we should take you to Doc Calvin? Get you checked out."

"That's not necessary," I insist.

"You look a little green around the gills," she tells me.

"Remind me to give you a raise."

Sue scowls at the road in front of her. I know I'm being stubborn. I know she's just trying to help. But I can't accept it right now.

"Why?" she asks moodily.

"So you can buy a new car."

She gives me a sharp look.

"What's wrong with this one?"

I crack an eye open and arch a brow but remain silent as the vehicle shudders around a sharp curve. She eases off the gas, letting it drop below forty until the shaking lessens.

"I'll have you know that I bought this car new, and it's never failed me, not once. I've never even been behind the wheel of another car since I got it." She raises her voice so I can hear her over the whistling coming from the moonroof. "What you need to do is find room in the budget to hire more staff."

I sigh heavily. She's right.

"Seriously, Maggie. You could have gotten hurt out there today."

"I know."

"You—wait. What?"

"I know, Sue." I draw a shaky breath. Try to push the thought of the picture in my back pocket, the evidence I know I shouldn't have stolen from the crime scene, much less be sitting on right now, from my mind as I say, "But it just as easily could have been you or Kal or some kid walking by after school."

Sue shivers. Grips the wheel a little tighter. She casts nervous glances in my direction while she waits for me to continue. When I don't, she asks, "What do you think happened?"

In those first few moments after the explosion, I thought I knew, but all that changed the instant I found that photograph.

Wesley Banks had been blackmailing my fiancé. Now he's dead.

But I can't tell Sue that.

"I'm not sure. Probably a meth lab gone wrong."

"You were still in your Jeep when it exploded?"

"Fortunately." I brace a hand against the dashboard and twist in my seat to look at her as she pauses at a stop sign. "Where are we going?"

"Where do you think? I'm taking you home."

"Why? There's no one at the department right now."

"Maggie."

"Sue."

She matches my irritated huff with one of her own. The turn signal ticks loudly as we face off, exchanging narrow-eyed frowns.

"Sue," I say again, a warning in my tone as she aims the vehicle toward my house and presses the gas.

"Listen, at the very least, you need to clean up a bit, right? If you still want to go to the office after that—instead of relaxing for the rest of the day, which we both know is what you *should* do—then you can bully Steve into driving you."

I fall quiet as we travel down the narrow, thickly wooded lane toward the house I share with my fiancé. Stare out the passenger window, hiding my expression, hoping Sue will be too preoccupied to notice that the driveway's empty as she makes the turn.

"Thanks for the ride."

I grab the door handle before she's even come to a stop, but she puts her hand on my shoulder before I can hop out.

"Maybe I should come in for a while. Just until Steve gets home."

I turn to face her, hoping I don't look as guilty as I feel as I decide whether or not I should lie to her. Sue takes my hand and squeezes gently. Gives me a patient smile. After a long, tense minute, I exhale heavily, my entire body sagging with the release like a deflating balloon.

"Steve's not here."

"Is everything okay?" Sue asks cautiously, like she's afraid of the answer.

"Yeah, everything's fine. He's just visiting his family."

"This close to the wedding?"

"Why not?"

I feel her studying me. Then, shrugging, she puts the car in gear, shifting from park to reverse. "Then we'll just swing by my place real quick and I'll pack an overnight bag."

"Uh, no."

I toss the door open before she can get the ancient rust bucket moving, suddenly relieved that Sue doesn't have a newer vehicle. I can only imagine how different things would be right now if she had one with that safety feature where you can keep children—or unruly police chiefs—locked inside.

"Come on. It'll be fun," she insists.

"Seriously, Sue. I appreciate the offer, but that isn't necessary."

"But—"

"Really." I lean across the car and wrap my arms around her. Her skin is velvet soft against mine. The smell of powder replaces the scent of smoke and sweat that's been assaulting my nose. I tighten my hold for just a second before pulling away.

"I appreciate the offer. I'm just going to take a shower and get some sleep, but if you could pick me up and give me a ride in tomorrow?"

Sue nods, too stunned to speak. I feel her watching me as I jog up the front steps and unlock the door. I turn and smile, give her a brief wave before vanishing inside.

But I suspect that I made a huge mistake. Because I've never hugged Sue before. Ever.

Hopefully she just assumes this uncharacteristic behavior is due to the close call I had earlier, or the fact that Steve isn't home, and I needed a moment of affection. Anything other than that something is wrong. Because I'm not yet willing to admit that anything is.

4

MAGGIE

I do my best to ignore the uncomfortable prickling sensation as sweat beads along my hairline. The way the red welted skin on my forehead and arms feels like it's being held to an open flame, having already been exposed to enough heat today. Shifting my weight, I try to get comfortable. Struggle to keep my eyes shut, even though doing so feels strangely unnatural.

This is supposed to be soothing. So why is it not?

I must be doing something wrong. I can't remember the last time I took a bath. I thought it was because I never had the time, but maybe I just don't enjoy them. Or maybe I'm incapable of holding still. Relaxing. Being alone with my thoughts. I should have brought a book to distract me.

I shift again, adjusting the knot of hair cushioning my head. Listen to the stillness of the house, the only sound the gentle sighs of the two dogs curled up on the bathmat beside me. It's too quiet. Too empty. Sue, as usual, was right. I shouldn't be alone with no distractions right now.

Because my mind keeps wandering. Images from this morning keep playing through my head. Entering the driveway. Coming to a stop. The blinding fireball of the explosion. The way my Jeep had rocked from the shockwave, then jolted with the impact of a corpse landing on my hood.

Details I didn't register at the time are now in acute focus. The front door slowly opening seconds after my arrival. A man's forearm appearing, hand on the knob. The way the pressure had changed, like I was on a plane and my ears needed to pop, seconds before the flash. The crack in my windshield made by the door handle clutched in a blackened fist.

I can't stop thinking about how different things would be right now if I had been even a minute earlier. Or five. How long had I been just down the street, stopped by the black canine in the road?

And had that really happened? It seems too fantastical now to believe, the logical, rational part of my brain doubting what I thought I saw. It's more likely that meth fumes had affected my brain, causing a delusion, than I had an actual rare wolf sighting that just happened to spare my life.

But had there been meth fumes? I'd been so sure that's what I'd find when I responded to the call, but now? I have no idea what's going on.

I think of the photograph that I'd found at the scene, now tucked away in my gun safe. I haven't confirmed my suspicions about the man's identity yet. I told myself that I needed to relax first, get into the right headspace, but the truth is that I'm scared.

Because if I'm right, what happened earlier might be only the beginning. Steve and I could be in danger.

What I told Sue earlier was only partially true. Steve is staying with his mother right now, but it's not for a family visit. He's in Massachusetts searching the rural backroads for the tree that he and Wesley buried a girl beneath after Wesley had run her down back when they were in college. The secret that Wesley was using to blackmail him.

Finding the burial site is something that Steve feels he has to do, not only to bring the girl's family peace and closure, but also himself. There's been a change in him over the past half year, though in the last few weeks it's become more pronounced. There's a haunted look in his eyes that I can't deny.

So when he came to me three nights ago and told me his plan, it was with relief that I agreed. Though our wedding is fast approaching, is, in fact, less than a month away, I gave him my complete support. He was gone the next morning. And though it's been lonely without him, I truly believed that it was for the best.

Now? I'm not so sure. I'd feel better if he were here. But would he be safer?

I keep telling myself that I might be worrying over nothing. That even if it is Wesley in the snapshot, there could be a rational explanation for how it came to be at the scene of a deadly explosion. Its presence doesn't necessarily mean that the dead man has some kind of connection to what happened.

And yet, I've never believed in coincidences. Show me any investigator worth their weight who does.

Which is why I have to figure out who that picture belonged to.

Of all the images from the explosion racing through my head on repeat, there's one that's plaguing me the most—right before the blast, the door had been almost completely open. I saw the man who was coming outside. And I can't shake the feeling that I recognized who it was that died. Yet no matter how hard I try, the answer remains locked uselessly inside my head.

My eyes burst open wide, as if trying to escape the shadowed corner of my subconscious I'd been searching. My gaze lands on my legs, flushed pink from the heat like a cooked shrimp. I don't know who I think I'm fooling. I'm not going to be able to relax, not like this or any other way.

An unexpected noise intrudes on the silence, startling me. I jolt upright with a gasp. Water sloshes, threatening to spill over the side of the tub. I look around warily, muscles bunched, ready to spring into action, searching for danger. Feel like a fool as I realize the familiar buzzing is my phone.

Both dogs are awake now, licking my face as I reach for my cell. Their affection is so exuberant that it takes my breath away —quite literally. I can't manage to draw air through the tongues lashing my face. Laughing, I praise them as I pull away and answer the call.

"Hello?"

"Hey."

My chest swells, my heart not sure whether to sink or soar. Tears threaten to invade my eyes. I blink them away and for the first time today, the tension in my body eases.

"Hey."

As if he could sense my need, or my thoughts somehow conjured him, Steve's voice fills my ear. "Everything okay? You sound like you've been running."

"Everything's fine. And hardly. I've barely moved in the last fifteen minutes."

"I find that hard to believe," he jokes. "Is someone pinning you down?"

"Nope. I'm in the bath."

"Really? So you're na—" I can hear it in his tone, flirtation turning to concern. "Wait. A bath?"

"Uh-huh."

"Is this going to be a new thing, then?"

"Probably not. It's pretty boring."

Steve chuckles. "I don't think it's supposed to be exciting. More like a destressing kind of activity."

"Yeah, that's why I decided to give it a try."

I realize my mistake the moment I make it, even before Steve's tense, "What happened."

It's not a question. He knows something is wrong.

I laugh nervously, trying to put him at ease. "Just another day at the office."

"Are you hurt?"

I've lost count of how many times the answer's been yes. Only, I never had to say it. He was there to collect the pieces of me, to hold me back together until I stayed that way on my own. I need to do the same for him now, because he's the one who's hurt. Maybe not physically, but emotionally, mentally, which is just as painful, if not worse.

I can't tell him the truth. But we promised each other—no more lies.

"I'm fine. But there was an explosion."

Steve curses.

"Again, not injured," I say, staring at my reddened skin. At the faint soot stains still marking my hands and arms. "Not even a scratch. I got a little dirty sifting through the wreckage." It's not a lie, more of a stretching of the truth. "I thought a soak might help."

"Did you see it happen?"

Thinking of my car, probably on its way to the state crime lab right this moment to be processed as evidence, I'm forced to concede, "Yes."

"How close were you?"

"Some debris fell on my Jeep." Perhaps a bit of an understatement, but still the truth.

"I'm coming home."

"No. Steve, don't be ridiculous. I'm fine. Honest."

He releases a heavy sigh. "You sure you're okay?"

"Yes."

The line falls silent again and I wonder if he's swallowing as many words that he wants to say as I am. I hope he's not keeping them in because he's afraid of stressing me out further—or worse, revealing how bad he's really doing. Which is why even though I know I need to tell him about the photograph, I can't, not until I'm sure—not just that it's Wesley, but that it means something. Because it could be the final straw, the one that breaks Steve's back.

"So. How's it going on your end?" I ask.

He makes a noise, half groan, half grunt.

"That good, huh?"

"It's just that I have no idea where to even start looking. What direction to go, or how far. I was unconscious when we left the party."

With hindsight, Steve suspects that his old friend had given him a drugged beer, with the full intention of performing what had happened. What he believed for years to have been a tragic accident was, in fact, murder. And not the only one Wesley Banks would commit.

"All you can do is try," I say, wishing I could think of something more encouraging.

"I know, it's just—" He exhales noisily, and I know what he looks like at this exact moment, the actions that usually accompany the sound. His hand running through his hair. His shoulders slumping. His nose squinching up in a partial wince. "I need to do this, Maggie. I have to."

"I know. I understand. Have you seen anything that looks familiar yet?" I ask.

"No. Everything's changed so much. Been built up. What if —?" I hear him swallow hard. As much as I had wished only moments ago he were here with me, I now wish I were there with him even more. "What if it's too late? What if I can't find her?"

"Then we'll think of something else. Another way to bring her family closure."

He doesn't sound convinced when he replies, "Sure." I know he's not when he changes the subject, asking about the dogs.

"They're great. They miss you, though. How's your mom and Grandpa Joe?"

"Grandpa Joe's not here. He went to some kind of reunion with some old war buddies of his, which means I'm facing the full brunt of my mother's attention alone."

"Yikes."

"Yeah."

"And Izzy?"

"Haven't seen her yet."

Steve sounds depressed and hopeless. My heart aches as we make small talk because I know exactly where he is right now mentally. I've spent too much time trapped in the pit of self-loathing under a crushing pile of guilt and despair to not recognize it.

I think I made the right choice, not telling him about the photograph I found today, but that doesn't make me feel any better about keeping a secret. Especially this one. And as we end the call and I emerge from the now tepid bath water, a sense of dread wraps itself around me along with my towel.

The pups trail me into the kitchen, where my laptop sits on the counter. I sit on a stool, pull the computer to me, and wake it. Stare at the screen, knowing that I need to get this over with. Drawing a deep breath, I bring up the Massachusetts Department of Corrections portal and type the name Wesley Banks into the search browser.

The results load, and I find myself looking into the same black eyes that sat across from me at the dinner table earlier this year. The exact dark gaze that burns out from the photograph I have locked in my safe. As much as I don't want to, it's time to admit—the nightmare might not be over yet.

5

STEVE

The click of stepping on the landmine is deafening. It fills my head, repeating over and over, echoing that little harbinger of death so loudly that it blocks all other sounds. Drives out all other thoughts. Odd, because at the time I didn't hear a thing.

Don't get me wrong. I knew that what was happening would change everything. Could feel the rift forming that would forever divide my life into a before-and-after. And though the guilt and shame, the disgust and self-loathing, were immediate and overwhelming, I did my best to block them out. And in the way that's a luxury provided only by the ignorance of youth, I succeeded.

Or so I thought.

But now, as I strain to recall the shadowy memories from that night. *Click.* As I think about the years a family's spent not knowing the fate of a loved one because of a crime I helped conceal. *Click.* As I look at the woman I love, knowing I don't deserve to have her in my life. *CLICK.*

Every second of my life is spent bracing for the blast. Which is why I have to do everything I can to make this right, while I still have the chance.

Spotting a vehicle trying to exit its spot, I breathe a sigh of relief. As small as it is, it's the first break I've caught during another fruitless day of searching, and I'll take it. Turning on my signal, I wait for the Mini Cooper to leave, then try to fit my SUV into the slot that the compact car vacated.

By the time I'm done, I'm in a full sweat. It's something that's been happening more and more lately, but it has nothing to do with the increasing heat as summer finally simmers on the horizon.

It comes from living in a constant state of fear.

I tell myself that what happened to Maggie earlier was just a fluke, not some kind of karmic comeuppance, the universe's way of evening the score for my deeds.

But we don't get to choose the way we pay our debts, do we?

I shake my head, trying to clear the thought. The clock is ticking down to our wedding. I need to stay focused. I have to put my past firmly behind us, once and for all.

I've been in Massachusetts two days already. Every morning, I drive west to Amherst, where Wesley Banks and I went to college, and start searching for rural roads that match the scraps of memory I have from that fateful night almost two decades ago. But whether it's the changes that have happened during that long stretch of time, my faulty recollection, or sheer bad luck, I haven't seen anything that looks familiar yet.

Nothing even remotely close to the towering oak that's seared into my brain, a goliath in the middle of nowhere, the sole landmark in an area marked by miles and miles of fields, though what type, I couldn't say. If I could, that might make this whole thing a little easier—not that I deserve for this to be easy.

But locating the right spot is just the first step in what seems an impossible feat. Because if I do manage to find that tree, I have to make sure that Georgia Pierce's remains are found. Her buried remains.

Maggie seems confident that we'll find a way to return her

to her family, but the more I think about it, the more I don't see how. It's not like I can claim that I pulled over for a picnic and found a human bone. The victim and I went to the same school. We were at the same party, the last place she was seen alive. Even I know that anyone investigating the case would find the connection odd.

How could I not be a suspect? And deservedly so.

I feel like I'm just prolonging the agony, both Maggie's and mine. If I had just turned myself in and confessed, this would all be over by now. Instead, we've sent out invitations to our wedding—a wedding I'm worried might not even take place.

Because I've promised myself that I'd become the kind of man worthy of being loved by a woman like her. And I'm worried that might mean having to find the strength to let her go.

I wait for traffic to break, then dash across the street, entering a familiar lobby. Step into an elevator where every single button, now all below shoulder level, had at one time been over the top of my head. I exit into a hallway full of ghosts, imagining I can see the print of my hand from where I once touched the ceiling while on my late father's shoulders.

The doorway of the apartment on my left is where I had my first kiss. And there, where there's a dip in the rug, is where Izzy once fell and scraped her knee. I remember scooping her up in my arms and carrying her home, drying her tears, speaking in funny voices until she forgot about the pain and her peals of laughter filled the room.

The memory reminds me that Maggie isn't the only woman in my life who's been affected by my poor decisions. My stomach tightens into a knot and I pause on the threshold, reluctant to put the key my mother gave me in the lock. Debating if I even should.

Maybe it would be better for everyone if I turned around

and got back in my car. Found a hotel to stay in. Try to keep my family separate from the mess I've created.

But before I can make up my mind the door opens, revealing my mother standing before me. She gives me a wide smile, genuinely happy to see me, and something inside my chest feels like it's breaking.

"I thought I heard you out here. Couldn't you find your key?"

"Just did," I say, holding up the piece of metal for her to see.

"Well, hurry up and come inside. You have just enough time to clean up before dinner."

"Mother, I told you not to go to any trouble."

"I didn't. Besides, how often do I get to sit down to a nice dinner with both of my babies?"

I swallow hard, feeling sweat prick at my skin as she ushers me inside. The lock turns behind me with a resounding click, making me feel trapped. I glance at the door as she pushes me toward my childhood bedroom, wishing I could make a run for it.

Clearing my throat, I try to steady my voice. "Izzy's coming?"

"She's already here, darling. Now hurry up and take a quick shower."

As much as I dread seeing my sister, suddenly, I need to.

"I'll take a shower later, mother."

She makes a noise of disapproval and gives me a slanted-eye look. I pretend not to notice and move around her, heading toward the kitchen.

My steps echo as I walk down the narrow hall. My heart mimics them, dull and hollow-sounding, as I approach the room where my sister and I made so many memories while growing up. I pause just around the corner, draw a deep breath to collect myself, fix a smile on my face, and continue forward.

Only to freeze the instant my gaze lands on the woman before me. The woman who only vaguely resembles my sibling.

"Great." My mother's voice rings with false cheer as she claps her hands together behind me. "Now that we're all here, let's eat."

Izzy makes no move to greet me as she lifts her darkly circled eyes from the drink before her to meet mine. There's no hint of a smile, of relief, of hatred, not even a sign of recognition as she stares at me, sloshing liquor on the table as she refills her glass without looking.

"Izzy, isn't it nice to see your brother?" our mother prods as she pulls dishes from a cabinet.

"How you doing, Iz?" I ask softly, settling at the table across from her.

Her sole response is to snatch her hand away as I reach to take it in my own, spilling more tequila in the process. The only part of me that was still whole breaks, shards of glass shredding my insides. Because the woman across from me is only a shadow of her former self. And it's clear that she blames me.

Why shouldn't she? What happened is absolutely my fault. She never would have found herself in that position, her back against the wall with an impossible decision to make, if it wasn't for me. I'm the reason she picked up the gun. It's because of me she pulled the trigger.

I'd thought that Izzy, with all her training as a licensed psychologist, would have the skills to get through this, but that's no excuse. I should have made more of an effort to make sure. I should have known before now that she wasn't okay. I should have sensed that she needed help. Instead, I've been so worried about myself, about disappointing Maggie, that I neglected my duties as a big brother.

I owe my little sister my life. But it looks like saving mine might be costing hers.

6

MAGGIE

Anxiety hums under my skin like a horde of bees. If I thought the ride into the office with Sue this morning, when she studied me like I were a slide pinned under a microscope, was tense, it's being rivaled by the drive back out to the blast scene with Kal. But while Sue kept up a relentless chain of probing questions, Kal is all stony silence.

But I need a distraction to keep me out of my head right now. I glance over at him as we round a curve in the winding mountain road. His shaggy eyebrows are creased in a frown, his hands curled into fists around the steering wheel.

"Everything all right?" I ask.

He jerks as if stung by a bee, turns to face me with a somewhat guilty expression.

"Yeah, why?"

I gesture toward his stranglehold grip on the wheel. He instantly loosens it.

"I was just thinking," he says.

"About choking someone?" I joke.

His smile takes too long to develop and never reaches his dimples, making me think I've struck a nerve. I wonder if there's something going on in his personal life. My lieutenant is a private person. I don't know much about him other than that he came up here after a failed engagement.

The thought—that you can have every intention of marrying someone and yet never make it to the altar—fills me with apprehension. I'm not naïve. I know it happens. And I know that marriages fail. But I find myself, in the midst of this overwhelming quietude between us, curious about the details of what happened in Kal's case.

Is there something he could share with me that could help me and Steve be one of the couples who beat the odds? I want to ask, but I'm afraid it would be prying. But I can't take being trapped in my head with my own thoughts any longer.

"I looked up the property records on the trailer last night."

Kal glances at me, eyebrows cocked. This isn't our case. Major crimes fall under state police jurisdiction in Maine. But I don't care.

Until I figure out why a picture of Wesley Banks was at the scene of an explosion in my town, what caused the blast, and whether there's a threat to those I care about, including myself, I'll step on whoever's toes get in my way.

"The address on file where the tax collector sends the bills is over in Jefferson."

"Really?" The curiosity in his tone makes it clear that he understands the significance of what I've said—that the owner may not have lived in the trailer.

"Yeah. I was able to cross-reference the address with the name on the title. Turns out the property was being rented out."

"You confirmed that?" he asks.

I give him a sheepish smile.

"I may have happened upon a phone number for the owner and tested it this morning to see if it was the right one."

"And?"

"And there's no lease, but the owner was able to provide me

with the name of the tenant who wrote him a check each month, Marie Bouchard. He said he'd never met the woman— he has a friend who lives nearby who handles renting the property out for him and who keeps a couple of junker cars in the yard, so at least they didn't all belong to people who were inside the trailer. He's going to have the guy give me a call," I say.

We round a corner and my attention drifts to the woods that line the road. I find myself searching the shadows as I add, "But he told me that in the three months she was his tenant he'd never had a problem with her, the rent was always paid on time, which seems surprising since she's only twenty-two and has a rap sheet a mile long."

"Any drug-related?"

"Over a half-dozen charges for possession of meth-amphetamine, all from different towns in Maine."

It was this information that I used to rationalize not calling Steve back last night to tell him about the photograph of Wesley. Because Marie had started renting the property right around the time when his old friend had come to town.

It's possible that the two felons had known each other. That the photograph had belonged to Marie. And that the blast was indeed an accident caused by a meth lab. If there's a chance that I can get this all wrapped up neatly without ever having to tell Steve about what I found, I'm going to take it.

The yard we pull into looks much different than the one I arrived at yesterday. Vehicles are squeezed into every opening big enough to park. Uniformed officials mill about. Two folding tables have been erected off to the side, one covered with food and water, the other with an assortment of evidence containers waiting to be filled and other tools of the trade. The most notable change, however, is that the spot the trailer once occupied is now a smoking ruin of charred debris.

My pulse quickens as I stare at it, anxiety rippling through me like a shockwave. My skin bristles, drawing uncomfortably tight. I'm struck by the overwhelming urge to run away, to leave this place and go somewhere safe. But I can't.

Swallowing down the lump of fear threatening to choke me, I force myself forward, tying up my hair as I weave my way through the firefighters and state police officers. Pause at a table and grab a pair of disposable slip-on booties, putting them on over my shoes before nearing the ruins.

Sweat dampens my shirt as I force myself closer to the wreckage, craning my head to inspect the rubble. A blob of what looks like melted glass draws my attention. My heart pounds as I inch closer, confirming my suspicion.

"Hey, Red. I was hoping you'd stop by today."

Though the voice is soft and low, I jump. My face feels like it's on fire as I turn to face Fire Investigator Larson.

"Everything okay?" he asks, frowning.

I quickly look away from the concern in his eyes, focusing instead on the man in slacks behind him, most likely the detective assigned the case.

"Chief Maggie Riley," I say, pretending like I don't feel on the verge of a panic attack as I step past Larson and extend a hand to his companion.

"Detective Ken Martin. You were the first on the scene yesterday, correct?" he asks.

I do my best to keep my voice steady. "Arrived just in time to have a front-row seat for the show."

"I heard about that. Close one. You ever respond to any calls out here before?"

I shake my head. "Not to this particular address, no. But according to the owner, the current tenant's been here only about three months. A woman named Marie Bouchard. Ran the name out of curiosity. She's been charged multiple times for possession of methamphetamine."

Martin's eyebrows rise. His lips purse as he gives me a side-long look. "Done a bit of legwork already, have you?"

I shrug and give him a friendly smile. Say, "It's a small town," even though that has nothing to do with anything I've discovered.

"Would you mind forwarding the information you found? No sense in reinventing the wheel."

"Of course." I accept the card he hands me, pocketing it for later. "Do you mind if I ask what you've found so far?"

Martin grimaces. "Body count's up to three."

My stomach churns. I try desperately to recall the face of the man I'd seen. I'm still drawing a blank, but I *know* I recognized him. Had I known the other people who died?

"Any idea who they were?" I ask.

"That's gonna take some time and luck. Doubt we'll be getting any prints off the remains we recovered. Two of them didn't have much soft tissue left."

"What about the cars that were in the yard? Did you run the plates?" I ask, realizing I should have done it myself yesterday, but I'd been too stunned to think straight. "According to the owner, a few were stored here by a friend, but there's a chance some of them belonged to our victims."

"I'll have to check. The CSIs had them towed before I got here. Cause of death seems pretty obvious to me," Detective Martin continues, "but we'll see what the autopsies turn up. Other than that, there's not much I can do until I have the official cause of the explosion." He shoots a pointed look at Larson.

"It's too soon to say," Larson says.

"The call you were responding to yesterday was because of the report of a rotten egg smell, right?" the detective asks.

"That's correct."

"Between that and the tenant's history, I'd say it's pretty obvious this trailer was being used to cook meth," he says.

"That's what I thought, as well," I say, trying not to betray how badly I want that to be the truth as I glance at the melted glass visible among the ashes.

"It's possible that the trailer could have been used as a lab," Larson admits.

Martin throws his hands up in the air. "See. Then what are we waiting for? Make the ruling."

The fire investigator clears his throat. "But even if it was, that doesn't mean it's what caused the explosion."

It feels like I'm trembling, but it could just be the surge of my pulse, the wave of dizziness crashing over me. I tell myself to stay calm, drawing a deep breath.

"Then what did?" Martin asks.

"I can't tell you that yet."

"Then what can you tell me?" Martin mutters.

Larson gestures toward the wreckage. "These things take time. It's not all going to get sorted in one night." His eyes burn into mine with the intensity of yesterday's flames as he says, "But I promise you, I'll get to the bottom of this. I'll find the answers we're looking for."

A queasy feeling takes hold of my stomach and squeezes. Though I want to retreat, I force myself to stand my ground. Because... Larson's words? For some reason, they feel like a threat. I just hope that it's the only one I'm facing.

7

MAGGIE

I need to get far away from here as fast as I can. I scan my surroundings carefully as I head back to the front of the lot, trying to commit as much as possible to memory, hoping to never return. Reaching the staging table, I remove the booties from my shoes and tuck them into the waiting bag so an analyst can process them later for any trace evidence they may have picked up as I walked around. Spotting Kal chatting to a couple of staties across the clearing, I catch his eye and we both start heading toward his cruiser.

"Hey, Red, hold up."

I spin to find Larson jogging to catch up with me. I kick myself for responding to a nickname I detest. Though instinct tells me to pretend I didn't hear him and hurry away, professionalism makes me wait. But the moment the distance between us closes and I find myself pinned by that intense gaze of his, I regret it.

He rubs the back of his neck, head dipping almost bashfully as he says, "I just wanted to check, see how you're doing."

I stare at him, looking for his angle.

"You know, after what happened to you, there's no shame in—"

"I'm fine."

My jaw tenses, teeth clenched together, because I'm not sure it's true. But either way, it's none of his business.

His voice is soft as he says, "I'm worried about you."

"Well, don't be. The only thing you need to worry about is figuring out the cause of the explosion."

"I'm working on that."

"Good."

"What are you doing later? After work?"

"Why?"

"I was thinking we could get dinner."

"I don't think that's a good idea."

"Why not?"

"I'm engaged."

"What's that have to do with eating?"

I close my eyes. Shake my head. It feels like I'm on the verge of a meltdown.

"Listen," he says in that low, soothing voice of his. "I'm just trying to help. You need someone to talk to right now and I understand what—"

"You really want to help?" I interrupt. Taking a deep breath, I force myself to relax my fists.

"I do."

"Good. Text any updates you receive on the case to my lieutenant, starting with whatever you have on the bodies that were recovered from the wreckage."

"But—"

"The only thing I need from you is information. Either ante up or back off."

I spin around and walk away before he has a chance to say anything else, struggling to balance on the thin thread that's left of my composure. Because something in those eyes of his tells me he does understand. Not just what it's like to relive the same moment over and over again every time you close your eyes, but all of it.

The things I try so hard not to think about—the loss and the pain, the solitude and what it feels like to be irreparably broken. Forced to wear a costume and live in a world you'll never fully belong in. And misery loves company.

That's why the man is dangerous.

"What was that all about?" Kal asks as he holds the passenger door open for me.

"Just a little experiment," I say. "We'll see if it pays off soon enough."

Kal's lips press together in a hard line. He gives me side-eye, maintaining the gaze through the windshield while he rounds the car. As he slips behind the wheel, his phone pings.

"What's this?" he asks, showing me the chain of texts he just received from Fire Investigator Larson.

"That," I say, "is victory."

"How so?"

I turn and look out the window so he can't see my face. Try my best to keep my voice emotionless, to not betray that there's a personal significance to what I'm about to say.

"Something funny's going on. Larson isn't ready to make a ruling on the explosion, which means he thinks it was caused by something other than a meth lab accident."

"Did he say that?"

"He didn't have to."

"What about the detective?"

"Seems more than willing to wash his hands of the whole thing and just do the bare minimum even though three lives were lost in the blast. If we leave it up to that guy, they'll probably never get identified."

"Three?"

"Unfortunately, yes."

He falls silent for a moment. I watch his reflection in the side mirror as he stares out the windshield, hands curled tightly around the wheel. "We'll find out who they are. And what happened to them."

"Yes, we will."

He casts a quick glance in my direction. Then another. I brace myself for whatever it is he's so reluctant to say before I face him.

"What?" I ask.

"What did you have to do to get Larson to send me all this?"

"Control my temper."

Kal struggles to keep a straight face.

"What?"

"That doesn't sound like you." I'm mid-eye roll when he adds, "It must be your alter ego, Red."

He looks scared for an instant as I pin him with the glare I've been working so hard to contain all day.

"Am I in trouble?" he asks.

"Not quite yet. I still need a driver."

But I can't keep from giving him a smile as he starts the engine and puts the car in gear. Admittedly, I'm not the best at relationships. I'm so focused on the job that sometimes I get tunnel vision.

It's easy for me to forget that the people I work with have more parts to them than just the professional. That I should know more about them than the way they like their coffee and how they do their job. But I couldn't even work up the nerve to ask him questions about himself on the drive to the scene.

Kal and I spend too much time together for that. I feel guilty for keeping the whole truth from him, for not telling him about the photograph I stole from the scene yesterday, but it's something I just can't share. It's not that I don't trust him, because I do.

I'd like for him to be—and hope that he considers *me*—a friend. It feels good to loosen up and exchange a little banter.

But what happened to Wesley? It's not my secret to tell.

And if it turns out that's what this explosion was about? I don't want Kal in the crosshairs with me. It's not his risk to take.

8

MAGGIE

Two hours later I'm fighting a bad case of eye strain and a neck that keeps going into spasm. I stretch, wincing against the tug in my too tight muscles, and try to rub out the knot in my shoulder that seems to be the culprit. A blinding jolt of lightning shoots up behind my ear as I strike a nerve, and it becomes apparent that all I'm accomplishing is making it worse.

I push back from the screen, wondering what Steve's doing right now. Hoping that he's having some luck, and not just for the sheer selfishness of having my personal masseuse back. I miss him, from that first groggy smile he gives me in the morning to the soft kiss he gives me every night before bed.

And I'm worried about him. About us.

About how we'll manage to find a way to move forward if he never finds Georgia Pierce's body.

Because he had made up his mind to turn himself in. To confess. And I'm the one who asked him to stay.

If I hadn't done that, he wouldn't be in his car right now traveling down backcountry roads in Massachusetts on the slim chance that he'll recognize the tree they buried the girl under.

He'd be in county lockup, awaiting trial. Or would he have waived his right to a trial?

Would he be in prison this very moment, in a maximum-security ward where the cells around him were filled with murderers and rapists, people who actually posed a threat to society? I shudder away the thought, am relieved for the distraction when a knock sounds on the door.

"Come in."

The door cracks open and even before I see the face I know it's one of the last ones I expected to see in front of me right now. The mound of teased blonde hair that precedes her gives her away.

"Hey, girl."

"CeCe, hi."

"Listen, I know you're working, so I won't take up too much of your time, but I've been so excited since I got the wedding invitation that I had to stop by."

The tiny woman hustles across the room and settles into the chair across from me, her cherry red lips spread wide. I try to focus on the feeling of having a friend who's happy for me, instead of the fear that something might happen that would keep me and Steve from saying our vows.

"So, I wanted to discuss options."

"I already told you I trust whatever you decide to do with my hair."

"Not about that, silly. Like there's any way I'd let you renege on that one. About your bachelorette party."

"What bachelorette party?"

"The one I'm gonna plan for you."

It takes me a moment to find my voice. When I do, I still sound breathless as I say, "CeCe, I appreciate the thought, really, but I'm not having one."

"Sure you are."

"No, I—"

"I'll help." Suddenly, Sue's in the doorway, pinning me with a look that tells me not to argue. But I do anyway.

"Absolutely not. I have zero interest—"

"Why's it got to be about you?" Sue asks, smirking. "What about what we want?"

"I guess because I'm the bride."

"Exactly. The party's not for you. It's for us, as our reward for putting up with you when you go all bridezilla on us."

"I'm not planning on doing that."

"Famous last words."

I study Sue for signs that she's joking, but there are none. Either she's been working on her poker face, or she thinks it's a possibility.

"I promise you. I don't even care about the wedding," I insist. "It's just going to be a simple ceremony in the backyard. Nothing to get super picky over."

"The term doesn't just cover going all control freak," she says.

CeCe nods as she turns to face Sue. "Mm-hmm. Personally, I got her pegged as a runner."

"A what?"

"Same," Sue agrees. "We're gonna need a whole team to help."

"Who were you thinking?" CeCe asks.

Suddenly I'm on the outside, watching helplessly as a strange phenomenon that seems entirely beyond my control occurs, a numb sensation taking hold of me as I realize what they mean by *runner*—they think I'm going to leave Steve at the altar. I wouldn't. I couldn't. Especially not after I asked him to stay and marry me, and... do I regret it?

Beneath the desk, my legs are trembling. I feel dizzy. I'm taking deep breaths but can't seem to get enough air. I think I'm having a panic attack.

"Definitely Margot," Sue says. I nod along, because Margot

won't put up with any nonsense. She'll make sure I stay right where I'm supposed to be. "And Dr. Ricky."

"Haven't met her," CeCe says.

"She's a little brusque, but trust me, we need her."

My heart is shimmying like a belly dancer's hips, pulse throbbing loud in my ears. Dr. Ricky is another good choice.

"What about Greta?" CeCe asks. Greta, our local librarian, is a six-foot-tall native German. I imagine myself trying to run past her. I don't see myself getting far.

I've never been in a wedding. My only close female friend before now, Linda, got married on a whim in Las Vegas. I wasn't there to see if she had any doubts, but the way Sue and CeCe are making it sound, second thoughts aren't abnormal. Maybe everyone gets cold feet.

"All right. I'm in," I say, the panic in my body slowly starting to recede. "Let's do it. I'll call my friend Linda to join us, too."

"And of course your future sister-in-law," Sue adds.

And just like that fear seizes me once again. I don't know Izzy Winters well, but there was a time when I was looking forward to gaining her as a sister. Now, I'm not so sure. It's not that my opinion of the woman has changed, if anything, I'm eternally grateful for what she's done. Only I'm not supposed to know she's done it.

Any relationship we have going forward will be built on us both harboring a secret. And if there's one thing I've learned, the more desperate you are to keep something concealed, the bigger the blast that's made when it comes to light. And if this secret gets revealed, it'll make what happened to that trailer look like it was caused by a popped soap bubble.

9

STEVE

Some battles are lost before they're begun. And some aren't worth the effort.

I slip out into the hallway, easing the door shut silently behind me. Feel like a teenager sneaking out in the middle of the night as I pause to listen for any sounds coming from the apartment I've just left, making sure my getaway's gone unnoticed. Ridiculous, considering I'm a grown man and it's light out, but try telling my mother that.

Her morning interrogations aren't exactly conducive to an early start, so here I am, creeping down the hallway like a prowler until I notice an older woman ahead of me, shuffling toward the elevator. The back of my neck heats. I check behind me, glad to find that no one has witnessed my awkward escape. Turn back around just in time to see the woman's toe snag on a dip in the rug.

She stumbles, a small gasp drifting down the hall. Her handbag falls to the ground, the contents spilling out onto the floor. I can feel her angst as she looks down at her scattered possessions.

"Are you okay, ma'am? Here, let me help," I say, jogging to close the distance between us.

I squat and right her purse, then start placing items back inside. A worn leather wallet, a packet of tissues, an assortment of hard candies. "They really should fix that carpet. My sister tripped on that same spot once, scraped her knees up. That was over thirty years ago and it's still causing issues."

Realizing she hasn't responded yet, I look up, worried that she's injured. Find myself struck speechless, staring into a familiar face.

"Steve Winters. I thought that was you."

I hastily shove the rest of the items back into the bag and stand. Take a step away as I hand it to its owner, trying to keep as much distance between us as possible.

"Mrs. Banks."

The woman before me is right around the same age as my mother, though you'd never know it. She looks so much older, frailer, more weathered. I wonder for a moment if she's sick, then realize it can't be easy having a murderer for a son, especially one who's disappeared without a trace.

And yet, her face wears a wide smile. Her hand shakes as it reaches out, settling on my arm. I fight the urge to pull away. For the first two decades of my life, this woman was like a second mom to me. What happened isn't her fault.

I worry about what Wesley might have told her. She must have wondered about our falling out. But whatever she thinks, she seems genuinely happy to see me.

"Come on," she says, turning away from the elevator and giving me a gentle tug toward her apartment. Wherever she had planned to go, it must not be pressing. "I'll make us some tea and we can catch up."

I open my mouth to make an excuse—only it's not really an excuse, I do need to go—but she seems so lonely, her eyes so hopeful, that I can't do it.

"I'd really like that," I say instead.

Her smile grows impossibly bigger. And yet I can't deny the nerves stirring inside my gut as I walk beside her, taking one stride for every four of her hesitant steps. What are we going to talk about? It would be strange if I didn't ask about Wesley, wouldn't it?

She releases me to search for her keys, and I find myself looking down the hall in both directions, praying for an interruption as she unlocks the door with palsied hands and totters inside, beckoning for me to join her. Swallowing hard against the bowling ball-sized lump in my throat, I do.

Everything looks exactly like I remember. Floral print wallpaper, beige carpeting, a crocheted blanket draped over the back of the couch. And on the walls around us, everywhere I look, Wesley's grinning face.

She gestures for me to take a seat at the kitchen table. I reluctantly lower myself onto one of the same vinyl chairs I used to sit on after school while she made snacks, purposely choosing the one that will leave my back to the photographs.

"So," I say, clearing my throat. Anything to break the silence being filled by the memories in my head. "How's Wesley?"

Her back goes rigid, brittle shoulders rounding. She turns to face me with a grimace. "I'm afraid I wouldn't know."

"He doesn't keep in touch?" I ask, forcing a note of sympathy into my voice, feeling like a villain because I know he doesn't. He can't. Not unless the dead can speak. The thought makes me shift uncomfortably in my seat.

"I'm afraid not." She eyes me like she's debating how much to say. Sighs heavily in defeat. "Wesley, well, I'm not sure how much you've heard over the years, but he's made some poor decisions in life."

She settles into the chair across from me, the tea forgotten. "I'd really hoped that this time he had learned his lesson. That he'd try to get his life back on track. He's still young enough, has plenty of good years ahead of him, but I'm afraid it just wasn't in the cards. I tried to cover for him with his parole officer as long as I could, but..."

Her body withers as she exhales. "He hasn't been home in months now. His parole's been revoked. When he turns up—if he turns up—he'll be going back to prison."

"I'm so sorry to hear that." I can't keep my eyes from flicking toward the hallway, to the closed door to Wesley's bedroom. "He was living here with you?"

She nods. "I had hoped it would help keep him out of trouble, but I guess the apple doesn't fall far from the tree after all."

Catching my confused look, Mrs. Banks colors, realizing her slip. She gives me an awkward smile. "My husband had similar issues with the law."

My pulse races like I'm on a roller coaster and not a chair in an old neighbor's apartment. I remember Wesley's father, but only vaguely. He'd been some kind of traveling salesman and had rarely been home. He'd left his family sometime while Wesley and I were in middle school. Or, at least, that's what I'd been told. Now it seems there's more to the story.

She smiles sadly. "I'm too old to put up with it anymore. I tried my best, I truly did, but some people— Anyway, I had the locks changed."

"So you don't think he'll be back?" I ask.

"He isn't welcome even if he does."

I glance again at the closed door to Wesley's bedroom, wondering what he might have left behind. And who might eventually find it.

"Would you like to take a look?" she asks, noticing my not so stealthy interest. "I'm afraid it's a mess. I'm having the super's son in next month when I get my next check to clean everything out, but you're more than welcome to anything you find in there. There might be some mementos that you'd like to have."

I rub my lips together, debating. Knowing that I have to do

it, no matter how much I don't want to. I try to tell myself that
my reasons aren't purely selfish as I take in my shabby surroundings. "You're paying someone to clean it out?"

"I am." The resolute nod she gives is the most confident
gesture she's made.

"I'm in town for a while longer. Why don't I do it for you,
save you some money?"

"Oh, I couldn't. I don't want to take up time you could be
spending with your mother during your visit." But she looks
eager at the suggestion.

"Please. I want to." I take a closer look at this woman who'd
once been such a large part of my life and realize it's true. Even
if I knew there was nothing incriminating in there, this is still
something I need to do.

"Well, if you're sure..."

I'm already thinking about the cash I'll just happen to find
somewhere in Wesley's room, suspecting the money will be
more of a help to her than I ever could be, as I say, "It would be
my pleasure."

"You always were a good one."

It's not true. But as she reaches out and pats my cheek with
a soft palm, I hope that it could be.

10

MAGGIE

There's about to be another explosion. It's not even 9 a.m. and I'm already ready to burst. Exhaling a deep breath, I stare at the plaque on my desk as I hang up the phone. The one that boasts CHIEF OF POLICE.

The title implies a certain amount of authority. The ability to take control. Handle any given situation. And get the job done.

Instead, I can't even get the rental car company to deliver the vehicle that was supposed to be here yesterday. I can't even manage to get a reason why it hasn't been delivered yet, or when I can expect it.

I imagine a world in which things were easy. I try to imagine myself in it. I can't.

Now I imagine showing up at the rental agency and having a conversation face to face with the snooty woman who just hung up on me. That doesn't end well either. How am I supposed to run a town, find out why I have three dead bodies on my hands and what a picture of my fiancé's dead blackmailer was doing at the crime scene, and save my impending marriage if I can't even get a customer service agent to do her job?

The phone rings and I snatch it up, hoping it's the woman calling to apologize. That she'll claim we got cut off accidentally, despite the very loud clank that sounded in my ear as the handset slammed against the receiver on her end. Sighing, I prepare myself for disappointment as I answer, "Chief Riley."

"I RSVPed to your wedding. Did you get it?"

"Dr. Ricky?"

"Yes."

"I did."

"Good. I'm looking forward to it. And your bachelorette party. I've never been to one before."

"Neither have I."

"In the movies, there are strippers."

I try imagining the tiny fiftysomething doctor with her serious expression, severe bangs, and thick glasses in an encounter with a stripper, but can't. Apparently, I've already tapped my imagination for today.

"I don't think there will be any at mine."

"I wondered."

Her expressionless tone leaves me debating whether she's disappointed or relieved.

"Anyway, that's not why I'm calling. I hear I have you to thank for securing the identity of one of the fire victims that you sent my way."

"You were able to confirm that one of the bodies belonged to Marie Bouchard?"

"I was, using dental records procured from one of the facilities in which she served time. She had quite a bit of work done for someone so young."

It doesn't surprise me. The use of methamphetamine is known for causing severe tooth decay.

"I'm still working on identifying the victim who was thrown from the blast," Dr. Ricky continues. "I wasn't able to pull any usable prints, and there are no other unique features present that could aid with ID. All I can tell you at this point is that he was male. I don't suppose you've had any men reported as missing since the explosion?"

"Unfortunately, no." I squeeze my eyes shut, once again summoning the memory of the trailer door opening, trying to latch on to details that might help. I get the same strange feeling of recognition, but the place where the face should be in my mind's eye remains blank.

"Hmm. I suspect it will be an interesting turn of events, should we find out."

"How's that?"

"The supposition is based on the identification of the second set of remains that were recovered from the fire."

"You have a positive ID for me?" I ask hopefully, pulling a pen from a holder and shoving my keyboard to the side, revealing a clear spot on my blotter.

"Perhaps."

I pause, my body freezing in place. "Perhaps?"

"I've made a tentative identification."

"Why only tentative?"

Dr. Ricky clears her throat. When she speaks, her tone holds an uncharacteristic lack of confidence. "I was able to match the serial number on a surgical rod used to repair a spiral radial fracture of the right arm."

"That's a pretty solid confirmation, isn't it?"

"Usually."

"Then what's the issue?"

"The woman, Ruby Anderson, had already been reported as deceased. Twenty years ago."

The ice holding my limbs hostage breaks, flooding my veins with slush.

"Any chance her bones were unearthed by the blast?"

"None. The state of her remains suggests she was alive at or very close to the time of the explosion."

"So what are you thinking, then? A mix up with the serial numbers?"

Again, she responds with, "Perhaps. It happens, but it's rare. Great care is typically taken when recording the serial numbers of an implant during a procedure."

I swallow a lump of frustration, frowning down at my desk as I wrack my brain for a way to politely urge Dr. Ricky along. I've worked with the woman enough times to know that we wouldn't be having this conversation unless she had something useful to share. But I also know rushing her is futile. So I do my best to practice having the patience that's always eluded me.

"All I know at the moment is that her death was ruled an accidental drowning on the death certificate. I've been unable to locate an autopsy report for her, so I'll need a copy of the police investigation for more details. I looked up the reporting officer. It was your predecessor. I don't suppose you have a copy of his files, do you?"

I swallow hard, trying to work up some spit, my mouth suddenly gone dry. "Going that far back? I'm not sure. I'll have to look."

"Please do. And anything else you can find on the woman, assuming she was a local to your area, would be helpful as well. I think that at this point, our best course of action would be to proceed cautiously and wait until I've been able to make a conclusive determination before contacting the family."

"Do you believe you'll be able to do that? Make a conclusive identification of the victim?"

"I don't see why not. There are a number of old injuries on the remains that would have required medical attention. It will take me a while to catalog them all, but there should be more than enough to match to her health records, assuming we can find them."

"What kind of injuries? Can you tell me what you're thinking?"

"At this point, any deduction would be a guess, and you know I don't do that. I'll forward my conclusion to you as soon as I make one."

"Thank you."

"And I'll see you soon, of course."

It takes me a moment to remember—the bachelorette party. Though it had been at the forefront of my mind, all concerns about the matter have now been shoved to the side, replaced by curiosity. I end the call with Dr. Ricky, preoccupied by the question: how does one woman manage to die twice?

11

STEVE

The office is small but neat, the lighting soft, the sound of harp music just barely audible over a water feature by the door that's no doubt meant to mask the sound of conversation from anyone sitting in the waiting room beyond. I take a seat in a plush leather armchair, the woman across from me nodding her approval and jotting a quick note on the pad sitting on the small end table beside her.

Setting the pen down, she interlaces her fingers and cups them around her crossed knee. Gives me a warm smile meant to put me at ease. It does just the opposite.

"I'm Dr. Curry. I see this is your first visit, Mr.—?"

"Winters. Steve Winters."

"May I call you Steve?"

"Yes," I say, even though it adds to my discomfort, the power imbalance of her calling me by my first name without offering her own. But if there's the possibility that she can help...

"What brings you in today, Steve?"

Perhaps it would be easier to answer the question of what doesn't bring me in today, though I don't make that my response. And I don't tell Dr. Curry how I spent the previous night researching doctor-patient confidentiality, followed by hours of research into the specialty I was seeking, until finally discovering one who offered online appointment booking and had availability today. Instead, I stare down at my hands and give her the answer I worked on during the two hours it took me to drive here.

"I've had dreams," I begin. "For a long time now. Since college. The same dream."

Her head bobs as her attention shifts, eyes finding the pad beside her as she makes another note.

"Recently, there have been more details, and I realized that the dream might be real. Like, memories of something that really happened."

"And what do you think happened?"

I swallow hard before confessing, "I think I watched my friend hit a girl with a car and bury her body under a tree."

Dr. Curry shifts her weight, lengthening her spine. She gives a long slow blink. Clears her throat and says, "Where were you when this occurred?"

"In the back seat. Sleeping. I think I may have been drugged."

"And why do you think that?"

"It's the only explanation that makes sense. For why I was so out of it, for the hazy memory..." And though I don't say it, I think, for not doing something to stop what was happening. Because that's the most inexcusable part.

If I had stopped Wesley that night, that girl would still be alive. He wouldn't have been able to try to blackmail me. I wouldn't have lied to Maggie. And my sister would be more than just a shadow of her former self. But there's no way to rewind time and go back. So I have to find a way to fix everything moving forward.

"Is there any evidence to support your belief that this dream you keep having is an actual memory?"

"There was a girl we—this friend and I—went to school with who disappeared that night."

"This was how long ago?"

"Almost twenty years."

"And you're just connecting the two occurrences—your dreams and the classmate who went missing—now?"

Something in my body language must give away the truth.

"I see. So what's changed?"

"I need to remember what happened. Where it happened. I need to be able to tell her family where they can find her."

"Why?"

I search her face to see if she's serious. It appears that she is.

"Because it's something I have to do."

"Again, why?"

My temperature rises, anger simmering deep in the pit of my stomach. "It's eating away at me."

"Is this a recent development?"

"It's been getting worse."

"Because...?" she prods.

She pins me with a gaze that makes me feel like an insect. Something about her demeanor, so cold and calm and detached, makes me feel reluctant to speak. I force the words out anyway.

"Because I'm getting married. I want to be a better man. Need to be. And my sister—" I catch myself seconds before I say too much. "It could have been my sister. Everything I told myself for years isn't cutting it anymore. No more excuses. I need to take action."

"You've told your fiancée?"

"Yes."

"Is she pressuring you to do this?"

"No. She doesn't even know I'm here."

"Then, again, I have to ask why—?"

I jump to my feet, ready to leave. My breath comes in ragged pants, hands curled into fists. My heart beats erratically, too fast and with no discernible pattern, and though I expect myself to be shouting when I speak, my voice instead comes out a near whisper. "Because I need help. Can you give it to me or not?"

"Do you think you can sit back down, Steve?"

I nod, shame burning my cheeks as I obey.

"I assume you're here because you saw that I specialize in regressive hypnosis. Specifically, in helping to retrieve repressed memories."

"Yes."

"There are no guarantees with hypnosis. While many of my patients make great strides in achieving their therapeutic goals, others don't. They're either not receptive or simply don't respond to the treatments. Above all, this is something you have to do for yourself. Not because it's what you think you should do."

"This is what I want. What I need."

"Then that's how we'll proceed. But I must caution you. Sometimes the memories I help my patients access come with unwanted consequences."

If only the doctor knew everything that's happened over the last six months. Then maybe she'd realized that the consequences can't get much worse.

12

MAGGIE

I wish I could ignore this foreboding in my gut. The one that keeps whispering danger. The one that makes me feel like I'm a fool as I set the phone back on its cradle.

Detective Martin was predictably agreeable to my offer to do a little digging after I updated him on Dr. Ricky's findings. The man seems to have already made up his mind about what happened at the trailer. Was all too quick to assume that whoever the remains belonged to, they were "just another junkie who fell prey to their addiction."

Even if that's true, that doesn't mean her death should just be dismissed. She was someone's daughter. Possibly a sibling or spouse, or even a mother. Those people deserve to know the truth about what happened to their loved one. They still deserve our best effort.

And I can't shake the feeling that there's more going on here than the drug angle he seems so fixated on. Whatever it is, it feels dangerous. I can't help thinking that it would be smarter to keep my distance on this one.

But I'm already too deep for that.

I need to find my predecessor's file with the report from the first time Ruby Anderson supposedly died. But it's not going to be an easy task.

A trio of five-foot-tall industrial beige filing cabinets have occupied the wall just to the left of the bathroom since I've worked here. When I first arrived, I tried thumbing through them to get an idea of the type of cases I'd be dealing with, but quickly gave up upon discovering the complete lack of organization.

The idea of having to search through that mess for a report that I may not find doesn't exactly fill me with joy. Sighing dramatically since there's no one to witness it, I stand and cross to the door. Hesitate with my hand on the knob.

Assuring myself that I'm just being silly, that nothing bad awaits me on the other side, I inch it open. Release a sigh of relief when the action isn't followed by a percussive bang. But the sound of the phone ringing as I step into the room sounds almost as loud to my frayed nerves.

The start I give doesn't go unnoticed. Sue frowns at me, quickly snatching the phone from its hook and answering, "Coyote Cove Police Department."

I give her a smile, doing my best to play it off, but that doesn't stop her from watching me like a hawk as I pass by on my way to Kal's desk. Keeping my voice low, I fill him in on what I've learned and what needs to be done, turning as I gesture toward the filing cabinets.

Sue's still staring at me, but now there's something else in her expression. Something unfamiliar. Whatever it is, I don't like it. I give her my full attention, waiting for the call to end.

"What've we got?" I ask.

"The call was from a Missy Anderson," Sue says. My toes go cold inside my shoes. I'm not psychic. I've never met Missy, but I can predict what Sue's going to say next, and it has nothing to do with the vein that's suddenly appeared on her forehead. "She wants to file a missing person report on her husband, Ronny."

I run the name through my mind, seeing if it will unlock the image of the face trapped somewhere in my brain, but I can't remember ever meeting anyone named Ronny. Or with the last name Anderson, at least not until Dr. Ricky told me about Ruby earlier.

"He's the assistant manager at the trading post," Sue adds.

I flash to a memory from last week, when the friendly employee who always insists on carrying my bag of dog food to the car for me asked me about my pups and told me he was thinking about getting one of his own. Though we've had numerous interactions throughout the years, I can't quite picture the details of his face other than a nice smile and dark hair.

Had it been Ronny? I suspect it had.

Then another thought occurs to me, one that makes my empty stomach feel curiously heavy. Is it possible that Ronny had somehow known Wesley? It would make sense, on Wesley's part. To befriend someone who was already part of the town, part of our lives, no matter how small a role they played.

"Want me to take it?" Kal asks.

"No, I'll do it." I hurry toward the door, stop and turn sheepishly. "Can I borrow someone's car?"

"I'll take you." Sue's already on her feet, purse in hand.

"Are you sure? I don't mind—"

"I'm sure. I need to get some air."

I trail her reluctantly to the little green Pinto in the corner of the lot, hoping it's the last time I have to stuff myself inside the tiny monster, though barring a miracle, which is what it would be if we came back to find my rental car waiting for me, I suspect it's not.

Buckling my seatbelt, I squeeze the strap across my chest as Sue cranks the engine two, three, four times before it finally catches. She glances tensely in my direction, then backs out of the space and pulls onto the road.

"Did you know Ronny?" I ask, curious if she has a personal connection to the man.

The muscles in her neck stand out as she frowns at the road before her. "I know who he is, but only because he works at the trading post."

"How about his wife?"

"Uh-uh."

I fall quiet, not sure if I should keep probing. The silence between us feels unusually awkward, the expression on her face abnormally tense.

"Are we going far?" I ask.

"Nope."

Sue reaches the end of town and takes a left onto a residential street. A row of houses stretches to either side, the buildings close together, creating a cluttered appearance, the narrow strips of green that separate each seeming more of an afterthought or a decoration than a yard. She pulls up along the curb in front of a pale yellow two story with faded blue trim.

"This it?"

She stares at the house a moment before nodding. I wrench the handle and elbow the door open, surprised when I hear the complaint of a second set of hinges behind me.

"You're coming?" I ask, turning back around toward the driver's seat in surprise, but I'm talking to myself. Sue has already exited the vehicle. I hurry to join her and repeat the question, this time over the hood of the car.

"Is that a problem?" she asks.

I'm not quite sure if it's appropriate, or even why she'd want to tag along for something like this, but before I can respond I hear the sound of someone approaching behind me. I turn and see a woman somewhere in her late twenties. I watch as she gathers her long brown hair into a ponytail that drapes almost all the way down her spine, then pulls the drawstring on the gray sweatpants she's wearing tighter.

Three stripes of her rainbow socks are visible before they disappear beneath a pair of dirty slippers that were once a pale shade of pink but are now mostly gray. She stops in front of me, crossing her arms over the front of her KENNEDY K-12 shirt. Though her posture says aggressive, the smile she gives me is friendly. "Wow, that was fast."

Returning the smile, I ask, "Missy Anderson?"

"For a bit longer, yeah."

I arch a questioning eyebrow.

"The divorce should be final by the end of the month, then I'll be filing the paperwork to go back to my maiden name. Fischer." She shrugs then says, "Anyway, as far as I know, Ronny's been couch-surfing for the last few months. Not sure which one of his friends is putting him up at the moment."

"Then may I ask how you know he's missing?"

"Got a call from the trading post this morning asking if I knew where he was. His boss said he hadn't shown up for his shifts the last three days."

"And would that be considered out of character?"

"Oh, yeah. Ronny's always taken himself too seriously. Once he got that assistant manager position, that job became his life."

"Is that why you're getting divorced?" Sue asks from behind me.

Missy hardens her eyes at the older woman. "I don't see how that's any of your business."

I give Sue a sharp look, silently signaling for her to let me handle it. You can't just jump right into touchy subjects.

"Have you made any calls to see if anyone knows where he is?" I ask.

"His boss at the trading post already did that before he

called me, on account of the divorce and all. Spoke with a few of his friends, left a message for his dad. No one has."

"May I ask why you're the one filing the report?" I ask, genuinely curious.

"I watch all those shows on TV. I know that the ex is always the main suspect. Figured I might as well get it over with." Missy smirks, the expression making her youthful face appear even younger. "You can come on in and take a look around if you want. You won't find any evidence of what happened to him 'cause I truly don't know."

"That won't be necessary," I say.

And it won't. I suspect I already know what happened to her soon-to-be-ex-husband, and it didn't happen here.

13

MAGGIE

There's a feeling I get when I'm working a case, when pieces start coming together and a picture begins to emerge. I'm not quite there yet. There is no image forming before me. But it has to be getting closer, because I suspect I've just found my first two interconnecting clues.

Adrenaline makes my blood feel like it's humming as Sue and I return to her car. The second the doors shut behind us, I take out my phone and dial Dr. Ricky. She answers before Sue manages to get the engine to crank.

"Hello?"

"It's Chief Riley. I've got a possible candidate for the unidentified explosion victim."

"I'm ready."

"Ronald Anderson. Goes by Ronny. Same surname as Ruby. His estranged wife just reported him missing."

The car jerks. My shoulder strikes the window. I glance over as Sue rights the vehicle.

"Any idea about a possible relation?" Dr. Ricky asks.

"Given the odds, I'd say it's likely. And the wife said his mother died when he was a child, so it seems they didn't know that Ruby was still alive—assuming that the remains in your possession are indeed hers. How quickly could you confirm?"

Without missing a beat, Dr. Ricky says, "That there's a genetic relationship between the two? Three days if I put a rush on it, maybe less if I visit the lab in person."

I hear a great deal of rustling in the background. I try not to picture what gruesome tasks she might be performing.

"Can you do that?"

"Collecting the first sample now as we speak."

"You're the best."

"I know. As for confirming the female victim's identity, I'm still waiting for any medical records for Ruby Anderson. I had my assistant cast a wide net, so hopefully we'll get a hit soon. If not, proving a familial connection to the male victim could be enough. This Ronald Anderson was a local?"

"Yes. According to his wife, he got regular cleanings at Gentle Dental over in Lincoln."

"Text me his date of birth and address. I'll have my assistant see about getting a copy of his latest films for comparison. As soon as I have anything worth knowing, I'll be in touch."

She ends the call without a goodbye. Pocketing the phone, I look over at Sue. The atmosphere in the car between us is strained. Should I say something about her behavior at Missy Anderson's?

I wait for her to glance in my direction, but she keeps her stare aimed out the windshield in front of her, fists clenched around the steering wheel at ten and two. Her lips are set in a hard straight line. She looks unnaturally pale other than two bright spots of color on her cheeks.

I wonder if she's feeling okay. Maybe she's coming down with something. But that still wouldn't explain the way she acted back there, refusing to stay quiet when I was taking Missy Anderson's statement, badgering the woman for details about the reason the couple was getting divorced. It's odd, because Sue knows better than to interfere.

Then again, this whole situation is odd: The entire encounter with Missy as I took the young woman's statement about her missing soon-to-be-ex-husband. That he shares a surname with one of the other possible victims of the explosion, a woman who was reported dead twenty years ago. That he was at a trailer far outside of town when he was supposed to be at a job he valued.

When I asked Missy about her estranged husband's family, she'd given me the names of his father and two siblings, mentioning that his mom had died when he was younger. If Ruby Anderson is indeed Ronny's mother, where's she been the last two decades?

She had three children that she left behind. According to the ages Missy gave me, the youngest would have been only four. Ronny, the oldest, was twelve. Had they believed their mother was dead? Or had they known she was alive?

Sue pulls into her space back at the department and exits the vehicle quickly, without saying a word. Her short pajama-clad legs have marched all the way up the ramp by the I time I get out and hurry after her, getting inside just in time to see her toss herself into the chair behind her desk.

I glance at Kal, barely visible behind a stack of files. More piles surround him on the floor. As he looks between me and Sue, his expression tenses like a child whose parents are fighting on Christmas morning.

"Is everything all right?" I ask her. "Are you feeling okay?"

"You know what, actually I'm not," she snaps.

I flinch, feeling slightly wounded by the sharpness of her response. I know I'm not always the most socially adept person. If I've done something to warrant this, I feel horrible, because I don't have a clue what it could have been. I'd hate to do anything to hurt Sue.

"Do you want to go home?" I ask.

Her eyes meet mine for the first time since we left Missy Anderson's. She shifts her gaze away quickly. "Yes."

I watch her gather her things, afraid I've done something wrong.

"I hope you feel better," I say. Sue pauses at the threshold but doesn't respond. A second later the door closes behind her. I turn toward Kal, confused. "I don't know what I did."

"Maybe she's really just not feeling well, and it has nothing to do with you," he suggests.

"I don't know. She seemed fine until we left. Maybe she's sick of driving me around already. I should probably check on the status of my rental again." But instead of going to my office and making the call, I slump into the chair in front of Kal's desk. Gesturing toward the towers of cream-colored folders strewn about, I ask, "What are you up to?"

"I sent a request for Ruby Anderson's medical records to both Dr. Calvin and Lincoln Memorial. I figured I'd find the case file while we were waiting, but..." He sighs heavily, shaking his head as he looks around at the mess. "I tried thumbing through them in the cabinets, but they were packed in so tight it was impossible. Since I had to pull them out to look, I figured I might as well try to organize them in case we ever have to do this again. Does alphabetical work for you?"

"However you want to do it, I'm grateful. Explain your system to me and I'll help."

Grabbing an armload of files from the cabinet, I settle onto the floor amid the chaos and start sorting. That's where I still am ten minutes later when the door opens. I cringe, embarrassed at having been caught sitting on the floor amid stacks of folders like I'm a kid building a fort.

My discomfort grows as a woodsy scent fills the room. I close my eyes and draw a deep breath. Keep them shut, sweat pricking to the surface of my skin as Fire Investigator Larson approaches behind me.

"Detective Martin left earlier today," he says.

Something about his tone makes my stomach drop. I tell myself I don't know this man well enough for five simple words to tell me so much, that the sentence could mean plenty of things. Yet, somehow, I do know.

"And?" I prompt, my voice barely more than a whisper, dreading what he's going to say as I turn to face him.

"I need to report a murder. Three of them, actually."

14

MAGGIE

The air whooshes out of my lungs. The pressure in the room changes, much like it had three days ago in the second before the explosion. I brace myself as if preparing for another blast. It doesn't come, but I feel the shockwave nonetheless. *Murder*.

For the first time I regret concealing the photograph of Wesley I'd found at the scene. Maybe there should be more heads trying to figure out what his connection to this case is than just mine. Especially if I was meant to be there for the blast.

"What caused that trailer to blow was intentional," Larson says. "It wasn't an accident."

"How do you know?" I ask.

"You mean how can I exclude a meth production incident as the cause of the explosion?" he asks.

"Yes."

"Well, for one, the chemical signatures from the samples I took showed minimal amounts of those associated with methamphetamine, suggesting that if the trailer was used for the manufacture of the drug, they weren't actively cooking at the time of the blast."

"Then what do you think happened?" Kal asks.

"I think that someone intentionally caused a propane explosion."

"So there were high levels of propane in your samples?"

"Well, that's not exactly how propane works."

"Then how does it?" I tap my palm against my knee, wishing he'd get to the point already. Pushing to my feet, I start pacing the room. "Plenty of people up here use propane as a heating source. And to fuel their appliances. How can you tell that the explosion was caused by propane and not that it was a secondary factor caused by the fire?"

Larson drops into the chair in front of Kal's desk. He looks tired, yet that same intensity burns in his eyes as they track my movements.

"Propane tank explosions are actually quite rare. I blame the media for making people think otherwise. Like if a tank tips over, you better run and hide. It's all sensationalism, really. Scare tactics to get people to tune in. Propane tanks have a number of safety features to prevent that from happening. Now, if some of those safety features fail or you have a leak, that's when you need to worry."

"Is that what happened?" Kal asks.

"Not exactly."

"Then what did?"

"Well, even if you have a propane leak, that alone isn't enough to cause an explosion. You also need an ignition source. And not just a lit cigarette like they show in the movies, but an actual spark, like from an electrical malfunction, or an open flame."

Larson becomes more animated as he speaks, his passion for the subject showing as he starts accentuating his speech with his hands, waving them around as he says, "You see, propane explosions are like a perfect storm, if you will. Everything has to line up just right for one to occur, and that really doesn't happen that often."

"Is that why you're ruling this arson?" I ask.

He shakes his head. "There was a thousand-gallon tank just beside the trailer. A fair amount of the gas was probably out of the tank by the time of the blast. That would explain the call you received about a rotten egg smell, though propane is actually odorless. The unpleasant scent is added so you know when you have a leak."

"Wouldn't the people inside the trailer have noticed the smell?" Kal asks.

"The leak wasn't in the trailer. It was outside of it. Of course, I had some help in making that assumption." Pulling his phone from his pocket, he scrolls through his camera feed until he finds what he's looking for. He holds the screen toward me and Kal so we can see. My eyes flick to Larson's to find his already on me, waiting for my reaction.

"Any ideas about what cut the fuel line?" I ask.

He scrolls to the next photo. This shot shows a large pair of blackened branch clippers half buried by dirt and debris. "Just sent one of my guys to the crime lab with these along with the end of the fuel line we recovered. I can't say for sure without the official results, but it sure looks like someone cut the gas line on purpose. And that, my friends, means murder."

Three deaths. A woman with a known meth addiction. Another who supposedly died twenty years ago but was really alive all this time. And her son, a seemingly upstanding local man. Marie Bouchard lived there, but what brought the other two to the trailer that day?

"Have you told any of this to Detective Martin?" I ask.

"No."

"Why not?"

"I tried calling but he didn't answer. Left a message that he hasn't bothered to return. Considering he took off during the middle of an active investigation, you'd think he'd be a little more responsive."

"It's still his case. A triple homicide definitely falls under state police territory."

"But it's your town," Larson says. "Should I not have come to you with this?"

"No, I'm glad you did. I guess I'm just wondering why."

Something about the look he gives me makes my stomach flutter. A surge of heat warms my face. I glance away, worried I might be blushing.

"I'm from a small town myself. I know how guys like Martin work. Five minutes with the detective and it was clear that he was more concerned with making it home for dinner than with finding out what had really happened. And I know you want this case solved as much as I do. I realize we'll have to keep him in the loop, but seriously, if you were me, who would you rather work with? So do we have a deal?"

I know he's right about Detective Martin. And if what he's saying is true, there might still be a killer in my town. What if they're just getting started? If I was one of the intended victims, then they're not done. And if there *is* some kind of connection to Wesley, it's better that I find it than risk another cop digging too deep.

So I agree, even though doing so causes a fresh surge of anxiety to crash against me. Because for some reason, the idea of working with Larson feels risky.

15

STEVE

I pull into the parking lot, wishing I didn't have to go inside. Reluctantly open my car door. And even though I haven't eaten all day, and the night air that wraps around me carries the scent of garlic and grilled meat, aromas that would normally have my mouth watering and my stomach growling, my appetite is nonexistent. The very idea of a meal makes me queasy.

It's been another long day on the road with no results. Well, I take that back. There's been one result, the same one, over and over. Failure.

Tomorrow, I have my first hypnotherapy session with Dr. Curry. She'd warned me not to get my hopes up. Told me that I might not be susceptible to hypnosis, or that it could take multiple appointments to achieve the breakthrough that I'm looking for, but still, I have to believe that she holds the power to unlock what happened that night.

I know the memories are there. I can feel them hovering on the edge of my consciousness every morning when I wake, before the weight of what I've done hits me, knocking me breathless. And though I fear the possible consequences that may arise from accessing the full knowledge of what happened, I know that it's something I have to do.

The interior of the restaurant is dim, long shadows stretching across the room. But when the hostess shows me to the table where my mother and sister already sit in stony silence, it does little to conceal the friction between them.

My mother gives me an annoyed look. "You're late."

I shrug. "I told you I might not make it on time. I tried."

"What are you so busy with all day that you can't be bothered to show up to dinner?"

Opening the menu, I pretend not to hear her. I understand why she's upset, but the fact is, I'm not down here for a family visit. Only there's no way to get her to understand that without telling her why I am here, and that's never going to happen.

I'm saved by the server as he comes over to take our orders. When he's done, I launch a preemptive strike.

"So, tell me about this reunion Grandpa Joe is at."

"There's nothing to tell, darling. Just Joe and some of the men he served with getting together to rehash the past."

"Where is it?"

"I'm not quite sure."

"When will he be back?"

She gives me a long look, one that says she knows exactly what I'm trying to do, and she's not falling for it, before saying, "To be honest, he's been rather evasive about it. It's like the two of you have been practicing together."

Ignoring the jab, I turn to my sister. "How was your day, Iz?"

"I got invited to Maggie's bachelorette party this weekend."

"Her what?"

"Bachelorette party."

"Maggie's?" I ask, not quite believing my ears.

"Do you have any other fiancées we should know about?"

"No, it's just, it's not like her, is all."

"I wasn't invited," my mother says in a hurt tone.

"No one wants their future mother-in-law at their bachelorette party," Izzy says.

"But you were invited."

"You're going, right?" I ask.

My sister shrugs, giving me a look that clearly says she's not.

"You have to."

"Why?"

"Because it'll be good for you. Both of you. It'll give you a chance to get to know each other."

"We did that."

"But better," I insist.

"Listen, Steve, I'm sorry but I don't feel like driving up to northern Maine just so I can spy on Maggie for you."

"That's not—"

I close my mouth as the server brings our salads. Keep it closed after he leaves. Picking up my fork, I stab at the lettuce on the plate. Because maybe that *is* why I want Izzy to go so bad. Why hadn't Maggie said anything to me about the party?

The answer comes on a wave of guilt that threatens to send the bite I just swallowed back up. Maybe she would have told me if I had done a better job of keeping in touch. Ever since I've been down here though… I don't know how to describe it. The best I can do is that I'm trying to keep the two worlds apart—my current life with Maggie, where our wedding is mere weeks away, and my old life, which has become a nightmare that threatens to haunt any future happiness I hope to have.

"—Do you think that Maggie would like that?"

"Huh?"

I look at my mother, unsure how much of the one-sided conversation I've missed.

"Don't say *huh*, dear, it's impolite. Say *pardon*."

Izzy snickers at the correction. Our eyes meet and we share

a smirk, giving me a flashback to my teen years, a reminder that most of my youth was good. It shouldn't all be forgotten.

Feeling a sudden wave of nostalgia, the tension in my body eases. I smile at my mother, a genuine one, suddenly thankful for the good I have in my life. I've been so wrapped up in the past, I've let it overshadow the present and threaten my future. I have to stop. I nod to myself, knowing it's true.

"Oh, fantastic!" my mother gushes. "I'll send it out to have it freshened up first thing tomorrow. You've made me so happy. Thank you."

I stare at my mother's hand, wrapped around my own on the tabletop, having absolutely no idea what I just agreed to, but knowing that whatever it is, I can't take it back. Because here's the thing about having something good—it can go bad real fast.

I glance over at Izzy, but my sister's already withdrawn back into herself, frowning down into her empty wineglass. In this lighting, the strain on her face is apparent. Fine lines I've never noticed before bracket her eyes and mouth. Two grooves form deep trenches between her brows. The light that used to shine behind her eyes is gone. I fear I may never see it again.

Your life can change forever in an instant. I learned that the hard way almost two decades ago, and again less than two months back. I still haven't figured out how to make it right. In fact, I'm pretty sure I keep making it worse.

16

MAGGIE

I hate this feeling. The uncomfortable, itchy one that I get when I have to rely on other people. The one that makes me worry that I made a deal with the devil. And though Fire Investigator Larson doesn't appear to be hiding any horns underneath that perfect hair of his, I can't shake the suspicion all the same.

It's a relief when he leaves to make the trip back to Lincoln for the night, but I know he'll be back in the morning. What he'll bring with him besides those intense eyes of his I can't quite say, though I hope it will be useful, because at the moment this investigation has me feeling like I'm running through cement.

So much of this case is out of my hands right now. Until Dr. Ricky is able to confirm Ruby Anderson's identity and determine if the third victim is Ronny Anderson, our missing person, there's not much I can do. We need Ruby's medical records. And we need to find my predecessor's report from when she supposedly died twenty years ago. Only one of those things is within my control.

Which is why it's almost seven before I tell Kal that we should call it a day. If it were just me, I'd keep at it all night until

I found the file, assuming it exists. But I need Kal to drive me home and feel guilty enough already for keeping him late.

As we make the drive in silence, I wonder if he had plans tonight. If there's something I'm keeping him from doing. If he regrets moving to Coyote Cove.

It's odd, because though I'd say that I know my lieutenant, I don't really. I know big things, like he's a good cop, but I don't know much about his past.

It makes me feel bad. Just because I don't like it when people pry into my history, that doesn't mean he might not appreciate it if I took the time to get to get better acquainted with his. But as we turn into the drive, I tell myself it will have to wait.

I can't help feeling a twinge of apprehension as Kal pulls up in front of the cabin and puts the car in park. It seems so strange. I spent my entire adult life living by myself until Steve and I moved in together. Even in college I never had a roommate, preferring the privacy and solitude of my own company. But now, with Steve out of town, it feels wrong being here.

I'm reaching for the door handle when Kal asks, "Are you sure you'll be okay?"

I answer before I have a chance to really contemplate the question. "Yeah, why wouldn't I be?"

He doesn't respond, just gives a one-shouldered shrug, but I can see it in his eyes, that there's something he isn't saying.

"How about you?" I ask.

"What about me?"

"How are you doing? I feel like maybe I've just assumed that you've settled in all right since you got here. Have you?"

"Yeah. Of course." But he doesn't look at me as he says it.

"I know firsthand how lonely it can be up here. It's a small town. Close-knit. It can be hard to make friends."

Kal raises a hand to cover his mouth, but not before I can

see the smile that's spread across his lips, making his dimples appear.

"What?" I ask.

"I'm just trying to imagine what it might have looked like. You trying to make friends when you first moved up."

"I never said that I tried. Just that I knew it could be hard."

We share a laugh, and though it seems a good way to end the conversation, it also feels like the opening I've been looking for. I might not get a better chance than this.

"I guess what I'm getting at is I want to make sure you're happy up here. That you're planning on sticking around."

"Why wouldn't I?"

"Why would you? I mean, there's not really much up here for you, is there? Not to mention that you're so far from your family."

Kal has a sister listed as his next of kin, but he never talks about her, or his parents. He's never asked for time off to see them, and I don't think they've ever visited him—that would be big news in a town as tiny as Coyote Cove.

"Did you ever think that maybe I like it that way?" he says.

I give him a sharp look, surprised. "No, I guess I didn't."

"Don't get me wrong," he rushes to say. "I love my family."

"No, you don't have to explain. I was probing. It was rude."

"Isn't that what friends do when they get to know each other?"

I'm surprised how pleased I am to hear him calling me a friend. "Yeah, I guess it is." I wait a beat, then ask, "Do you miss them?"

"I do. The four of us have always been close. My parents and an older sister. They're all in southern Maine. And all doctors."

"Oh."

"Yeah. It hasn't always been easy. I mean, I know that, ultimately, they just want me to be happy, but still. There was always that little part of me that felt guilty because I knew I was disappointing them, even if they never said it."

I feel like I should say something, share something about myself in exchange for all he's told me. "I think my parents always expected me to follow in their footsteps and become a professor."

"Really?" He squints at me as I nod. "I suppose I could see that."

"They always referred to my career as 'the cop thing,' like it was some kind of phase I'd get sick of."

"Mine finally stopped sending me brochures for medical schools when they thought they were going to get grandchildren instead, but... you see how that turned out."

I do. The failed engagement, the reason he came up here in the first place. The cause of which I've become more curious to learn the closer I get to walking down the aisle myself.

"Do you mind if I ask what happened?"

"*That* I don't want to talk about," he says softly, staring out the window.

I nod, even though he's not looking. Say the only thing I can think of to change the subject. "You know, anytime you want some time off to go visit—"

Kal shakes his head. "I'm not going back there."

"Why not?"

His face tenses. He gives me a smile, but it doesn't reach his dimples. "You know what they say. You can never go home again, or something like that, right?"

That's not true and we both know it, despite whatever some adage might say. There's a reason he doesn't want to go back, and I suspect that it has to do with his ex-fiancée. What could have possibly happened between them that was so bad?

But he's made it clear that the topic's off limits. I wrack my brain for something to fill the silence that's growing awkward between us. "Then why don't you invite them here? They should come up for my wedding. I'd love to meet them."

"I appreciate the offer, but I don't think so."

"Really, you should."

Kal's jaw clenches, his hands tightening around the steering wheel. It's obvious I've made him upset.

"I'm sorry. I shouldn't have pushed," I hurry to say. "It's a bad habit. I'll see you tomorrow."

I hop out of the car before he has a chance to respond and jog up the front steps, letting myself into the house and closing the door behind me without a backward glance. I turn the lock before sinking to the floor and gathering the pups in my arms, using them to soothe away the strains of the day.

Maybe it's this case. Or the stress of the upcoming wedding, of Steve being out of town, of the photograph I found of Wesley Banks, or any of a dozen other reasons that have me feeling so unsettled.

But there's a niggling in my gut that's telling me that my lieutenant, the man who I at times trust with my life, is hiding something. And though I know that the absolute last thing I should do if I value our friendship is to dig until I find out what it is, I'm not sure if I can just let it be.

I know that everyone has their secrets. And I know that I should respect that. But it seems like the people closest to me have a habit of keeping ones that are deadly.

17

STEVE

My stomach churns like it's a pit filled with writhing snakes. The steering wheel feels sticky beneath my clammy palms. My mouth is dry, no spit to spare, and yet I can't stop swallowing, throat clicking with each dry push.

My first hypnotherapy session is later today. I'd been so excited, so hopeful, but now that the time has come, well, I'm not sure what I am anymore, but whatever it is, it doesn't feel like anything good. More like a trip to the doctor when you know they're going to tell you that lump you found is cancer.

And that's exactly what having this secret locked inside my mind is like—a deadly black growth slowly eating away at me, replacing my cells with poison.

Checking the time, I debate for a moment, then place the call. It's still early, but I need to remind myself of what I stand to gain if I make it through this nightmare.

"Hey."

Already my breath comes a little easier. A smile replaces the tense frown I've worn since waking. Keeping my voice low so it doesn't betray my nerves, I say, "So what's this I hear about a bachelorette party? Am I invited?"

Maggie laughs. I still remember the first time I heard the sound, the way my heart felt like it had given an extra beat. The quickening of my pulse as I'd hurried away from my car toward the road so I could see who it belonged to.

That first glimpse of her is forever seared into my brain, her face limned by the sun, the light catching her hair, throwing sparks like fire. I don't know if love at first sight is a real thing, but I felt more awake in that moment than I had in years.

"Good morning to you, too. And only if you sit next to Margot."

"Margot's going to be there?"

"Who else do you think I have to invite?"

"I'm not sure, but now I'm worried."

"Why's that?"

"Because if Margot's there, the party's definitely going to get out of control."

She laughs again. Serenity washes over me, making me feel like everything is going to be okay.

"I'm afraid you might be right."

After that first time I saw Maggie, I spent as much time as possible in my front yard, waiting for the opportunity to meet her. Wearing comfortable shoes, dressed in clothes I could hike in, hoping to join her while she walked her dogs if given the chance. Because there was something about her—the need to get to know the woman I'd seen was unexplainably over-whelming and all consuming.

Weeks passed. My car had never been cleaner. There wasn't a stray fallen leaf in the yard. And yet, there'd been no sign of her.

I started to fear that she'd only been visiting the area. That I'd never see her again. It felt like I was in mourning, grieving the loss of a person who I'd never even met.

Then, just when I'd given up hope, it happened. I was out getting my mail when a Jeep appeared down the road, slowing as it approached me. The window rolled down as it came to a stop. And there she was, behind the wheel.

"Are you my new neighbor?" she'd asked.

I'd dropped my mail in my haste to hurry over, wiping my hands on my pants, wishing I hadn't just propped a palm on top of the pollen-dusted box.

"Steve," I'd said, grinning like a fool.

"Maggie. Have you been here long?"

"No, just moved in."

"How do you like it so far?"

"It's... quiet. Kinda creepy."

I cursed inwardly, telling myself to shut up, but she simply laughed and reached into the car beside her.

"I'm glad I'm not the only one who thinks so. But if you ever get too spooked, you can give me a call."

It wasn't until she'd disappeared down the driveway opposite mine that I looked at the card she'd given me. Saw that she wasn't just a cop, but the local chief of police. And though I knew that I should keep my distance, I didn't stand a chance of staying away.

I hear her opening and closing drawers on the other end of the line. She grumbles to herself.

"What's going on?"

"I don't suppose you've noticed one of my uniforms somewhere odd, have you?"

"Like where?"

"Anywhere not in the bedroom. I thought I had a spare in my Jeep, but when I cleaned it out before the techs took it, it wasn't there."

"Out of clean laundry already?"

"I'll get to it."

"Don't forget to check your pockets first," I remind her, grinning as I think of all the odd tidbits I've found over the years.

"I know how to do laundry." There's a long pause. She

sounds unsure as she adds, "At least, I'm pretty sure it will come back to me."

I think of the washer and dryer in the basement. What a headache it was to get them down there. How much abuse they'd be able to take before one of them might need to be replaced.

"Maybe you should ask Sue to help," I suggest.

Maggie doesn't answer. If I couldn't still hear her rustling around, I'd think the call had dropped. I wait for a reply, but it doesn't come. Eventually, I break the silence.

"Is everything all right?"

Her reply comes after a pause and sounds unsure. "Yeah, why?"

The peace I'd felt evaporates. I want to ask her what's really going on. What she isn't telling me. *Why* she isn't telling me.

My muscles tense as I answer my own question: Because she doesn't want to. Does she not trust me? Or is there another reason?

"I don't know. Just checking, I guess."

"How are things going there?"

It's my turn to be evasive.

"Fine."

"Are you having any luck?"

"I... I'm pretty sure today's going to be the day."

"Really?"

The hope in her tone makes my heart clench. I clear my throat, trying to disguise the hitch in my breathing.

"Yeah. Hey, listen, my exit's coming up. I'm going to have to let you go."

"Oh. Okay."

I ignore the disappointment I hear in her voice as we say goodbye, knowing that I need to focus and get my head in the game. I have to make this work. There's too much at stake to fail.

18

MAGGIE

I lean against the side of the house and stare out at the lake, watching the hazy mist that hovers over its surface slowly burn away as the sun rises over the mountains in the distance, chasing away the shadows. The morning holds the kind of stillness that only exists when it's still early. But no matter how peaceful the world around me is, inside me it's pure chaos.

Steve's keeping something from me, I could hear it in his voice as he rushed me off the phone. And though I'm trying to tell myself that it might be something good, like he really is making progress there and will be home soon, that I should trust this man who I've chosen to marry, there's this tiny little part of me that's whispering not to be so stupid.

I don't have a good track record as far as relationships are concerned. I've always been preoccupied with not getting caught by surprise. Prided myself on the fact that I'd never be one of those women who trusted enough to get cheated on without knowing. It was more important to me to save face and not get tricked, even if it cost me the relationship.

But I let my guard down with Steve, and like a self-fulfilling prophecy, once I allowed myself to be vulnerable, I was caught by surprise. It feels a bit like a slap from karma.

How many men had I driven away? How many more slaps should I expect?

A sudden thud shatters the stillness, sending a flock of birds into flight. I flinch, a gasp catching in my throat. Though I place the sound as a car door, knowing the cause does little to soothe the sudden rush of my pulse, nor the irrational fear flooding into my veins.

But at least the distraction interrupted my thoughts before they could turn too dark.

I follow the dogs as they race around the side of the house, wondering who in their right mind would show up unexpectedly so early in the morning. Slow my pace as I see a woman wearing khakis and a polo shirt standing in front of a shiny SUV, a sedan idling behind it. The pups sit politely before her, sniffing the air to see if she's brought treats.

"Ms. Riley?" she asks, peering down at the clipboard she holds.

Normally I'd just say yes, but I recognize her voice. This is the lady at the rental car agency who's been giving me such a hard time. The one who hung up on me.

"Police Chief Riley," I say.

She shifts nervously, not meeting my gaze as she holds the paperwork and a pen out to me. "Sorry about the delay. I just need you to sign here and we'll be all set."

If I wasn't so relieved to finally have a vehicle at my disposal again, I might be tempted to give her a hard time. Instead, I scrawl my signature beside the X, take the key and duplicate copy of the rental agreement from her, and watch her retreat into the car driven by her coworker, waiting for them to disappear before calling the dogs to follow me to the rear of the house and back inside.

I needed this—for one thing to go right.

I shoot off a quick text to Kal letting him know I won't need a ride in today, my relief at not having to get in a car with him after the awkwardness I caused last night so overwhelming that I'm almost giddy.

One way or another, I'm going to get some answers today.

Checking the time, I see it's late enough, but just barely. The local doctor's office opened only minutes ago. As the sole medical facility in town, they're probably dealing with the morning rush, trying to process the patients with appointments and those utilizing the walk-in clinic. It's likely the worst time to ask for a favor. I scroll through the contacts in my phone and call anyway.

"North Country Medical Center, can you please hold?"

"Actually, no. Karen this is Chief Riley. I know you have your hands full, but I need a favor."

"Chief! Hold on just a sec." I hear her instruct someone to fill out all the highlighted portions of a form, then her chipper voice is back in my ear. "All right, then. What did you need?"

"There should be a subpoena headed your way—you might have received it already—for any medical records you have for a woman named Ruby Anderson. I'm sure you've already received the request from the state medical examiner's office, but there's been an update on the case. It's been confirmed as a crime, and the woman is believed deceased, so there shouldn't be any HIPAA issues."

I know for a fact that Karen Edmunds, receptionist, nurse, and town selectman, has played fast and loose with HIPAA rules before, to my benefit, so under these circumstances, what I'm asking for shouldn't pose a problem.

"Is there any way I can get you to bump the request to the top of your list? If she was a patient, she probably hasn't been in for at least twenty years, so it might require a bit of digging, but we're kind of at a standstill until the ME can confirm ID, so..." I trail off, fingers crossed that she'll pick up the conversation with the response I'm hoping for.

"That long ago, I'll have to go search through the physical files in the storage room."

"Is that an issue?"

"With the appointments we have today and the number of patients already filling the walk-in waiting room? There's nothing I'd rather do. Is this an official request?"

"It is."

"Then Dr. Calvin's going to get to see firsthand why we need that assistant I've been asking for. If I find anything, should I send it to you or the ME's office?"

"Can you do both?"

"Of course."

"Thanks, Karen. I owe you one."

"Then I can count on your vote?"

I forgot that it was an election year. But even if she wasn't doing me a favor, Karen would still have my support. She's been lobbying since I got to the Cove to get the police department the budget to hire a third officer.

"Without a doubt."

I end the call feeling hopeful. With Karen looking for Ruby Anderson's medical records, and Kal searching for Chief Parker's investigation from when she was originally reported dead, I might finally make some progress on this case.

Then my phone starts buzzing. I suspect I was optimistic too soon.

An uneasy feeling stirs inside me as Fire Investigator Larson's name appears on the screen. Taking a deep breath, I try to swallow down my anxiety as I answer.

"Chief Riley."

"Red, we've got a problem."

My stomach tenses, my hand cramping as my grip tightens on the phone.

"What kind of a problem?"

"The clippers I sent for analysis? The ones I figured had cut the fuel line? The results came back inconclusive."

"Already?"

"Yep. There was damage to the cutting edge caused by the blast. The analyst took one look at the surface and said there was no way it was a match for the clean cut."

"So it wasn't just inconclusive, then. It was a negative."

"I was hoping you wouldn't catch that. It's not quite as cut and dry, though. They could have been what was used, there's just no way to prove it since the cutting edge got damaged and no longer matches the impression on the line. Which means we no longer have proof of arson."

I curse, the sick feeling in my stomach increasing. "What can we do?"

"I need you to help me find something else to prove the explosion was intentional."

"Me?"

"I've had a full crew out there processing the scene for days already. Now that the case has been downgraded, my manpower's been slashed."

"By how much?"

"To just me."

Bile threatens to rise up my throat. This is what I get for being hopeful. You'd think I would have learned my lesson by now.

"Is there any way you and Kal can meet me out there and help me look around?" he asks.

"For what?"

"I'm not sure exactly. But there's got to be something we missed. Something that will help prove arson."

"What makes you think we'll be able to find something that your crew has missed?"

"Because we have to."

Four simple words, but they speak volumes. Without proof that the blast was caused intentionally, it will be ruled accidental. Accidental implies that the deaths were that as well—which means not homicide.

While it's possible that the fuel line was cut by a sharp piece of debris during the explosion, it's not likely, especially considering that one of the victims might be a woman who's supposedly been dead for the last twenty years.

Or maybe I'm reaching. Dr. Ricky hasn't made a conclusive determination on ID yet. Maybe the serial number on the surgical rod found attached to the unidentified female's remains really had been recorded to the wrong patient. Maybe Ronny Anderson simply took off. And maybe that photograph of Wesley... yeah, I still don't have a good explanation for that.

I have to see this through to the end, which means finding out the truth about what happened. I'm not going to be able to relax until I'm sure that whatever threat Wesley—and those from any friends he might have had—is over.

"Have you called Detective Martin?" I ask.

"I tried him first. Figured he'd have a bigger team at his disposal."

"And?"

"He thinks we're chasing our tails on this. So are you in? Can you guys meet me at the blast scene?"

I pull my phone away from my ear and check the time. See that I've received a text from Sue informing me that she still doesn't feel well and won't be in today. Someone has to be at the office in case anyone comes in. Kal's probably already there. Should I send him out into the field with Larson?

What about the medical records? It's a fine line—if this isn't a homicide, then Karen shouldn't be forwarding a copy of Ruby Anderson's records to the department, especially if she hasn't received the subpoena yet. And we shouldn't be wasting man-hours searching for Parker's accident report. But we're in too deep now—or, at least, I am. I need to know what happened to Ruby.

So even though I'm willing to walk the line, would Kal be? Should I be putting him in the position to have to choose? Right now, that's the only answer I do know.

Reluctantly, I tell Larson, "I'll see you there in thirty."

It's the last thing I want. But it's the only thing I can do.

19

MAGGIE

This feels wrong. Like Sue with her Pinto, I can't remember the last time I drove something other than my Jeep. The rental car is strange and unfamiliar. The wheel beneath my hands is too thin, the vehicle itself too light, seeming unstable on these winding mountain roads, like it might lose traction around the corners. It has an unsettling effect, leaving me strangely disconnected from my surroundings. Ungrounded.

Though it's not unusual to not pass any other drivers on Old Mill Road, today it's unnerving. I stay well below the speed limit, eyes scanning the surrounding woods. Slowing whenever I reach a clearing or the narrow gap of a driveway.

Though I've returned to the scene of the explosion before, Kal was in the car with me. There's something different about being alone. It too closely mirrors what happened that day.

And it's with that insight that I realize what I'm looking for. The wolf.

I still don't know if what I saw was real. I'm not sure what to believe. But had I not stopped that day, I might not be here now.

Goosebumps rise to the surface of my skin, making my arm hair stand on end. I open my eyes a little wider, peer a little deeper into the shadows surrounding me. Feel a rush of gratitude as I spot an approaching vehicle, glad to no longer be out here alone, even if the company is only temporary.

As the distance between us closes, I slow my speed even more, not trusting my twitchy grip on the foreign steering wheel coupled with the narrow road. Hugging the outside edge of the pavement, I prepare to pass, glancing from the lane ahead to the man inside the truck.

Our gazes meet through the windshield. His eyes stay locked to mine, our heads turning until we're looking directly at each other through our side windows. The moment seems to last a lifetime. A ripple of unease makes my muscles tense. And then it's over.

I check my rearview mirror, watching as he disappears into the distance behind me. Release a heavy sigh as I spot the mailbox planted in its five-gallon bucket up ahead. Turning into the pitted driveway, I experience a strange sense of relief to see that Fire Investigator Larson is already here.

I'm not used to feeling so anxious. I don't like it. Unwilling to show any signs of weakness or vulnerability, I summon fake confidence as I exit the car.

"Hey, Red."

"Inspector Larson," I say, nodding.

"You can call me Dean, you know."

I ignore the offer. "Where do we start?"

He raises his arm and gestures toward the ruins dramatically.

"Can you at least tell me what we're looking for?"

"Anything that shouldn't be here."

Though my thoughts are pretty insistent that *I* am one of the things that shouldn't be here, I stride forward, approaching the wreckage. Larson follows too closely, yet I can't deny that his presence brings a strange sense of comfort as I skirt around the edges of the blast site, searching the charred rubble with a wary gaze.

The air still reeks of smoke and burned plastic, the ground still muddy from the spray of the fire hoses, clumps of ash floating on top of shallow puddles. The area appears to have been abandoned by local wildlife, not a chipmunk or a bird or even an insect in sight.

"This is about where the clippers were discovered," he says, breaking the silence.

I look to where he's pointing, at some scrubby brush about ten feet from where the end of the trailer once was. The bushes are singed. There's a large area that's been crushed, most likely from flying debris.

"It seems odd that that's where they were left," I say. "The perpetrator had to have known they'd be recovered that close to the scene."

"Unless they thought the blast would be bigger than it was. Maybe they thought the entire area would burn," Larson suggests.

I nod, conceding his point, but it still seems strange to me. Why go to all the trouble of causing an explosion if you didn't want people to think it was an accident? There are easier ways to kill someone.

"The gas line would have entered the house somewhere about here," Larson points. "And the propane tank was right here. Not far enough away, per code, not that anyone seems to pay attention to things like that up here."

There's a small pit in the ground below where the tank once sat that I don't remember seeing before.

"Will the gas company get in trouble?"

Larson shrugs. "Probably not. They might not have even placed the tank. Sometimes the homeowner owns it, sometimes the gas company. And this was a larger tank. Codes change from time to time. With a place this size, who knows when it was last filled."

I can't stop looking at the spot where the tank once sat. Something about it is odd, making my memory feel disjointed.

"Did you guys excavate where the tank was?" I ask.

"No. Even though it was empty, it still weighed too much for the techs to lift. They had to get some heavy equipment out here to move it. A special truck to put it on to haul it to the lab. They just got it done yesterday, after I left. Why?"

"It doesn't fit with what I remember. I guess because the tank was still here."

But even with the explanation, something's still niggling at the corner of my mind. I scan the destroyed trailer. The singed black of charred wood maimed by the flames. The pale gray of fluffy ash. Unidentifiable items twisted and melted into grotesque shapes. Everything has been distorted from its prior form.

Everything except—

"Red, watch out!"

I lift my head toward the creak overhead. A second later I'm on the ground, pinned beneath Larson's body, a large tree bough crashing to the earth where I'd just been standing. I stare at the branch beside us with wide eyes, the gnarled, burned end as big around as my waist.

"You okay?" he asks.

"Yeah." My voice sounds weak. Shaky. Breathless.

I force myself to look away from the chunk of wood, knowing I should thank Larson for getting me out of the way, but I can't—my pride feels crushed enough already as it is. I need to get out of here, but I'm still trapped beneath him, the weight of his body against mine making my cheeks burn with embarrassment. I glance around desperately, looking for an escape, and spot something that makes me forget all about my discomfort.

"What's that?" I ask, pointing to the charred mound where the propane tank had been, the anomaly that had caught my eye right before the branch fell. I push Larson off me and crawl forward for a closer look. Whatever the artifact had once been, it looks like it was made of smaller, squarish objects.

"What *is* that?" Larson frowns as he squats next to the edge of the pit. "I don't have any gloves on me or—"

"Here." I fish out one of the nitrile gloves I always carry in my pocket and pass it to him. "Let me take some pictures first."

I get to my feet and circle the pit, using my cell phone to document what we've found from every angle, focusing my attention on the unidentified objects as Larson pulls the glove on and gingerly picks up one of the pieces between his thumb and forefinger.

He turns back to me with a lopsided smile. "Nice catch, Red."

"What is it?"

"Exactly what we were looking for. You have any evidence bags in your pocket, too?" Pulling out my wallet, I remove a small rectangle of folded plastic and hand it over. He shakes his head, grinning. "Where do you keep your marker?"

"In my Jeep, which is at the state crime lab. You're going to have to handle that one on your own."

"Fair enough."

He heads back around the ruins to the front yard. This time I'm the one following close behind.

"Are you going to tell me what that is or not?" I ask.

"I believe it's charcoal. Same as you'd use for your grill to cook up a couple of nice steaks on your day off. And if it is, it's also the proof we need that the explosion was intentionally set."

"So you think someone cut the propane line to the house and, what? Dug a hole under the tank and set a bag of charcoal on fire as an incendiary device?" I ask.

I feel a rush of relief, because if it's true, then there's no way the blast was timed for my arrival, which means I wasn't an intended victim, and the photograph of Wesley I found really is just some sort of strange coincidence.

"That's exactly what I think. I had initially assumed that the ignition source had been someone inside the trailer using an open flame, but looks like I was wrong. Whoever cut the line arranged their own." He holds the baggie up for me to see. "Thanks to this little guy and his friends, this is a homicide investigation again."

20

MAGGIE

It's a relief to leave the blast site, even if driving the rental vehicle still feels like wearing a shoe embedded with the impression of someone else's foot. But the case is back on track. Larson is stuck at the scene until a forensic analyst arrives to document and collect our find, which means he'll be occupied for hours. Now if only Steve were back, and things weren't so awkward with my coworkers right now, I might get to breathe easy.

But even as I think it, I know it's not true. Because there's a killer on the loose. Someone purposely caused an explosion in my town. Three people are dead as a result. I need to discover who, and I want to know why.

Pulling into the CCPD lot, my eyes are drawn to the empty spot in the corner that Sue's Pinto usually fills. The need to hear her voice is overwhelming. I should check on her. Scrolling through my contacts as I walk up the ramp to the front door, I look for her home number. Though I have her cell memorized, I know she doesn't keep it on her when she's at her house.

I'm still looking as I walk inside. In an instant, I know that something is wrong. Kal spins to face me from the middle of the room, his expression a mix of misery and relief. He tries to smooth down his hair, standing in clumps from where he's run his hands through it. And by the looks of it, maybe tugged at it a bit as well.

"Chief, I think you should sit down."

I stare at him, knowing that whatever it is that he has to tell me, it's going to be bad. Is Sue's illness serious? Has something happened to her? Or Steve. He's been so tired, so strained lately. And he's been doing so much driving. People are crazy on the roads, and he's worn down. What if he's been in an accident?

I swallow hard, feeling lightheaded as I sidestep to the chair behind Sue's desk and take a seat.

Kal's head twists back and forth as he looks between me and his desk. Stacks of files still cover its surface. The ones on the floor have grown into towers, leading me to believe that he must have managed to empty the metal cabinets of most of their contents. Finally, he makes a decision, snatching a folder from the top of one of the piles before approaching me with it clutched in his hand.

My phone rings as he reaches me. I glance down and see Dr. Ricky's name on the screen.

"I should take this," I say, trying to buy time though I'm not sure why. Except that his expression suggests that I don't want to hear what he's going to tell me.

"That can wait a moment," he says.

I laugh nervously. "Have you met Dr. Ricky?

"Maggie."

This is going to hurt, I know it is. He pulls the guest chair from the far side of the desk over next to mine and settles beside me, the file still clutched in his fist.

"Chief, we have a big problem. I found the file for Ruby Anderson's case."

I exhale a huge breath. A wave of relief rushes through me,

trying to flush out the poisonous fear that had been weighing my limbs down only a second before.

"That's great news."

Only, the look he's giving me says that it's not.

"And?" I prod.

"Her body was never recovered."

"Which makes sense, since she was possibly alive this whole time. What supposedly happened to her, anyway? Dr. Ricky said her death certificate stated she had drowned—"

"I'm getting there."

I bite my tongue, doing my best to remain quiet.

"There aren't many specifics. It seems Chief Parker was a man of few words. But apparently, Ruby was kayaking at a place called Great Sparrow Falls when her vessel tipped. Since her body was never recovered, the ruling was made based on the accounts given by two people who witnessed the woman's death. This is where it gets tricky."

"Because the witnesses either gave a false statement or were incorrect?"

Kal grimaces. "Yes. And because one of the two witness was Sue."

My spine strikes against the back of the chair like I've been shoved. Air whooshes out of my lungs with the invisible blow. I stare at the file in Kal's hand like it's a grenade with the pin pulled, unsure whether to throw it and take cover or simply accept the fate of what's to come.

I think of the petite woman I've worked with for the last five and a half years. The one who has an endless supply of cartoon character pajama pants and knows how I like my coffee even better than I know myself. The woman who didn't hesitate to drive her rickety old car out to a rural crime scene to take me home because she knew that was what I needed.

The one who's become the closest friend and confidant I've

made since moving to the valley. No, more than that. Sue's become like family, my surrogate mother.

There must be some kind of mistake.

But what if there's not?

I thought I'd done something to upset Sue, but what if it wasn't me? Thinking back, her mood had shifted when she received Missy Anderson's call to report her husband missing. A man whose mother had supposedly died when he was still a child. Who may have been killed in the same explosion as a woman who has tentatively been identified as one Sue reported as dead two decades ago. An explosion that had been intentional.

"Chief?"

I clear my throat. "Who was the other witness?"

"A woman named Michelle Sanders."

"We need to locate her immediately. What else can you tell me? About the details surrounding the woman's death?"

"Not much. Just that Ruby had gone kayaking that day. And that Sue and Michelle Sanders were with her."

"Also kayaking? At Great Sparrow Falls?"

"That's what the report says."

The falls, a class-three rapids, is at the very edge of my jurisdiction, about two hours north of town. It's a popular spot for outdoor enthusiasts. Which, to my knowledge, Sue has never been. Try as I might, I can't imagine her manning a paddle out on the water. But would she have twenty years ago?

"Like I said, the details are sparse. The report states that Sue picked up the other two women that morning and drove them all out to the falls. That all three women were paddling in their respective kayaks when Ms. Anderson's tipped. When Sue and Ms. Sanders reached the vessel and righted it, it was empty. They searched their immediate surroundings, then later returned with help to scour a larger area, but their friend was never found."

"How soon after this happened was Ruby Anderson ruled deceased?"

"Immediately."

"What? That can't be right." Typically, without a body a family must wait seven years before petitioning for a death certificate.

"Yeah. I found that strange as well," Kal says. "But the date on the photocopied death certificate in the file is less than two weeks after the date the report was written."

A long moment of silence stretches between us.

"What do you think it means?" he asks.

"It could mean nothing," I say, wanting to believe it. "It's a small town. Maybe there were some details that were left out of the report to spare the family."

But the growing ache in my gut tells me there's more to it than that. That someone didn't want questions asked. But who? And what were they trying to hide?

Was the explosion a desperate attempt to keep that secret concealed? And perhaps most concerning—what does Sue have to do with it?

21

MAGGIE

Sue reported that she witnessed Ruby Anderson lose her life in a kayaking accident twenty years ago, but Ruby was still alive as recently as this week, until she died in the explosion. No, not died. Was killed. There must be a rational explanation. One other than that the woman I've grown so close to over the years purposely filed a false report.

I squeeze my eyes shut against an approaching headache and think about Sue's recent behavior. She had seemed fine when she picked me up from the scene the day of the explosion. Likewise, when she drove me to work the next morning. Or had she?

Now that I think about it, she'd kept a close eye on me the entire drive. Peppered me with endless questions. Had what I'd taken for concern really been something else?

No, I can't believe that. Not about Sue. But there's no denying that something strange is going on with her.

"Sue was on the phone when I told you that Dr. Ricky had tentatively ID'd the victim," I say, slowly working through the chain of events to help me process my thoughts. "She didn't start acting oddly until she took the call from Ronny's wife. She was probably just upset because an old friend's son was missing. That would explain why she was so pushy when I was talking to his wife, asking her own questions. Even then— Oh, I'm an idiot."

Covering my face with my hands, I groan.

"What?"

"On the drive back I called Dr. Ricky and told her I had a possible match for the unknown male in the explosion. Gave her Ronny's name. And requested that she test his DNA against Ruby's to see if there was a familial match. No wonder Sue reacted the way she did. She must have been in shock."

"Because Ronny might have been killed?" Kal asks. "Or because she believed Ruby was dead all these years?"

"Possibly both."

I ignore the tiny whisper coming from the dark corner of my mind suggesting an alternative—that Sue's response was guilt, not shock. Or even fear. Because if you'd spent two decades thinking you'd gotten away with a crime, only to discover that you hadn't... I shake the thought from my head and offer an alternative that doesn't make Sue a criminal.

"Dr. Ricky told me it would take her a while to catalog all the old injuries on Ruby Anderson's bones. What if those injuries were caused by being tossed about the rapids? She could have sustained a head injury, maybe even had some sort of amnesia."

"And, what?" Kal asks. "She just remembered who she was and came back to town now, after all these years? Then just happened to be killed in an explosion that was purposely set?"

The muscles in my neck draw tight, pulling my shoulders up under my ears. "You're right. That is a little too coincidental."

"Sorry."

"But it's not impossible. It's too soon to rule anything out."

What I can't understand though is why Sue didn't speak up

when she heard me say Ruby Anderson's name. If she really believed her friend had died all those years ago, like she reported, wouldn't she have had questions upon learning otherwise? It's more than a little suspicious.

It makes me think that Sue knew that Ruby was still alive. Or worse, that she knew Ruby had been one of the victims of the explosion. Could her startled reaction have been because she was surprised Ruby had been identified?

And when I asked her if she knew Ronny, she said no, only who he was because of his job at the trading post. But Ronny was twelve when Ruby supposedly died. Surely if Sue had been friends with his mother...

She lied to me. But why? What could she possibly stand to gain by being dishonest?

Or is the better question what does she stand to lose by telling the truth?

"Why don't we just talk to her?" Kal suggests. "I'm sure there's a perfectly reasonable explanation if we just ask."

He's probably right, but I can't, not yet. I've been hurt so badly by people who I've trusted before in the past. People who I loved. And I'm afraid that Sue's about to become one of them.

And if she's not? How will she feel when she finds out that I suspected she was? No doubt devastated.

Balling my hands into fists, I dig my nails deep into the flesh of my palms, resisting the urge to scream. I need more time, more details, before making a decision.

"Let's see what else we can find out first. I want to speak with Michelle Sanders, see what she has to say."

I look away as I say it, ashamed. Does Kal think that I'm treating Sue not as a friend, but as a suspect, already trying to build a case against her? Or that I'm trying to spare a friend's feelings by not questioning her when I should, even if it's at the risk of hindering the investigation?

Either is unprofessional on my part.

And though I'm hoping more than anything that any evidence we find will exonerate Sue, not implicate her, saving me from having a delicate conversation that I'm sure to botch, the realization that this is what I'm doing leaves me feeling slightly ill. Because I shouldn't be concerned with anything other than solving this case. I shouldn't let my personal feelings interfere with me doing my job.

Yet that's exactly what I'm doing.

Swallowing the lump in my throat, I continue. "We need to get our hands on Ruby Anderson's medical records. What if... maybe it wasn't even her in the explosion?"

Even as I say it, I know I'm grasping at straws. Kal gives me a strained look.

"A fax came in earlier from Karen over at North Country Medical Center. I was so worked up, I barely glanced at it."

"That must have been why Dr. Ricky was calling," I say. "I better phone her back."

I'd been anxiously awaiting her conclusion less than a half hour ago. Now I'm dreading it, because if the remains belong to Ruby, I have to consider Sue a suspect, no matter how much I don't want to.

Standing on shaky legs, I pretend I don't notice Kal's look of concern as I walk to my office, closing the door behind me. I need a few minutes alone to collect myself before making the call.

I have to figure out what I'm going to do if it's confirmed that the statement Sue gave reporting Ruby Anderson's death was false. I need to prepare myself for the possibility that I'm going to have to investigate my friend, but for what, I'm not yet sure.

Perjury? Obstruction? Or—though just the thought of it makes me ill, my breakfast rising in my throat, threatening to make a reappearance—murder?

22

MAGGIE

I settle stiffly behind my desk, my body feeling like it went ten rounds in a boxing ring and lost. I haven't been sleeping since Steve left. The worry of what will happen if he fails—or succeeds—in the grim task he's set out to do is a sinister force in the darkness that I can feel. Because either way, it's going to cost us both something. I'm afraid to find out what.

And I haven't wanted to even close my eyes since the explosion, the image of the blast, of the charred corpse that landed on the hood of my Jeep, seared onto the back of each lid. The knowledge of how close I had come to being a victim of what happened is a tender bruise I can't stop poking, a constant reminder of what a dangerous place this world is, both to myself and those I love.

Now this.

Sue was the first—and for a long time the only—person to welcome me to Coyote Cove. She ignored my prickly exterior and looked past any jabs she received, patiently waiting for me to come around and realize she wasn't my enemy. It didn't happen overnight.

Most of the residents of this tiny Maine town weren't happy

when an outsider—a woman, no less—took over as their chief of police. Many were outspoken about the way they felt. It was a bad situation, dangerous at times, made worse by my own behavior. It wasn't just that I lacked the charisma and social skills that could have helped disarm my detractors. There were times when I purposely antagonized them.

I was such a mess when I came here, eyes only on my long-term goal, a suicide mission of sorts. Sue was the one who stood by my side while I waged a war against myself. The one who held the predators at bay while I did so. Eventually, she came to fill the void left by the family that abandoned me and helped ease the loss.

I can't fail her now. I need to be at the top of my game. Because unless Sue has drastically changed over the last two decades, she isn't the type to make a mistake of the kind that's come to light. The more I think about it, the more convinced I become that she knows exactly what happened to Ruby Anderson twenty years ago—which means she lied.

Filing a false report is in itself a crime. But what else has she done? How serious is her offense?

If I lose her, I don't have much left.

I'm galloping toward the altar with Steve when I should be taking the time to reassess, all because I'm so desperate to hold on to what we have. I stopped him from turning himself in. Was that selfish of me? Foolish? Wrong?

Am I in danger of making a similar bad decision now? I'm supposed to uphold the law, not decide who it does and doesn't apply to. Yet here I am, already preparing to see whatever my friend might have done in shades of gray.

It's not the first time I've used my position to bend the law to suit myself. Hadn't I done the very same thing when Wesley Banks was killed? Now, I've found a photograph of the man at a crime scene, and I can't let anyone else investigating the case know out of fear that they'll discover the truth about what happened. What I've kept concealed.

And would I do it again? Absolutely. Which means I've learned nothing.

The phone wavers in my vision as my eyes go dry from staring at it so long. I know I need to pick it up and make the call. But which is the right one?

Removing my cell from my pocket, I check my notifications. Breathe a sigh of relief when I see I've received a response and open the thread.

Who is this woman having a bachelorette party? Do I know her? JK, of course I'll come!!! Can't wait!!!

I imagine Linda's surprise when she read my text about the party. She's right. It is out of character. But maybe that's what I need right now. To not be so much like myself.

Though I can't say which it is that puts a smile on my face—the knowledge that I'll get to see my best friend soon, or the idea of being someone else—it's a relief to not feel quite as broken as I was only a moment ago. I tap out a reply.

Any chance you could come early? I have the house to myself.

I hit send before I have a chance to overthink it. Place the cell face down on my desk, pick up the office phone, and dial Dr. Ricky at her extension in the autopsy suite, suspecting that's where I'll find her. Afraid of losing my momentum, the second I hear her voice I launch right in.

"Sorry I missed your call. I know you received Ruby Anderson's medical records from our local doctor's office. Was it enough to establish an ID?"

"Hello to you, too, Chief Riley. And yes, it was."

"So it's her."

"It is."

It's the answer I've been wanting to hear, only now I wish it weren't true. The moment I learned of Sue's involvement with Ruby's case, I started hoping that the remains belonged to someone else. That Sue and her friend Michelle had been correct, and Ruby Anderson had died that day at the falls twenty years ago.

"Have you made any progress cataloging her injuries?" I ask.

"I have."

"We located the police report. The victim was believed to have lost her life in a kayaking accident. Is it possible being thrown against the rocks in rapids would account for what you found?"

There's a long pause. Only the noise she's making on the other end of the line lets me know she's still there.

"Hello?"

"I heard you. Hold on a second."

My foot taps beneath the desk as I wait for her response. This could all be so simple. A rational, if unlikely, explanation.

Finally, Dr. Ricky grunts into the phone. "Sorry to disappoint you, but no. Both arms had suffered spiral fractures. That type of injury occurs due to a pulling or twisting force upon the bone, not blunt impact."

"Could they have been caused if she was grabbing at the rocks, trying to hold on to them?"

"In my opinion, that would be highly implausible. And I'm unable to confirm if the breaks occurred at the same time."

"You had said there were a number of old injuries you needed to catalog. What did you find besides the broken arms?"

"There was remodeling on multiple ribs. Those breaks could possibly have been caused by impacts against rocks while the victim was swept down the rapids, but a majority of the injuries were concentrated to the facial bones."

I think about being carried along, caught in a current. You'd have your arms out, even if they were broken, to keep your face from smashing into any obstacles. It's possible she was unconscious, but then her neck would be limp, her head to the side or angled down, not face-first.

"Then what do you think caused Ruby's injuries?"

"In my opinion? The woman was beaten."

A bubble of bile rises up my throat, coating my tongue in acid. My voice is barely above a whisper as I choke out a question. "How severely?"

"Quite."

"Can you tell when the injuries occurred?" I stare down at the crossed fingers in my lap, feeling foolish. But maybe they happened when Ruby was a kid. Or it's possible that they're more recent.

"Several of the injuries were within areas considered growth plates, but did not affect the development of the bones, leading me to believe that they happened while she was an adult. That said, given the state of remodeling, I'd say that they were quite old, possibly even decades. Considering the age of the victim, it's possible they occurred near the time she went missing. I'd need to consult with a physical anthropologist to give you anything more specific than that."

"Is there anything else?" I ask, though I'm only half listening, most of my mind occupied by my own thoughts.

"Yes. Ronald Anderson's dental records came in. They were a match for the male remains that were recovered, so I'm able to confirm ID on him as well. I've yet to receive the results of the DNA test you requested to confirm a genetic relationship, but you should know that I took the liberty of submitting a sample from the third victim of the explosion on the off chance that there's a familial connection there as well."

"That was a great idea, thank you."

"Yes, well, I'm anxious to see if it pans out. I'm planning on heading over to the serology department a little later today and staring at them until they complete the task."

On any other day, I'd laugh. Being under Dr. Ricky's watchful eye would be enough to make anyone work a little faster. And while I appreciate her efforts, I'm not sure they're necessary anymore.

Chances are the results will show that Ruby is Ronny's mother, and the third victim, Marie, who would have been born before Ruby was reported dead, is unrelated. Then again, this case has been full of surprises so far—maybe I shouldn't be so fast to assume what the findings will be.

After all, Ruby's youngest daughter would be right around Marie's age now. Given the oddities already surrounding this investigation, it's possible Dr. Ricky's foresight will reveal another unexpected turn of events.

"After you push that DNA test through, is there any chance you could come up here early?"

"Why would I do that? Don't you think my time would be best spent getting you as much information as I can about the case before your party?"

I feel bad because I told Linda we'd have the house to ourselves. Now I'm going to try to put her to work while she's here. I should at least ask before volunteering her. But I do it anyway.

"Because I have one. A forensic anthropologist, I mean. She'll be at the party, but I've asked her to come early."

"Sounds like this get-together will be more fun than I anticipated." In usual Dr. Ricky fashion, I can't tell if she's being genuine or sarcastic. "What should I bring?"

An image of her arriving at the house with a box full of bones flashes through my mind.

"Just the X-rays, detailed photographs, and your notes. Nothing... physical."

"I meant for the party," she says.

"Oh. I don't think you need to bring anything."

"I'll call Sue and ask. She'll know."

I suck in a sharp breath, barely able to draw air. Because Dr. Ricky's response? It's the same reaction I usually have. The same person I usually turn to. Is all that about to change?

Anxiety wraps around me, tightening in knots. Though I try to focus, I barely pay attention as we exchange parting pleasantries.

Am I numb? Or is it the opposite? Am I feeling so much that I can't process all the sensations? Each individual excruciating pain.

I stare into space until my vision grows fuzzy. The phone starts making a noise of complaint, reminding me to put it back on the hook. What have I done?

Dr. Ricky can't definitively say that Ruby Anderson's injuries happened around the time that Sue reported the woman dead. But Linda? She reads bones. It's what she does. Every muscle attachment, abnormality, and past injury tells her a story others would never see.

Someone physically assaulted Ruby Anderson, perhaps even injuring her badly enough that they thought they had killed her. What am I going to do if Linda determines that the age of the injuries coincides with the timeframe when Sue reported her dead?

23

MAGGIE

I feel frozen with indecision. Sickened by it, actually.

This technically isn't my case. I'm under no obligation to investigate the explosion—in fact, I shouldn't be. And though I've never let that stop me before, maybe I should let it now. I can forward Dr. Ricky's findings and the police report from when Ruby Anderson was first reported dead to Detective Martin and turn my back on this whole mess.

But as I think about what that future might look like, never having to approach Sue with questions about her innocence or guilt, not risking our friendship, yet at the same time no longer able to trust it, always wondering yet not truly knowing what happened all those years ago, I know that I can't.

I need the truth, no matter what it costs.

Shuffling through the clutter on my desk, I find the file I started with Ronald Anderson's missing person report. Grab it and stand, scroll through the contacts in my phone, and press dial. Kal glances up as the door to my office opens. I lean against the threshold as the call is answered.

"Yes, Detective Martin, hi, this is Chief Riley up in Coyote Cove. I wanted to let you know that I just spoke with the medical examiner, and she's finishing up her report as we speak. All three victims of the explosion have been identified."

I repeat the detective's question for Kal's benefit.

"Yes, the second set of female remains has been confirmed as Ruby Anderson's. I'm calling because the male remains belong to a local." I purposely don't give a name, though I do nod in response to Kal's questioning look. "Would you like me to make the death notification to the family, save you the drive back up here?"

He answers exactly how I expected him to.

"No, I don't mind at all. I'll get right on that then. Uh-huh, you, too."

Kal's already crossed the room and taken the case file from me by the time the conversation has ended. I watch as he types an address into the GPS on his phone.

"Thirty-two minutes," he says, handing the folder back to me. "You want me to text you the route?"

"I'd like you to come with me on this one."

Kal's eyebrows rise high, creasing his forehead. He knows I hate having the department closed during business hours, but I want him along for this visit, and without Sue here, there's no other choice. I can't help wondering if this is going to be a permanent predicament as I place the sign with my cell number in the window on the door, follow Kal outside, and lock up.

I get in the passenger seat of his cruiser, buckle my seatbelt as he starts the engine. Kal is silent, but I know he's aware of what's really going on.

Though I called Detective Martin under the pretense of notifying Ronald Anderson's next of kin about his death, what I really got was permission from the investigating officer to speak with the family. Ruby Anderson's family. And if what happens when we reach her husband's house seems more like an interrogation, well, that's just my poor delivery of bad news.

"Who are you going to start with?" Kal asks, glancing over

at me as he turns onto North Mountain Highway, taking us out of town.

I pinch my lower lip as I think, because this is going to be tricky. How do you break the news that a loved one believed dead for the last twenty years was actually alive all that time? But there's no chance for a happy reunion because now she really is dead? And, oh, yeah, by the way? Your son is, too.

Yet, if I inform the man about his son's death first, he might be too distraught to have a useful conversation, the fresh loss surely more painful than one two decades old. But I don't think I have a choice.

"The son," I say, wincing. "Don't you think?"

"I do."

The gentle drum of tires on asphalt fills the space between us. Ahead, a long stretch of road snakes its way through the valley. To either side, an endless wall of trees pens us in, smears of brown and green blurring together as we speed past.

"We should take turns," Kal suggests. "I can inform him of his son's passing, you can tell him about his wife."

There's logic behind the tactic. If Mr. Anderson reacts poorly to finding out about his son, chances are he'll associate the bearer of the news with his grief and anger. He'll be less likely to cooperate with that person. If that person is Kal, it gives me a better chance of successfully questioning the man about the details surrounding his wife's supposed death.

"Deal. We also need to try and get contact info for Ronald's siblings," I say. "According to the wife, he has two sisters, Rachel and Rene, but she didn't have their addresses."

"She didn't know where his sisters live?"

"She said she thought they were both still local, but wasn't sure."

"Sounds like maybe they weren't that close."

I don't respond, studying my lieutenant's profile instead. I'm the last person who should judge another family's relationship, but that doesn't mean I can't be curious. Because Kal had told me himself that he *was* close to his family. That he missed them. Moments later, he got upset and clammed up when I suggested ways for him to see them, because he didn't want that to happen.

Families are strange. They all have their private languages. Some of them use those languages to communicate their love. Others, to conceal their crimes.

24

STEVE

Just as I'm crossing the threshold, I'm struck by an overwhelming sense of danger. My heart thrashes inside my chest like I'm standing at a precipice, like one more step will carry me over the edge, crashing onto the rocks below. I take that step anyway.

The room is dim, lit only by a small desk lamp that sits at Dr. Curry's elbow. A floral scent hangs faintly in the air. I listen to the tinkle of the water feature by the door, the tick of the metronome as the pendulum rocks back and forth.

"I'd like you to close your eyes for me, Steve. Good. Now, as you breathe in, I want you to concentrate on relaxing. As you breathe out, I want you to release the tension in your body. Imagine yourself melting into the cushions."

I listen to the doctor's soothing voice, doing my best to follow her directions as she guides me through the process until we're down to my toes. I feel strange, like I'm outside my body, watching myself sleep.

The doctor sounds distant as she says, "Now I want you to focus on one single night from your past. Do you know which one I'm talking about?"

I'm in a crowded apartment, standing by myself against the wall, a red Solo cup in hand. Watching as my best friend, Wesley, chats up a girl across the room. "Yes."

"And which one is that?" Dr. Curry asks.

The girl laughs at something Wesley says. His face darkens, jaw tensing as his eyes narrow. He wasn't trying to be funny.

"The night Wesley killed Georgia."

"Yes, good, Steve. I want you to travel back through the years to the night Wesley killed Georgia. Are you there?"

"Yes."

"Good. Tell me what's happening. What do you see?"

I stare down at my dirt-caked hands in my lap, feeling ill. Though my stomach is empty, I have the sensation of being overly full, so stuffed with guilt and shame, remorse, and horror, that I fear I might erupt.

Wesley clears his throat from the driver's seat beside me, but I don't look at him. I can't. Instead, I pretend I'm alone in the car. Lift my eyes and gaze out the window at the darkened night beyond.

I shouldn't be here. But where can I go?

A building appears in the distance. A store. I squint, trying to make out the wording, hoping it might be a place to take refuge.

"What does the sign say, Steve?" she asks.

"McAllister and Sons."

"Good. Can you see any other signs nearby? A street sign, maybe?"

"No."

"Do you know where you're going?"

"Home."

"I need you to go further back, Steve, to before you got in the car to go home. Can you do that for me?"

The scrape of the shovel sets my nerves on edge. I can feel it in my bones, in my teeth, in the hairs at the center of the goose-

bumps peppering my body. I stand with my back to the noise, staring out at the field of wheat, the stalks bobbing gently on a breeze I'm too numb to feel. The scent of freshly turned soil fills my nose.

This can't be happening.

And as the night falls silent, just the gentle rustling of leaves from the giant oak towering over me, I can almost believe it isn't. It's just a dream, a bad one. After tonight, I can forget all about it.

I squeeze my eyes shut, trying to block out the muffled grunt of exertion. The hollow thud as the body lands in the hole. My breath is coming too quick, too loud, almost blocking out the sounds of the shovel getting back to work. I wrap my arms around myself, rocking back and forth on my feet, trying to wake from this nightmare.

Then he's beside me.

I flinch, startled. Wesley's eyes flash in the moonlight as he gestures toward the car with his head. We start the return journey across the field.

"Is he saying anything?" Dr. Curry asks.

"No."

"What's he doing right now?"

"Holding out his hand."

"For?"

I tell her. Then add, "The one he gave me to use."

"For what? Did Wesley tell you what to do with it?"

"No. I just knew."

Catching sight of my now empty outstretched palm in the glow of the moonlight, I come to a stop in the middle of the field. Squat down and grab a fistful of dirt, rubbing it against my skin until I can no longer see the red stains.

"What did you do, Steve?"

Straightening, I take a final glance over my shoulder, knowing I'll never be the same again.

"What did you do?"

I sit up with a start, blinking at the room around me. My gaze lands on Dr. Curry, rigid in her chair, staring at me with wide eyes.

"Did it work?" I ask. "Did I remember?"

She swallows hard. Her voice cracks as she tries to respond. She coughs to clear her throat, then says, "No. I'm sorry. You couldn't access the memory."

"I couldn't remember anything?" I ask, leaning forward.

She jumps to her feet. Her hands twist each other.

"Only that you passed a store called McAllister and Sons on your way back. And that you think the field may have been wheat."

Her hands pull apart and she beckons toward the door. I ignore the gesture, hoping for more answers.

"Is that normal?" I ask. "If I remembered that much, shouldn't I have been able to remember more?"

She backs across the room.

"Not necessarily, no."

I stand reluctantly as she opens the door, walks out of her office and into the waiting room.

"I'm sorry, Mr. Winters. Hypnosis doesn't always work for everyone," she says as she stands beside the exit, waiting for me to join her. "But I wish you the best of luck."

I step over the threshold into the hall beyond. Turn back toward her to finish the conversation. But the door is already closed. And as I stand there, staring at it, debating whether or not I should go back inside, I hear the lock click.

25

MAGGIE

Sometimes things are difficult for a reason, to keep your from doing something stupid. I can't help but feel like this is one of those times.

We have to turn around several times before spotting the claustrophobic tree-lined drive barely visible from the main road. There's no marker. No mailbox. Just a narrow gap in the woods barely wide cnough for a vehicle to squeeze through.

A disquieted feeling forms deep in the pit of my stomach as we pull into the pine-needled drive. This is not a place that someone is just going to stumble onto. It was extremely well hidden. Yet, despite that, someone has gone to the trouble of posting NO TRESPASSING signs every thirty feet or so along the way.

Whoever lives here is not someone who wants visitors.

We continue on anyway, winding through a quarter mile of forest until the drive opens up onto a small clearing. A run-down house sits at its center. The cedar shingles are rotting, the scalloped trim and paneled shutters need a fresh coat of paint, and the flowerboxes are filled with weeds instead of splashes of color.

Exiting the cruiser, Kal and I pass through the remnants of a picket fence and onto a cobbled walk mostly hidden under dirt and dead leaves that leads to the front door. Was this the effect that Ruby's death had on her husband? Had her loss caused him to withdraw from the rest of the world? Let his home fall into disrepair?

If that's the case, what's going to happen when he learns about his son? Or that he's lost his wife a second time? Though I'm not looking forward to finding out, I knock on the door without delay.

Immediately, an angry voice yells from inside, "Don't know who was stupid enough to ignore all them signs, but I got a shotgun here with both barrels loaded that's gonna make you regret it."

Kal and I take a step apart to either side, sheltering behind the threshold framing. The pop of him unsnapping the strap on his holster echoes mine. Though my right palm rests on the grip of my firearm, my left holds a finger up, signaling for him to wait.

"This is Chief Riley from the Coyote Cove Police Department. I'm here with Lieutenant Kishore. We're here to speak with Nathan Anderson. We have some news for him. I'd appreciate it if he'd come outside so we could talk. Without the shotgun, please."

The request is answered by silence. I shift uncomfortably as we wait, nerves ratcheting. Wondering what he's doing. Debating whether one of us should sneak around to the back of the house, or if it's smarter for us to stick together.

"Sir?" I call.

"Yeah, yeah." The door opens, releasing the stench that had been trapped inside, a nauseating mix of ripe trash and unwashed body. I take an involuntary step backward, away from the odor, as a man appears before me. He scratches his ample belly through a yellowed undershirt, eyeing me suspiciously as he says, "Figured you'd probably want me to put some pants on."

"I appreciate that. Are you Nathan Anderson?"

"Yeah, that's me. Now you gonna tell me what you're here for?"

Kal moves closer to the man. "Sir." Clearing his throat, he says, "We regret to inform you that your son has been identified as one of the casualties in a recent incident that happened just outside of town. An explosion out on Old Mill Road. Don't know if you've heard about it?"

"Sure I did. That was Ronny?"

"One of the victims, yes. I'm very sorry for your loss, sir. Please accept my sincerest condolences."

The man shrugs like he wasn't just told his son was dead. Mutters, "Stupid SOB."

Unsure if I heard him right, I ask, "Excuse me?"

He turns his jowled face my direction, tiny beady eyes peering out from beneath a heavy brow. "World's not suffering much of a loss. More of a favor if you ask me."

I've seen grief handled in a variety of ways, but never like this. I sharpen my focus, searching for a sign that his bluster is just a show to cover his sorrow, but there's nothing. His coloring, posture, and respiration have remained the same. I take that as my cue to proceed.

"Do you know the woman who was renting the trailer where the explosion took place? Marie Bouchard?"

"Can't say the name rings a bell."

"Can you think of a reason why your son would have been out that way?"

"No idea."

"Have you heard anything we might find interesting about what happened?"

The question is answered by a shake of his meaty head. "Nope."

"How about your daughters? Can you tell me where I can find them?"

"Whatcha want to do that for?"

I don't give him the real reason I'd like to speak with his surviving children. Instead, I say, "I'd like to inform them of their loss."

Anderson snorts. "Doubt they'll see it that way, but it's your time. Last I knew, the older one was living in some dump out on Route 3 with her litter of kids and some fella named Raymond."

"Is that his first name or his last?"

"Beats me."

"What about your youngest daughter? Rene, is it?"

"No clue. You'd know about that one better than I would."

"What do you mean?"

He scowls at me. "What do you think I mean? Girl can't keep herself out of trouble. You'd think at least one of the three would have been worth the time it took to make them, but the whole lot is useless. We're done here."

"Actually, sir." I take a step forward as he takes one back. I brace myself against the stench as I say, "There's something else we need to discuss with you."

His already narrowed eyes turn into slits.

"We found your wife, Ruby."

"Well, did you now? Where'd she finally wash up?"

I watch him closely as I say, "Actually, sir, her remains were discovered inside the trailer that exploded. She was the third victim."

"This some kind of joke?"

"No, sir. I'm aware that your wife was presumed dead after a kayaking accident twenty years ago, and I realize this must be a shock, but we're sure. Ruby died in the same explosion that killed your son."

His eyes drill into mine, hardening into stone as he barks out a harsh laugh, the sound of it sending a chill up my spine and down my arms. "Well, you don't say. She always was a willful one. And he was always an ungrateful little momma's boy."

"So you aren't surprised?"

His fingers curl into fists, knuckles cracking as he says, "Oh, no, I'm surprised. I guess I just don't much care. As long as she's dead now, that's all that matters."

Kal muffles a cough, choking on his reaction. I force myself to swallow mine down and ask, "Do you have any idea where she's been all this time?"

"Not a clue."

"Does she have any relatives she might have—"

Nathan Anderson interrupts me by rudely holding his hand out in front of my face.

"It's time for you to leave."

"Mr. Anderson—"

"I'm not interested in hearing anything else you got to say. That woman's been dead to me for a long time. It's best you just forget those questions of yours. Trust me. You don't wanna press your luck on this over a woman no one ever missed."

"Is that a threat?" Kal asks.

"Nope. It's a guarantee."

With that, he slams the door in our faces. Kal starts speaking, but I quickly raise a finger to my lips and gesture toward the car. He nods his understanding, waiting until we're settled inside and traveling back up the driveway toward the main road before saying, "That was strange, wasn't it?"

I shrug, unsure what to say, because there's something scratching at the back of my mind, but like an itch in the very middle of my back, it remains just out of reach. It has something to do with Nathan Anderson's reaction. He'd seemed to genuinely not care when informed of his son's death—he hadn't reacted at all.

But when I told him about Ruby, his hands had drawn into fists and his jaw had clenched—he'd been angry. Why? Did he feel tricked? Betrayed? Or was it something else? And how dangerous could that something be?

26

MAGGIE

I need to speak with someone I can trust. Someone who's lived in Coyote Cove long enough to know the ins and outs and secrets of this little town. Usually in this situation, I'd go to Sue, but I can't do that now, can I? Not with her somehow wrapped up in what happened to Ruby Anderson.

But what exactly did happen to the woman? And how is Sue involved?

I wish I could believe that she was above suspicion, but if there's one thing I've learned, it's that no one is. Everyone is capable of committing unspeakable acts. Corner them, threaten their loved ones, make them desperate... Or sometimes it's as simple as having—or jeopardizing—something they want.

Nathan Anderson still harbors a great deal of anger toward his wife after all these years, and I can think of only one reason for why that could be that would also involve Sue. Had Ruby gotten involved with Sue's husband and somehow been injured as a result of the affair? If that's the case, who would Sue have lied to protect?

Nathan? Doubtful. Her husband? Maybe. Herself? Probably. Her kids? Definitely.

But there's no way. I've met Sue's children. I'd have an easier time believing that I blacked out one night twenty years ago, found my way to Maine, and attacked Ruby myself than I would that either of Sue's kids were capable of doing something so violent at such a young age, even if their motivation was to protect their family.

But what if the child she was protecting wasn't hers? Sue's definitely a mother hen type. She even tucks me under her wing, though I don't fit, a prickly emu added to her nest of downy baby chicks.

Ronny was twelve when his mother went missing. Could he have had something to do with what happened, both then and now?

He'd been leaving the trailer when the explosion occurred, that's why the door was opening, how he got blown onto the hood of my Jeep. Had he been the one to set the blast, miscalculated the timing and still accidentally been at the scene when it blew?

Matricide is rare, but it's not unheard of.

We hit a pothole, jarring me from my thoughts just as we pass a battered mailbox leaning on a post beside a rutted drive. I scan the road ahead of us to either side, but other than the asphalt beneath us and the occasional glimpse of power lines strung between poles hidden by the trees, there's not another sign of civilization in sight.

Coyote Cove is beyond what one might define as rural. Like many of its residents, the Andersons lived on the fringe. There's no telling what truly lies at the end of the occasional narrow lanes that lead into the darkness of the woods.

What if I've got this all wrong?

Whatever happened to Ruby Anderson, the woman was missing for twenty years. Could she have been kept somewhere, held against her will this whole time? The thought causes a shudder to quake through me. Maybe Sue didn't speak up about Ruby not because she was guilty, but because she was scared.

Only, the Sue I know doesn't scare easily. I have a hard time believing she'd allow herself to be intimidated into keeping quiet. Unless the risk wasn't to her. Maybe someone threatened her family. I glare at myself in the side mirror, knowing I need to stop going in circles inside my head in a desperate attempt to figure out a way for Sue to be innocent and find a way to get some actual answers instead.

"You okay?" Kal asks.

I glance over at him, catch his eye, and offer a tight smile.

"Fine. Just thinking."

"You want to talk about it?"

"Not just yet."

As Kal turns onto Main Street, I assure myself that whatever the future brings, I'll survive it. I'm too stubborn to do anything else. Pretending that Steve's face hasn't appeared in my mind beside Sue's, I push all my personal concerns aside. "Turn here," I say.

The car bumps into the parking lot, coming to a stop as we pull into an empty spot.

Unbuckling my seatbelt, I say, "I'll walk back."

Kal casts a curious look in my direction. "You want me to come with you?"

"Not this time."

"I can wait," he offers. I shoot a pointed look at the clock on the dashboard, where the digital display shows it's fast approaching five o'clock.

"Go home and get some rest. A little fresh air will do me good."

I flash what I hope is a reassuring smile and exit the vehicle. Wince at the sharp tone of the bell that announces my arrival as I push my way inside the office of Margot's Motel. Organize my thoughts as I cross the empty room. Though I hear rustling coming from the back, no one comes out to greet me.

"Hello?" The murmur of a hushed conversation carries through the closed door. I glance up at the camera mounted to the ceiling, suspecting I'm being watched. Leaning across the counter, I raise my voice and call, "Margot? Is everything okay?"

"I'll be right there."

I look around the room as I wait. The rack of pamphlets mounted to the wall on my right has recently been refilled, information on skiing and snowmobile rentals replaced by brochures advertising guided moose tours and boat cruises on Beaverhead Lake. A stack of mail sits unopened on the corner of the desk. A cable-knit sweater is draped across the back of the chair behind it.

The sweater is one I recognize. My lips lift into a smile. It grows into a smirk. I push it away, so it won't be heard in my tone, replacing it with a stern expression as I say, "Margot, when you come out, you can bring Joe with you."

The door creaks open, one of Margot's dark eyes appearing through the gap. "I don't know what you're—"

I gesture toward the sweater, struggling not to show my amusement as she blushes. Sighing dramatically, she tosses the door open the rest of the way, calling over her shoulder, "Really, Joe? We might as well just take out an ad in the local paper if you're gonna leave clues everywhere."

Steve's Grandpa Joe emerges from the back grinning. Rounding the counter, he presses a kiss to my cheek. "Still wouldn't be able to pull anything over on this one."

"So this is what a reunion looks like?" I ask wryly.

"Nah. That looks like a bunch of old guys sitting around drinking beer and talking about their youth like their lives are already over. Got boring real quick, so I took off early and came up here instead."

"Does your family know where you are?"

"Not exactly."

"And I assume I'm not supposed to mention that I saw you?"

"I'd appreciate it if you wouldn't." He gives me a wink, then grows serious. "I know I shouldn't ask you to keep any secrets. And I'm going to tell them, just not quite yet. So if you could maybe just forget to mention it..."

Rolling my eyes to the ceiling, I shake my head. "You were never here."

"Thanks, Maggie. Best future granddaughter-in-law ever." He squeezes my shoulder as he turns to Margot. "I'm gonna go grab us some takeout, give you two girls some privacy."

Margot sighs happily as the door closes behind him, wearing a dreamy smile. It vanishes when she notices me watching her. "What?"

"Nothing."

"Why are you here, anyway?" She drops into the chair behind the desk, crosses her arms, and eyes me with suspicion.

"Do I need a reason?"

"Yes. You looked stressed."

"Do I ever not look stressed?"

She doesn't meet my eyes as she shrugs. "Is this about Steve?"

"Why would you think that? Did Joe say something?"

"Only that he's down in Massachusetts right now. Seems like with your wedding right around the corner, he should be sticking closer to home. If y'all don't hurry up, me and Joe are gonna beat you to the altar."

"It's that serious?"

"At our age, everything's serious. So why are you really here?"

"What can you tell me about Rufus Parker?"

"You mean that bozo who called himself the chief of police before you came to town?"

"Yes."

"Why do you want to know about him?"

"I just do."

Her eyes narrow at me, disappearing into the folds of her face.

"Okay, fine. I'm working a case that seems to overlap with one of his old ones, and it's looking like maybe he botched his investigation."

"Save yourself some time and just assume that he did."

"Was he really that bad?"

Margot snorts.

"Then how'd he the keep the position for so long?"

"Because he wasn't just a member of the good ol' boys club, he was the president. Knew how to scratch the backs of those around him, when to look the other way. You know the type."

"Are you saying he was corrupt?"

"Can't say for sure. But what I can tell you is that his family has deep roots in the area. Deep, rotten roots."

"How rotten?"

"You know that stench when—"

I put up a hand to cut her off before she can finish. "Can you tell me any particulars?"

"Let's just say that the dynasty's biggest problem was women's rights. Mainly that they got some."

Given the way I've been treated by some of the men since coming up here, Chief Parker—the few times I've been unfortunate enough to run into him—among them, I find the statement believable. But that doesn't necessarily make them rotten. "Can you elaborate?"

"From what I heard, his daddy ran around on his momma so much that any time he liked a girl, little Rufus had to run the name by him to make sure they weren't related."

The thought sickens me.

"You know why the building the hardware store is in is a historical landmark?" she asks.

"No, why?"

"Because it was one of the first buildings built in Coyote Cove, back when it was nothing more than a bunch of logging camps. Used to be the Howling Boy Saloon. Give you one guess what really went on there. Give you another as to the family who owned it. Made their fortune as pimps."

Maine has an interesting history with prostitution—mainly that it recently became the first state to decriminalize it, but only for those of age selling services, not the buyers. And those forced into it against their will is still an issue. Not to mention that human trafficking is a huge problem this far north. Being so close to the border makes it easy for predators to get their prey out of the country.

Could that be what happened to Ruby Anderson? Where she's been all these years? I add it to my growing list of possibilities, the one I should be narrowing down instead of expanding.

"You think he still has a hand in the old family business somehow?" I ask.

"I suspect you'd know about it if he did."

"How so?"

"The man is completely inept. Did you know the CCPD used to be over twice as big before he ran it into the ground?"

"Seriously?"

As a member of the town council, Margot is technically one of my bosses. And as the most intimidating person I've met in Coyote Cove, I suspect the one who managed to get a woman hired for my position.

"You ever hear of having a police chief for a department of two? The budget used to be over quadruple what it is now. He blew our state funding. The man refused to bust one of his buddies. All his revenue came from tourists until they caught on and stopped coming, and you know how much the Cove depends on their money. The whole town was on the edge of collapse. How do you think I got enough votes behind me to get him out?"

"I thought he retired."

Margot snorts. "That man would have kept taking a salary for doing nothing until his dying day."

"No wonder he's been such a pal to me," I say wryly.

"That the kind of friend you want?"

I wince, thinking about friendships. About allowing yourself to be vulnerable enough to trust someone. About Sue.

"No."

"Didn't think so."

I debate for a moment before asking, "What can you tell me about Ruby Anderson? Or her husband, Nathan?"

"Never heard of them."

"What about Michelle Sanders?"

"Now her I did know. Not well, but enough to feel bad about what happened."

A strange sensation takes hold. I lick my lips, doing my best to ignore the rapid beat of my heart as I ask, "And what was that?"

"She died. Hit and run."

"When?"

"Not long before you came here, actually. You'd already been hired for the job, so what... less than six years ago?"

It feels like an ice cube's been dropped down the back of my shirt. I shift uncomfortably, the chill spreading through my body. Is it possible that Michelle had been killed because someone needed to silence the woman before the new police chief came to town? Was her death part of some kind of cover-up?

Margot had said Chief Parker had a habit of looking the other way when his friends broke the law—now I'm curious if the same would extend to employees, too. Because Sue had been his receptionist long before she'd been mine. She'd worked with him for almost thirty years.

What had their relationship been like? The Sue I know isn't one to curb her opinion, but she's never once mentioned to me the lackadaisical way he'd run the department. Was that because she was okay with it? Benefitted from it, even?

A darker thought occurs, one that leaves me feeling gutted: Has the friendship I thought we shared really just been an act? A ruse to keep me influenced and under control?

My chest feels so tight I'm afraid my words might choke me. I push them out anyway. "Did they ever find out who did it?"

"I don't think so." Margot picks up a pen from her desk, frowns as she taps it against her leg. "It was real sad business. Left behind a little girl. Well, a teenager, but still. Couldn't have been easy for the kid."

A long moment of silence stretches between us, turning into two, and I can't help wondering what Margot would say if I told her what was happening. The case, my fears, my suspicions. But I know I can't.

"Thanks, Margot," I say, backing toward the door. "I appreciate it. I'll get out of your hair now."

"He's a good man, you know."

I stop midway through my retreat. Slowly lift my eyes to hers.

"What?"

"Joe. He's a good man."

"Oh. I know that." For some reason I thought she'd been talking about Steve. Or maybe I'd just been hoping. Because finding out that she wasn't leaves me feeling strangely disappointed.

"He hasn't told his family yet because I've asked him not to."

"Why?"

"It's kinda hot, feeling like we're sneaking around. It makes me feel young again."

But the sad pinch to her expression tells me there's something else, another reason why she doesn't want Joe to tell Steve and Diane and Izzy where he is this week.

"And what else?" I prod.

Her thin lips purse. Her gaze hardens. Just when I think she's going to dismiss me, the tightness in her features relaxes. Her voice is uncharacteristically timid as she says, "What if they don't like me?"

"Who wouldn't like you?"

"Uh, most people."

"That's because they don't know you."

"Except for the ones who do. They tend to dislike me the most."

"I don't."

"You're different."

"Well, so are they. They seem to like me, and my anti-fan club is even bigger than yours."

"True. When you put it that way, I suppose I have nothing to worry about. Don't let me keep you."

She brushes her hand through the air in a shooing motion, refusing to look at me. I'm guessing she's embarrassed. Margot's the last person I would have expected insecurity from. Seeing her vulnerable side seems surreal.

I pause in the doorway on the way out, glancing back over my shoulder at the older woman. Though she still won't look at me, there's something odd to her expression. And though I can't say what it is, I feel the strangest sensation that I have yet another friend I have to worry about losing.

27

MAGGIE

This is a truly horrible idea, but I don't let that stop me. The sun has sunk behind the mountains, tangerine rays streaking a darkening sky with the last dying embers of day by the time I pull into the driveway. I don't know what I had expected, but it wasn't this.

Maybe something darker, more sinister, the kind of place that kids run past. Instead, hunter green shutters gleam in the fading light, framing the bright white exterior of a single-story ranch-style home that appears in immaculate condition.

A small wishing well sits in the middle of the yard next to a fake wooden bridge, both surrounded by statuary, smiling frogs and dogs with wagging tails frozen in time. It looks like a miniature Disneyland. The front door opens, and suddenly it all makes sense.

The woman who appears gives me a friendly smile, smoothing the apron covering her dress as she prepares to come greet me. But she's taken only a single step over the threshold when she stops. She glances behind her. Her shoulders rise and her head lowers. She gives me a quick apologetic look before retreating.

A moment later, Rufus Parker appears, scowling at me as I close the distance between us. I return the man's unfriendly glare with one of my own.

"Would have thought you'd be long gone by now," he says. "This town ain't no place for a princess."

"Well, if I see one, I'll let her know."

He sniffs hard, throat rattling as a chunk of phlegm knocks against it. I don't bother to hide my disgust as it shoots past me, landing on the nearby grass like a bright green garden slug.

"What brings you out this way?"

"I wanted to talk to you about one of your old cases."

"You have questions, read my report."

"I did."

"And?"

"I didn't find the answers I was looking for."

"That supposed to be funny?"

"No. It was your report that's the joke."

"Listen here—"

"You can talk to me, or you can talk to a detective from the state police, your call," I interrupt.

He sighs heavily and jerks his hand through the air like I'm some gnat he's trying to shoo away. There's a distinct lack of enthusiasm in his voice as he asks, "Which case?"

"The disappearance of a woman named Ruby Anderson. Do you remember it?"

"I do. Enough to know that you need to work on your reading skills. The woman didn't disappear. She died."

"See, the funny thing about that is, it's true. But her death occurred only a few days ago. So whatever you thought happened, it wasn't the truth."

His jaw tenses, eyes narrowing.

"That's a pretty big mistake—"

"Hey, now. Don't you go pointing fingers. I did my job. Investigated what happened."

"Did you?"

He stares at me for a long moment. If looks could kill, I'd be on my way to Dr. Ricky right now on a stretcher. Finally, he asks, "What did Sue tell you?"

"What do you think she told me?"

He glances over his shoulder. Takes a step closer to me before hissing, "You listen here. I don't know what trouble you're trying to start, but this is one hornet's nest you don't want to kick."

"And why's that?"

"Because I know my rights. And I know that if that woman got killed, then it's the staties' case, not yours. They probably wouldn't be too happy to find out that you're sniffing around their murder investigation."

"I never said she was murdered."

His eyes flash.

"Get off my property."

I shrug and give him a smile. "Okay, sure. I was just trying to extend a little professional courtesy, see if you wanted to clear up any mistakes. I mean, you have to admit, it was a pretty big error, especially considering that a woman was declared dead based on your report. Makes me wonder what else I'd find if I looked at more of those old files of yours you left behind. Bet there's plenty the state's attorney would find interesting."

His stricken expression tells me everything I need to know —the man is scared. He has something to hide.

I return to my rental car, hold it together until I've backed out of his driveway and driven far enough down the street that his house is no longer in sight, then I pull over onto the side of the road. My hands tremble on the steering wheel, my torso convulsing with the force of the sobs I refuse to release.

As the first tear escapes and slides down my cheek, I smack the dashboard. I pound on it again and again until my palm is so far past throbbing that it's grown numb. Until I can swallow down the scream inside my chest and function again.

I feel hollow as I pull back onto the road and continue my drive home, like a part of me has been removed. That was a stupid, stupid thing I just did. I don't know what I was thinking.

Only, I do.

After talking to Margot, I'd been convinced that Rufus Parker was the exact type of man Sue would have delighted in tormenting. I'd gone to see him sure that his animosity toward my friend would show through, leaving no doubt in my mind that there was any chance that they'd cover for each other, providing the confirmation I needed about Sue's innocence.

But that hadn't happened. If anything, it's just left me more open to the possibility of her guilt.

28

MAGGIE

We walk around in life pretending to be safe and secure, but the truth is, it's a lie. At any moment the world we've constructed for ourselves could come crashing down around us, and there's not a thing we can do about it. It's a humbling thought. And a frightening one.

I sit on the couch, picking at a plate of pasta. Cooking had seemed like a good idea at the time. It kept me busy, required me to keep my thoughts on what I was doing, literally instead of figuratively, and I needed to eat. But I haven't been able to choke down more than a bite, and it has nothing to do with my limited culinary skills.

Tempest whines beside my right foot. She pitter-pats her front paws, dancing with the strain of behaving. I glance over to Sullivan on my left. He licks his lips and gives me a hopeful smile.

Abandoning the plate on the end table, I slide onto the floor between them. Wrap my arms around them as they step onto my lap, squirming excitedly against me. Close my eyes and relish the feel of their warm bodies as they give me kisses. I imagine staying in this moment, where I feel loved and safe and things are simple, forever.

But I can't. I have a job to do.

I wish I could call in sick tomorrow.

Wouldn't that be a luxury? One I haven't had since I came to Coyote Cove. I know there are certain perks that come with being the boss, but I can't remember what those are right now.

Groaning, I give the pups a squeeze and wiggle out from under them. Put my dinner on the ground for them to share, then settle back on the couch, this time with a thin stack of folders on my lap—and an imaginary one in my mind with Wesley Banks's name on it.

I open the file from when Ruby Anderson supposedly died, struggling to decipher Chief Parker's barely legible scrawl as I read the incident report for the dozenth time, knowing that I have to be missing something. There's no way that Ruby's death certificate would have been signed so soon based on the information before me.

That morning, Sue picked up Ruby and their friend Michelle Sanders to go kayaking. The three women went out on the rapids at Great Swallow Falls. Ruby's kayak tipped. When Sue and Michelle reached the vessel and turned it back over, Ruby wasn't inside.

When I get to the end, I begin again. And again. And again. Each time I hope to spot the clue I'm looking for, the detail that will crack this case open. But the words don't change.

Maybe I need to go about this a different way.

Despite growing up in Florida, I've never been much of one for watersports. Pulling out my phone, I google kayaks. Done with my dinner, the dogs jump up onto the couch, settling against me as I scroll through the results. Clicking the link to a large store that specializes in outdoor recreational equipment, I start reading sales descriptions. I had no idea there were so many different kinds and variations.

Selecting a model used for whitewater, I skim the features. I'm rubbing at the tension in my forehead, feeling completely overwhelmed by the time I reach the bottom of the page. Feel a small glimmer of hope when I notice the video that's been imbedded and press play.

The clip is short, less than thirty seconds, but it gives me an idea. I exit back to my browser and enter a new search. An instant later, a list of results populates. Three seconds after that, I'm waiting for a video posted by a user who calls themselves Great Swallow Guru to load on YouTube.

My heart quickens as the opening frame shows a view that I recognize as Great Swallow Falls. The iconic rock resembling a swallow taking flight that juts from the rushing water just before it spills down a fifty-foot drop to the river below is unmistakable. This is it, this is—the phone rings, Steve's name flashing across the screen.

I feel a moment of hesitation about answering it, then immediately feel guilty. I press the green button to accept the call.

"Hi, stranger."

"Hey."

Something about Steve's tone makes the hope I'd been feeling just a moment before vanish. My brows lower so much I can see them along the top edge of my vision.

"What's the matter?"

"Nothing." He speaks the word too quickly. "Just calling to say good night."

"What's going on there? How was your day?"

"Fine. I'm just really tired."

It's a lie, and every cell in my body knows it. I don't doubt the tired part, but something most definitely is not fine. We'd promised we'd stop this—lying to each other.

But that's exactly what I'd done when I told him about the explosion. Underplayed what happened and omitted the part about finding a photograph of his dead blackmailer so he wouldn't worry. Is he doing something similar now? If so, it has the opposite effect, making my concern skyrocket.

I want to reach through the phone and pull the truth out of him. I want to know every detail of what's happening. But maybe... maybe I should trust him.

It goes against who I am, what everything my experience in this life has made me be. But how can I expect our marriage to work if I hold him to a different set of rules than I hold myself? Which means I need to let him know what's really going on here.

"Steve?"

"Yeah?"

"I need to tell you something."

"You were hurt in that explosion, weren't you?" he asks, a note of panic in his voice.

"No, but... I found something while I was there. Something that shouldn't have been." I listen to the steady sound of his breathing on the other end of the line while he waits for me to continue, but I can't figure out how to tell him. This is harder than I thought it would be. Finally, I just spit it out. "There was a picture of Wesley."

"Wesley Banks?"

"Yes."

He's inhaling too quickly now, exhaling too forcefully. I'm worried that he's hyperventilating. Or having a panic attack.

"Are you okay?" I ask.

"What do you think it means?"

"Honestly? I'm not sure. The woman who rented the trailer had a prison record. It's possible she knew him. Or he might have known one of the other victims—the assistant manager from the trading post."

Steve curses. "There's a difference between knowing someone and having a photograph of them. I mean, who even prints out pictures anymore, anyway?"

"Inmates. That's why I really don't think it's anything to worry about. I'm sure it's just a coincidence."

"I don't like this. You should have told me, Maggie. I'm coming home."

"No, Steve—"

"Yes."

"No. Listen, there's no need to worry. I just, I wanted to be honest and let you know, because we promised we wouldn't keep secrets from each other anymore. But everything's fine here. Really."

He makes a noise that sounds like a growl.

"Tell me how you really feel," I joke.

"I just don't want to see you get hurt."

"I won't."

"You don't have a very good track record in that department."

"I realize that." A tense silence stretches between us. It makes me wish that I hadn't told him. And I definitely can't fill him in on the whole Sue thing now. Squeezing my eyes shut, I say, "I'll be extra careful. And if it makes you feel any better, I've been bringing Kal with me on interviews."

"I still don't like it."

"I know, but it's my job."

"I love you, Maggie. I don't know what I'd do if anything happened to you."

"I don't plan on that being something you'll ever have to find out."

His breathing has slowed back to normal. "Good."

"And everything's okay with you?"

I pretend not to notice the pause before he answers. "Yeah. Of course."

"Talk tomorrow, then?"

"Uh-huh. Good night. I love you."

"I love you, too."

And then he's gone. I focus on the little things. Pulling air into my lungs. Pushing it out. My heart as it slows from its too rapid beat. Relaxing the muscles in my face until it stops feeling like a crushed soda can. Finally, I open my eyes.

They land on the phone clenched in my hand. The screen is still on. The YouTube video is paused, the rushing waters of Great Swallow Falls as still as the rock that resembles a bird in flight. But this time, I notice something in the image that I missed before.

I press play, watching as the video pans the scenic view. Rewind the clip and watch it again from the beginning. Whoever's recording must be standing just outside the driver's door of their vehicle, filming over the roof, because as the image moves from left to right, they capture more than just the sky and the trees and the water and the rock. They capture the top of their kayak, held on its side in a roof rack.

I pull the folder with Parker's report out from beneath Tempe's fuzzy bottom and flip it open. Find the words I know are there. Even though this is the break I was looking for, it doesn't feel like a victory.

It doesn't matter how difficult or easy it would be to fall out of a capsized kayak. What type of kayak was being used. Or even what level of experience the rapids required.

Because according to the official report in front of me, on the morning of the accident, Ruby Anderson was picked up in a vehicle driven by Sue Bailey and already occupied by Michelle Sanders.

Sue drove them out to the falls. The same Sue who refuses to get a newer car because she's so attached to the ancient Pinto she drives now. The only vehicle she says she's been behind the wheel of since she bought it new. The hatchback with the whistling moonroof.

I do a quick search and discover they stopped manufacturing Pintos in 1980, over twenty-five years before Ruby

Anderson's supposed death. Which means it's the vehicle Sue had when they drove to the falls. The big problem with that is, there's no way they drove two hours north of here with three kayaks strapped to the tiny sliver of Sue's hatchback's roof—the car simply isn't big enough for that.

It's proof that Sue and Michelle told at least one lie that day. But how many more lies were there? And is it just a coincidence that only one of the women who were there that day is still alive to know that answer?

29

STEVE

Darkness presses in around me from every side. Out here in the
woods, far away from the city, the blackness of night is absolute.
It's enough to make you think you've been swallowed. To make
you worry that you'll never see light again.

I pull into the drive and stare at the house before me, drying
my sweaty palms on my jeans. There are no signs of life. Every
window is dark and empty. The place looks abandoned. And
though that seems reasonable considering it's two in the morning, I find myself battling the irrational fear that the little
niggling voice in the back of my head is correct, and no one is
here.

That I'm in the wrong place. Or I don't belong. Maybe I've
been imagining things, my life the way I wanted it to be, not the
way it is. That at any moment I'll wake up in a strange bed in an
unfamiliar room to find that it was all just a dream.

Though I keep telling myself the odd sense of uneasiness
I'm feeling is a remnant from the appointment I had earlier with
Dr. Curry, some kind of hypnosis hangover, or disappointment
with the lackluster results, I can't help but suspect that it's more

than that. And despite having the entire five-and-a-half-hour drive to think about it, I still haven't come to any conclusions.

Because there was something odd about how the doctor acted after I woke from my trance. The rather cold way she hurried me from her office into the waiting room, guiding me to the door.

According to her, I hadn't recalled much while I was under, only that I thought the crop planted around the oak tree was wheat, and that we had passed a shop called McAllister and Sons on the way back, but something about her behavior has me paranoid that I said more, maybe something that changed the way she thinks about me.

And she didn't have me make an appointment for a second session before I left. I guess she thinks that if those two minor details are all I could come up with during an entire hour, another would probably just be a waste of time. But there's no denying that the whole thing has left me feeling uneasy.

How worried should I be?

Very.

That's why I'm here, isn't it? My session with Dr. Curry aside, something else is going on, and whatever it is now involves Maggie.

The photograph of my former best friend that she found at the scene can't be a coincidence—but Wesley Banks is dead. I saw him die with my own eyes. Felt the unnatural weight of his lifeless body, the waxy texture of his blood-leached skin as I helped roll him into a ravine. There's no way I'm mistaken about that.

So then, is it supposed to be some kind of message? If so, I have no idea who sent it. And I'm afraid of what it means.

Because if Maggie's theory is right, and Wesley was friends with the woman who lived in the trailer, or the guy who worked at the trading post, who else had Wesley befriended in the area?

To what purpose? And if any of those cohorts are still alive, what else might they be planning?

Nothing good, I'm sure.

Exiting the vehicle, I creep up to the house. The sky above is dark, clouds of indigo velvet concealing the moon and stars. The only sound is the soft whisper of the grass beneath my feet, a branch cracking under the weight of a nocturnal creature somewhere in the surrounding trees. The mournful howl of a coyote in the distance.

Silently, I climb the porch steps and let myself inside. Tiptoe through the darkness of the house. Hear the unmistakable click of a gun cocking as I enter the living room.

I freeze, once again filled with the irrational fear that I'm in the wrong place, that I'm trespassing.

"Steve?"

I can just barely make out Maggie's form through the shadows. She releases the dog she has pinned under each arm and lowers the gun, uncocking the small revolver she keeps in her ankle holster. The dogs run over, jumping up to greet me.

"What are you doing here?" she asks.

"What are you?" I flick the light switch, illuminating the room.

She winces against the sudden brightness from her spot on the couch. Her face looks blotchy, her eyes puffy and red, like she's been crying.

"I must have fallen asleep," she says.

"And the gun?" I ask.

"You startled me—you're lucky you didn't get shot. What were you thinking?"

I cross the room and take a seat beside her on the couch. Wrap my arms around her, pulling her close. The tension in my body evaporates as she returns the embrace, melting against me. For the first time in days, I can breathe easily.

"I was thinking that I had to see you, make sure you were okay with my own eyes."

"I told you—"

"I know. I'm sorry. I just… I missed you."

"I've missed you, too."

I bury my nose in her hair. She nuzzles against my chest.

As much as I don't want to ruin the moment, I have to. "I don't like this whole thing with the Wesley photo. It makes me nervous."

Her body goes rigid in my arms. "Yeah."

"You really think it could just be a coincidence?" I ask.

"What else could it be?"

I'm afraid she'll think I'm crazy if I voice my thoughts—that maybe Wesley somehow recruited an army among our friends and neighbors, the people we share this tiny town with. That we're both in danger. So instead, I just say, "Trouble."

She lifts her head against my chest until our eyes meet. "I don't want you worrying about it."

"How can I not?"

"You've got enough on your plate already. And there's no use wasting time or energy on this when we don't even know if it's an actual problem yet."

She looks away as she says it, a melancholy note to her voice, and I can't help questioning if her words are for me, or herself— and if we're even talking about the same thing anymore.

"Is everything all right?" I ask.

"Yeah, why?"

"I don't know. You seem kind of sad."

"I'm just tired." She gives me a small smile. It looks forced. "Are you staying the night?"

I grimace. "I shouldn't. I finally have a lead on where to look for the tree. I just wanted to come check on you first."

"Oh."

She sounds disappointed.

"But I don't have to leave just yet. I can stick around for a while if you want?"

"No, that's all right. I don't want you to hit rush hour on your way back. And I have a busy day tomorrow. I should probably get some sleep."

"Are you sure?"

"Yeah, it's fine. Besides, the sooner you wrap this up, the sooner you're home for good, right?"

"Right."

Maggie stands, pulling me to my feet, and as I follow her out of the living room and toward the front door, I push all worries and concerns out of my head other than not messing this up. What we have—there's no replacing it.

And though the last thing I want to do right now is leave her alone, I don't have a choice. If there *is* someone who Wesley was working with, then once I find Georgia's body and turn the location over to the police, that will end whatever leverage they think they have on me. It's the only way to keep us safe.

30

MAGGIE

I jolt awake, gasping so hard I'm left panting, trying to catch my breath. My body is tensed, braced for danger. But besides a headache, I don't think my alarm poses an actual threat.

Feeling around on the nightstand until I find my phone, I jab sightlessly at the screen until the annoying noise stops. Lie there with my muscles ticking and twitching as the adrenaline coursing through my veins fades, not wanting to start my day just yet.

Steve's unexpected visit last night seems like a hazy dream, *felt* more than remembered. And while it provided a distraction of sorts from my obsessing over Sue's connection to the Ruby Anderson case, I'm not sure how helpful it was. Because the respite was too brief.

It left me feeling even more desperate. Even more convinced of how alone I am. Because in the end, he left.

When you have only a handful of people in your life, the loss of just one of them can be felt profoundly. The desire to hold on to them, even when you shouldn't, is hard to resist.

I wish he had stayed.

If I had asked him, he would have. Instead, I lied and said I was okay. I smiled and told him to go. And now I can't help feeling bitter that he couldn't read my mind and see the truth.

Because I'm not okay.

How could I be, with what's going on? I might be losing one of the most important people in my life.

My whole friendship with Sue—or what I thought was a friendship—might have been a lie constructed for the sole purpose of concealing a past crime.

Or is it crimes? She worked with Chief Parker for almost thirty years. How close were they? Are they still? How deep does this cover-up go—was Michelle Sanders' death truly an accident, or was it murder?

I'm not going to get the answers I need lying around.

I force myself out of bed. Stumble to the bathroom, wash up, get dressed, and let the dogs out.

When they come inside, I make my way to the kitchen. Stopping at the threshold, I stare at the empty coffee maker, sighing exhaustedly. My stomach growls.

If I lived somewhere normal, there'd be plenty of restaurant options for breakfast. But in Coyote Cove, only Em's is open right now, and because of that, there's bound to be a line out the door.

I'm considering the cholesterol-laden offerings at the gas station when a knock at the front carries through the house. My breath catches, but at least I don't jump. Hopefully this whole skittish thing has run its course.

Or maybe not. Because when I peer through the peephole and see Kal standing on the front porch, I want to hide.

My lieutenant lives right down the street from the police department. If he drove so far out of his way this early in the morning, something must be up. My already bubbling stomach roils as I open the door.

"I brought breakfast," he says, balancing several Tupperware containers.

I stare at the food, wondering what blow it's meant to soften. Hoping that he's not here to quit. And praying that at least one of the plastic bins holds something with cheese or sugar in it.

"Come on in." I step back to make room. Kal passes one of the containers to me as he enters. I open it and peek inside. Inhale deeply as I find my prayers answered. "French toast?"

"Do you like it?"

"It's exactly what I need. Thank you. You didn't have to go to all this trouble."

Kal shrugs. "Couldn't sleep."

I lead the way to the kitchen and set out silverware. Brew some coffee. Take a seat beside him at the island. I pick up my fork, stab a bite of French toast drowning in syrup, yet I don't eat. My mouth waters, but the tightness in my throat suggests I won't be able to swallow. Not until I know why he's here and what catastrophe I'm going to have to deal with next.

"You aren't here to give your notice, are you?"

"What? No."

My anxiety eases enough that I try a bite of food. The sugar heads straight to my bloodstream, giving it a much needed boost. The carbs wrap in me a hug.

"But we do need to talk."

I force myself to keep chewing, though the flavors that had been so comforting just a moment ago have gone sour. I raise my eyes to his.

Kal's gaze holds mine, an unspoken conversation taking place, and suddenly I get it, why he's here right now—so we have a chance to talk before we go to the station, just in case Sue shows up today.

I release a sigh that leaves me slumped over the countertop. "I brought Ruby's file home with me last night. Thought if I read it enough times that I'd find something in there that would... I don't know, exactly."

Kal makes a noise deep in his throat. "Honestly, I've never seen such a shoddy report before. There isn't enough in there for Parker to have conducted an actual investigation."

"There's enough to prove that Sue lied," I say softly.

My lieutenant's eyes widen.

Dropping my gaze to my hands in my lap, I say, "In the statement Sue gave, she said she's the one who drove them to the falls that day. In Michelle's, she states that all three of them were in separate kayaks. There's no way that they got three kayaks up there on top of Sue's Pinto."

"Maybe she had another car back then?"

"She's so attached to that thing because it's the first car she ever bought. The only car she's driven since. And she got it new, we were just talking about it the other day."

"Maybe she exaggerated about that. She could have driven someone else's vehicle."

"Possibly. But even if she did, Sue is tiny. And Ruby was, too. I was looking at kayaks last night online. It would have been a stretch for either woman to get even one of the smaller, lighter models on or off the roof of anything taller than the Pinto. Maybe Michelle Sanders was tall enough to do it, but if I want to find out, I'm either going to have to get my hands on a copy of her autopsy report or ask her next of kin."

Kal's mouth drops open, jaw slack. He stares at me, not blinking.

"It's true. I found out last night when I was talking with Margot. She was the victim of a hit and run."

He runs a hand through his hair as he processes the information.

"It could have been an accident," I say. "But it also could have been on purpose, a way to keep her from sharing a secret someone didn't want told. Either way, it leaves Sue as the only surviving witness of what happened all those years ago."

"Don't you think it's time to talk to her?" he asks. "Nothing formal, not an interrogation. Just to ask her version of what happened."

I shake my head. "Not yet."

As a tense silence descends between us, I know Kal doesn't understand. My lieutenant tends to believe the best about people until they give him a reason not to. I like that about him. I need it, to balance out my always-suspect-the-worst mentality.

And I appreciate that he seems to be on Sue's side. After all, he could be right—it is possible that she drove a different vehicle to the falls that day, one better suited to transporting kayaks. That she really did think that her friend had died out on the rapids.

But if I believed that, I wouldn't be feeling so gutted right now, would I? I wouldn't have made the decision to put off talking to her until I have more of the facts, so I can get my questions right the first time without giving her the opportunity to cover her tracks if she lies to me.

I tear off two small pieces of French toast and hold them under the table. I know I shouldn't. I've been giving the dogs way too much people food lately, and it's not good for them. I just so badly need to feel like I'm making someone—anyone— happy. As their little tongues lick my fingers clean, I know I've succeeded. I just wish I had faith that I'll be able to manage the same with a human again. Including myself.

"I talked to Chief Parker last night."

"You what?"

I avoid Kal's gaze as I shrug. "After speaking with Margot, I was sure he and Sue must have hated each other. I thought if I talked with him, I don't know... It was a bad idea."

"What did he say about her?"

"Nothing. Only asked what she had told me."

It breaks my heart to see the questions in his eyes. Questions about Sue, ones that didn't exist for him two minutes ago. But now I know he's wondering: Did Sue lie because Parker asked her to? Or is it possible that Parker fudged his report to help her?

"How long did they work together?"

"Almost thirty years."

It's a long time. Longer than most marriages. Is it possible to not feel some sense of loyalty to someone who you've spent that much of your life with?

He clears his throat. His voice is thick as he asks, "So what's our next step?"

"It seems like someone went to a lot of trouble to keep the truth about what happened to Ruby Anderson—and possibly Michelle Sanders—concealed. I want to talk to their kids, find out what they know, see if they remember something that might shed some light on the truth. We need to locate the youngest one, Rene."

"I'll see what I can find out."

I nod, staring off into the distance through the kitchen window. "While you do that, I'm going to pay the other two a visit, starting with Michelle's daughter. I want to get her take on what happened to her mother, try to narrow down exactly how many crimes we're dealing with here. And I want to make sure the woman's actually dead."

"You think she could still be alive like Ruby was?"

"At this point, I don't think we can rule anything out. But if she is still alive, I want to find her before it's too late to keep her that way."

Kal nods. Stands and carries his plate to the sink, taking an unnecessarily long time to rinse it before putting it in the dishwasher. When he turns back to face me, his jaw is set with determination.

"For what it's worth," he says, "when we get to the bottom of this, I think we're going to find that Sue's innocent."

I try giving him a smile, though I'm not quite sure I succeed. "For what it's worth, I really hope you're right."

And I do. I need it to be true, because I'm not sure I can handle losing Sue from my life right now.

But my job isn't to look for what I want to find. It's to look at the facts. And right now, the facts look pretty grim. So as much as I'm wishing for the best, I'm preparing myself for the worst.

31

MAGGIE

My entire body is tied into knots. It makes it difficult to swallow, hard to breathe. But it's no less than I deserve, because I'm a horrible person, a terrible friend.

I keep asking myself why I can't just trust myself to confront Sue instead of sneaking around behind her back like she's guilty. And I keep answering myself: because she *is* guilty. I'm just not sure of exactly what yet, and until I am, I can't risk tipping my hand until I get a better grasp on what's going on here. If keeping my distance is the only way for me to stay objective, then that's what I have to do.

Still, as I leave the CCPD parking lot, averting my eyes from the noticeably vacant space usually occupied by Sue's Pinto, an ache forms deep in the pit of my stomach.

Though I might not trust Sue's truthfulness on Chief Parker's report, I trust—or at least I trusted—her in terms of our relationship, and that doesn't come easily for me. I have to believe that our friendship is true, that she really does care about me the way I care about her.

And I can't stop worrying that something might actually be

wrong. What if she's really sick and needs help? So I can't help sending her a quick text asking how she's doing.

Feeling a bit better but not 100% yet. Thanks for checking.

Her reply comes so fast that I know that the woman, who despite being able to type sixty words a minute on her computer pecks painfully slow at her phone's keyboard, already had a response ready to go—she was just waiting to hit send.

I don't let myself think about it too closely, instead focusing on the task at hand, turning down a side street just on the edge of town. Scanning the numbers affixed to the front of each building, I pull up in front of a long two-story apartment complex, park at the curb, and draw a deep breath.

Thanks to Kal's efforts alphabetizing Chief Parker's archives, we were able to find the report for Michelle Sanders' accident relatively easily. Much like his report on Ruby Anderson's supposed death, the file containing his investigation into Michelle's hit and run was depressingly slim. There wasn't much besides a copy of the autopsy report, but that in itself told me plenty.

The woman had been hit from behind, suffering open breaks to both fibulas and the left tibia. Her left femur was fractured. Soft tissue damage was extensive—had she survived, she would have required surgery and extensive rehabilitation just for those injuries alone.

Cause of death was a traumatic subarachnoid hemorrhage. In Michelle's case, blood leaked into the space in between the brain and the membrane that covers it, an area normally filled with cerebral fluid. The increased pressure displaced vital brain tissue. With the nearest hospital equipped to handle such an extensive injury over thirty minutes away in Lincoln, the poor woman never stood a chance.

From a pathological standpoint, Michelle had been a healthy fifty-five-year-old woman until an automobile had rammed into her from behind. Though Chief Parker had believed that the injuries were caused by a car, considering the height of the injuries on Michelle's body, chances are good that she was struck by a vehicle with a higher bumper, like a truck or SUV.

A truck or SUV driven by someone who hit a woman from behind and then drove off, leaving her broken and alone, dying in the middle of the road, instead of getting help.

I check the apartment number on my phone one last time before pocketing the device and exiting the vehicle. Though Chief Parker's report had failed to include the name of Michelle's daughter, she was mentioned in the scant obituary I found online.

Katherine Sanders was listed as Michelle's sole survivor. It makes me feel even worse for what I'm about to do, but I don't let that stop me from entering the enclosed stairwell at the side of the building and climbing up to the second floor.

Walking quickly down the narrow breezeway so I don't have time to think too much about the painful memories I'm about to stir up for some poor young woman, I stop in front of unit 205 and knock. The smell of burned food carries on the wind. A TV plays too loudly, blasting the sound of a basketball game. And the door opens.

My mouth drops as I stare at the twentysomething before me. "Kit?"

"Hi, Chief Riley." The friendly smile on her face falters. "Um. Why are you here?"

This is a small town. I should have realized I might at least recognize Michelle's daughter, but the name Katherine hadn't rung any bells. Kit, however, who I now realize must go by a nickname, is more than just a familiar face.

The young woman, who can often be found behind the register at the local gas station, knows how many times a week I sneak the soda I tell myself I shouldn't be drinking. The potato chips I tell myself are an adequate lunch. And the Reese's Cups I use to self-medicate.

"Kit," I say again, trying to buy a little time to collect myself. "Are you also known as Katherine Sanders?"

She nods warily.

"And your mother was Michelle Sanders?"

"What's this all about?"

"I'm so sorry to bother you, but I was hoping I could ask a few questions about your mom."

"Why?"

Not wanting to tell her the truth, I lie. "I've been going through some of Chief Parker's files and saw that her case was still open."

Kit's expression relaxes. She exhales heavily and a fraction of the smile she wore when she first saw me returns to her face. "Oh."

"I'm afraid there wasn't much information in the file. I wanted to stop by and ask if you knew whether Chief Parker ever had any suspects in mind or not?"

"If he did, he never told me."

"What about in the days and weeks leading up to the accident. Had you noticed anything strange? Or did your mom mention anything unusual?"

"No."

"No threats, then?"

Kit's head shifts until she's looking at me from the sides of her eyes. They narrow slightly, her gaze hardening. Her hand wraps around the molding, knuckles turning white, but whether she's propping herself up or barring me from the doorway I couldn't say.

"None."

"Did she have any enemies?"

"Of course not. Why are you asking all this? I thought what happened was an accident."

"It most likely was," I assure her. "There's just been some..."

Her face has turned pink. Unshed tears fill her eyes, threatening to fall. And it's all my fault.

"Listen, Kit, I'm going to be honest with you. Your mom's name was mentioned in conjunction with another case. She didn't do anything wrong," I assure her, "but it has raised some questions."

"And you were hoping I had answers."

"Yes."

"What did you want to know?"

"Was your mom friends with Chief Parker?"

The look she gives me lets me know that they weren't.

"Any reason in particular?"

"Have you met the man?"

"Unfortunately." I flash her a brief smile. "What about Ruby Anderson? Did your mom ever mention the name?"

Her brows furrow as she thinks. She sounds unsure as she says, "No."

"But?" I prod.

"But I remember playing with Rene and Rachel Anderson when I was little. Were our moms friends?"

"I think they might have been."

Her frown deepens, a shadow passing over her face.

"What are you thinking?" I ask.

"I was just trying to remember their mom... I can't, though. But I don't think their dad was very nice."

"Why do you say that?"

Kit shrugs. "I'm not sure. Just a feeling."

Given the exchange I'd had with him, I'm under the same impression of the man, but I don't say so. Instead, I ask, "What about Sue Bailey?"

For the first time since I started this conversation, Kit gives me a genuine smile. "Yeah, I know Sue."

"She and your mom were friends?"

"Best friends. Growing up, Sue was like my second mom. She was the one to bring down the hammer whenever I started acting up. Kept me on the straight and narrow. She still checks up on me."

I feel my insides loosen a little. That's the Sue I know. The one I trust. The one who wouldn't cover up a crime. And yet...

"I have one more question, and it's going to seem like a really strange one."

Kit laughs nervously. "They haven't been strange so far?"

"Not comparatively speaking, no."

She swallows hard, but nods. "Shoot."

"Are you absolutely sure that your mom is dead?"

Her eyes widen, nostrils flaring. She looks at me like I've knocked on her door trying to sell her a cockroach as a house pet. Any rapport we'd had just a moment ago is gone. Her voice is cold, dripping disdain as she says, "Yes. I identified her body with my own eyes."

I'm not surprised when she shuts the door in my face before I can finish apologizing. I can't imagine what it must have been like, to have been the one to identify a loved one who lay broken and lifeless, and it kills me that I probably made the image return fresh to her mind.

But it had to be done. I had to know for sure. Because I've already had one woman come back from the dead. I needed to know if I should expect another.

32

MAGGIE

I lock the car door, but don't feel safe. Hold my breath as I start the engine. It's almost a shock when nothing happens.

I had enough enemies already without alienating yet another person in this tiny town. Was adding one more to the list worth it? No.

The only interesting thing to come from my awkward conversation with Kit was that she used to play with Ruby's daughters—and that she thought Nathan Anderson wasn't nice. It's not strange that she doesn't remember Ruby. Doing the math, Kit couldn't have been more than four or five when Ruby supposedly died. Plenty of kids don't remember their friends' parents from when they were that young, the adults simply faceless beings in the background.

So what had Nathan Anderson done to make him so memorable—and leave Kit with a bad impression?

I need to speak with Ruby's children.

Kal's working on finding out what he can about the younger daughter, but if the older one, Rachel, is still local like Nathan believed, then she shouldn't be too hard to locate. There can't be too many Rachel's living off of Route 3.

I type her name and Coyote Cove into the search bar on my phone. The first result is a newspaper article about the girls' track team at the local school. The second is her mother's obituary. I click the link, reading the brief paragraph twice.

It doesn't mention any service being held in Ruby's memory. It doesn't say anything about where to send flowers, donations, or gifts. The only thing it contains is a list of the family members who survived the deceased.

It's a pitiful summation of a life, but would mine be any better? I don't even have a family to name, just two pups, an overstressed, preoccupied fiancé, and a career that's seen better days. This is exactly what I don't need to think about right now.

Exiting the page, I return to my search results. The third link is to a white pages listing. Scrolling down the list of women who share the name Rachel Anderson, I stop when I spot one the right age. The address is local. I copy it, paste it into my navigation app, then exit the parking lot without a second thought.

I find myself the lone driver on the highway, the empty road snaking limply ahead of me like a dirty ribbon abandoned by a cat. On my left, a solid curtain of trees keeps me pinned against the rock wall that soars above me on my right. I feel like a mere speck lost among a sea of vegetation and stone.

Coyote Cove is vast, the mountain valley a seemingly endless expanse of wilderness. Yet at the same time, it's also small. Two-thirds of the people here know each other. Families go back generations. The gene pool is shallow, but the secrets are deep—and no less wild than the forest that contains them.

I slow as the arrow on the screen shows my turn approaching. Pull into a driveway that's a crumbling mess of broken asphalt and park in front of a drab manufactured home between a battered minivan with a missing rear bumper and an ancient station wagon.

Exiting the vehicle, my boots raise a cloud of dust as they hit the ground. It follows me to the front, where tears in the window screens and the smell of mildew signal the first stages of neglect.

I knock, wincing as a baby wails somewhere inside in response. The sound grows louder, reaching a crescendo as the door before me opens. I know I've earned the dirty look aimed at me from the woman standing there, trying to soothe the child.

She appears harried as she shushes the baby, casting a worried glance over her shoulder as she slips outside, forcing me to take a step back. Two children exit the house with her, clinging to fistfuls of her baggy jeans as she eases the door shut behind them.

"Are you Rachel?" I ask.

"Who are you?" The woman again looks anxiously behind her.

"Chief Maggie Riley, Coyote Cove Police Department."

She visibly pales, almost losing her grip on the squirming baby perched on her hip as she hurries to adjust her hair, bringing it forward over the left side of her face.

"What happened there?" I ask, gesturing to the fading bruise that she's trying to conceal.

"Nothing. I just bumped into an open cabinet." She laughs nervously, though it rings hollow. "Forgot to close it when I was cooking."

But the area is larger than the corner of a cabinet door. Rounder. About the size and shape of a fist. I force a smile, letting her think I believe her.

"Are you Rachel?" I ask again.

She nods. "Listen, Miss—"

"Chief. Police Chief Riley."

"Right. What did you want?"

"Have you heard from your father lately?"

Her expression tightens as she shakes her head. "Why, what happened to him?"

"Nothing that I'm aware of. But I'm afraid I have some bad news for you."

She glances again at the closed door behind her. Wipes at the sweat beading on her brow, then gestures toward the shade of a tree nearby. I follow, waiting patiently as she settles the baby in a bucket swing hanging from one of the boughs.

As soon as her arms are free, she turns toward the other children, gently removing her clothes from their fists. "Go play."

The little girl gives her a woeful look before trudging off to a dingy, dirt-stained kitchen set. But the larger child, a little boy, refuses to listen.

"You heard me," she says. "Go play with your sister."

"Up," he demands, pulling on one of her arms.

The child is half her size. There's no way he should still be carried, even if she were able to lift him.

"Not right now."

He jerks her arm roughly. Her body folds at the waist. The sound of the smack made as the boy strikes her face is shockingly loud. A bright red handprint immediately forms over the bruise I had noticed before. Yet she doesn't even wince.

The child gives her a filthy look before stalking off to join his sister. I watch as he snatches the toy frying pan she'd been playing with from her hand and slings it away.

Rachel gives me a wan smile as I turn to her, but I can't make myself return it. This isn't the first time I've wanted to discipline someone else's child, but that doesn't make it any easier to stomach. A part of me feels like making the offer. But I let it go. With behavior like that, I expect I'll be meeting the kid again soon enough.

"So," she says wearily. "What's the bad news?"

"It's about your brother."

"Ronny?"

"Yes. His body has been identified as one we recovered

from an explosion on the outskirts of town a few days ago. Please accept my condolences. I'm very sorry for your loss."

She blinks heavily. Stares at me for a long moment, then asks, "Are you sure?"

"I'm afraid so."

"But how? How do you know it was him?" Her voice gets louder, her tone more upset.

"He was identified using dental records."

"Ronny went to the dentist?" Rachel gives a shocked laugh as she rubs a palm against her cheek in a self-soothing manner. "I'm sorry, it's just such a surprise. We weren't close, but still... And the boy I grew up with would barely even brush his teeth. I guess it just goes to show how much I didn't know him."

"Had you seen him recently?"

"No."

"What about your sister, Rene?"

Rachel takes a step backward, toward the house behind her. "They didn't get along. I don't think she's seen him in years."

"What about you? Do you two keep in touch?"

"No."

"So you don't know where she is?"

"I'm afraid I don't."

"Is the name Michelle Sanders familiar to you?"

Though I see a flicker of recognition behind her eyes, she shakes her head.

"What about Sue Bailey?"

"Yeah, I know Sue. She used to try and come around and check up on me."

"Why'd she stop?"

Her eyes dart hard to the side. "Don't know. Guess she realized I was old enough to take care of myself."

"Were she and your father friends?"

"No."

"What about your mother?"

"What about her?"

"Did Sue know her?"

"What does it matter? She's been gone a long time."

"Rachel." I speak slowly, keeping my voice soft. "About that. I'm not exactly sure how to tell you this, but your mother died in the same explosion that killed your brother."

The blood leaches from her skin, leaving the woman deathly pale. "That's impossible."

"I'm afraid it's true. She was identified by the serial number on a surgical rod that had been used to repair a broken arm. Do you remember her ever having a broken arm?"

Rachel's eyes flash nervously. She snatches the baby from the swing so abruptly, she startles the child. Its face turns purple, screws up until it's all cheeks and open mouth as it releases a sob that makes my toes curl in my boots.

"Hush," she pleads. Then to her other children she barks, "Get inside."

The kids scurry ahead of her.

"Wait, Rachel—"

"No. You need to leave."

She hurries off, leaving me standing by myself, staring at the closed door. That's not the response I imagined getting when I told her that the mother she thought had been dead for the last two decades had been alive until earlier this week

But Rachel's surprise had been overshadowed by something else—fear.

I don't know what's going on, but I'm starting to suspect that Sue isn't the only one keeping secrets. Ruby's family is hiding something.

33

MAGGIE

I can't shake the feeling that something bad is going to happen. It hovers around me like a bad smell, thick and oppressive. And though my stomach aches with the nerves that fill it, I know I need to eat something to keep my strength up.

I stop at the gas station on my way back into town, hoping to grab a snack, but as I pull into a parking spot, I catch sight of Kit inside, working behind the counter. Does she usually look so pale? Are the fluorescent lights washing out her complexion, or is it a result of the stress I caused her earlier?

Suddenly, the idea of forcing food down feels impossible. Even if it weren't, there's no way I can go in there. Maybe ever again.

I eye the kids who loiter around the side of the building, wondering if I'll have to pay one of them to grab a snack for me the next time I need a junk food fix. Or maybe I should just go inside and apologize. Try to make things right.

I doubt she'd want me to—I'm probably the last person she wants to see. And as good as my intentions might be, I know that if I go in and talk to her, there will be more than an "I'm sorry" coming out of my mouth. Because I still have so many questions, and I'm getting desperate for answers.

Which is exactly why I should speak with her again, here, where she can't run or close a door in my face.

I watch the steady stream of customers come and go, waiting for the store to empty out. Am I a horrible a person for ambushing her at work, where she can't escape? But when a rare lull in the near constant activity finally occurs, I don't go inside. I can't bring myself to do it.

Kit looks so sad, and I'm the one who did that to her. Just like I'm the one who upset Ruby's daughter Rachel so badly that the poor woman ran into her house to escape me. I feel like I'm floundering, any knack I once had for this kind of thing long gone.

I used to be relentless in my pursuit of the truth. If I upset the people I questioned, I didn't let it bother me. It certainly never made me feel as emotional as I do now.

Is it an age thing? Maybe it has something to do with the way every interaction in such a small town, especially one where everyone is interconnected and you're just starting to be accepted, can set off a chain reaction?

Or is it something else? Something in my personal life, perhaps?

I'm debating the answer when a knock sounds against the glass, startling me. I hurry to compose myself, hitting the button to lower the passenger-side window, where Fire Investigator Larson stands bent at the waist, looking in at me.

"You're a hard woman to track down," he says.

I shrug. "Didn't know you were trying."

"I've driven by the department a few times today."

"My lieutenant didn't tell me."

"He didn't know. When I didn't see your rental there, I kept driving."

"Anything you need me to know you can tell him. He'll relay the message."

"But I wanted to speak with you. Is everything all right?" Resting his arm along the window opening, he leans against the door, closing the distance between us as he looks at me with something bordering on concern.

"Yeah." Afraid that my expression is giving away the truth, I add, "Why do you ask?"

"Because I've been sitting in my car for the last ten minutes watching you stare off into space."

"I wasn't staring off into space."

"Then what were you doing?"

"Working up my nerve for a difficult conversation."

I lift my chin in Kit's direction. He follows the gesture.

"Friend of yours?" he asks.

"A friendly acquaintance until earlier today."

"But not anymore?"

"Probably not."

"Want to talk about it?"

"No." But I do. Just not with him. But since he's the only one here and I need to get it off my chest, I say, "I had to ask her some questions about a case earlier, and I'm afraid I upset her pretty badly. Seems like I've been doing a lot of that lately."

"But you're just doing your job."

"Yeah, but I need to find a way to do it better, so I'm not leaving so much carnage in my wake."

"Sometimes it can't be avoided."

I give him a hard look, wanting to argue. "Why were you looking for me, anyway?"

"To thank you."

I raise my eyebrows, waiting for him to elaborate.

"The substance you found at the blast scene? Forensics has made a positive ID that it was charcoal. Not only that, but high traces of an accelerant were detected on the sample, confirming that a fire was deliberately set. It was definitely arson. We're back in business."

I nod, still not understanding why the update would require an in-person conversation.

"Anyway, I wanted to take you out. Buy you dinner."

"Why?"

"To say thank you."

"You just did."

He glances away, running a hand through his hair. "And also... I thought that maybe we could get to know each other better. That maybe you might need to talk."

"I don't."

"But I think maybe you do."

I exhale loudly, out of patience. "You just don't quit, do you?"

"No. Not when I'm trying to help—"

"—Well, you can stop, because I don't need any. I'm fine."

"Are you?"

I glare at him, pressing the button to close the window. He straightens and takes a step back, his gaze never leaving mine. And though he exudes strength and confidence, I can't shake the feeling that there's something tragic hiding behind that strong jaw and the brave firefighter front.

Or maybe I'm just imagining it, projecting.

I put the car in gear, back out of my space, and exit the parking lot. But as I glance in my rearview mirror before the gas station fades from view, I can still see him standing there, watching me drive away.

Whatever this is, whatever he thinks he's doing, it needs to stop. Maybe he's just bored and this is how he likes to pass the time, but I... I'm feeling too vulnerable right now to deal with something like this.

My phone buzzes beside me. I don't think I've ever been so

grateful to receive a call in my life. Snatching it from the middle console, I hesitate when I see the CCPD number.

"Kal?"

"Yeah."

I swallow down my disappointment. As unlikely as it seems right now, I'd really been hoping it was Sue.

"I just had a call come in. We got a body."

My pulse sharpens, needling at my skin.

"Where?"

"Railroad Street. You want me to take it?"

Railroad Street is the worst area of this tiny town. Tucked away in a dark corner shadowed by a mountain, it's home to three medium-sized apartment buildings, each one more run-down than the last as you get farther into the darkness.

If the first building houses those barely making ends meet in a place where jobs are scarce and opportunities even scarcer, and the second those who are desperate and struggling to survive, the third is home to those out of both options and hope. I suspect I know where on the street I'll find the body.

"I'll do it. I'm right down the road." Checking traffic, I pull a U-turn. "Did the caller leave a name?"

"No. They just said there was an overdose on Railroad Street. Told me the guy was dead and then they hung up."

"Male or female?"

"Honestly? I couldn't tell. They might have been trying to disguise their voice."

I'm more surprised that someone took the time to report the body than I am that the caller doesn't want to be identified. It's why I leave the strobing light in my glove box and keep my siren off. If any of the residents know I'm coming, there'll be zero chance I'll find a witness.

But as I pull onto the street, I realize I'd held out too much hope—it's a ghost town. Of course it is. They must have known I'd be coming.

"ETA?" Kal asks.

I pass the first two apartment buildings, zeroing in on a form lying on the crumbling sidewalk in front of the third.

"I'm here."

"Want me to call in for a transport?"

"Not yet. Hold on a sec, let me confirm."

Pulling to the curb, I grab the duffel bag containing the supplies I normally keep in my Jeep from the back seat of the rental. Fish around until I find the Narcan. I hurry out of the vehicle and squat beside the man.

His skin is ashen, his chest still. Bile has dried at the corner of his mouth into a thick yellow crust. A glass pipe lies in the palm of his limp hand.

I know I'm too late even before I pull on gloves and press my fingers into the flesh of his neck, feeling for a pulse, so it's no surprise when I don't find one.

His skin is cool but not yet cold. I take him gingerly by his wrist and bend his arm at the elbow. Rigor hasn't set in yet. He hasn't been dead long.

"We've got an adult male. No apparent wounds or trauma. Drug paraphernalia present. Go ahead and make the call," I say.

"I'm sorry, Chief."

"Yeah, me too. You know where you can find me for the next few hours."

Ending the call, I take a closer look at the body. The man's clothes look clean, his skin unblemished. The teeth visible through his slack mouth appear healthy. Plenty of people use drugs without their appearance betraying their habit, but my gut is telling me that something here's not right.

Bringing up my camera app, I start taking pictures of the scene. The decedent's clean clothes. His clear skin. The dried vomit on his face. More notably, the absence of vomit on the ground around him.

I study his posture. He doesn't look the way you'd expect if someone sat down and passed out. Or even if they fell. His limbs are splayed oddly, his head unnaturally bent on his neck. He looks like a ragdoll tossed across a room.

I'd bet my badge that this body was dumped. Which means that glass pipe in his hand? Somebody put it there. This was staged.

I bag the pipe as evidence and lock it in the glove box, then return to the body. My knees crack as I kneel. I draw a deep breath, steeling myself for what I'm about to do. Admittedly, this isn't my favorite part.

I work my hand into each of his pockets, checking for an ID. All I find is a crumpled rectangle of paper, a receipt from Armory Attic, an army-navy surplus store over in Lincoln. On it is a single purchase. One two-hundred-foot length of fuse paid for with cash.

I take a quick picture, then bag the receipt. Stare at it through the clear plastic as I make a call.

"Hey." The voice that answers is hopeful. "Change your mind?"

Ignoring the question, I ask one of my own. "The charcoal that was used in the explosion. Would the perp have used a fuse to light it?"

Sensing the gravity of the situation, Fire Inspector Larson's voice grows serious. "If they were smart. Not that what they did was. But yeah, if it were me? I'd make sure I was as far away as possible by the time the flames hit that gas."

"Thanks."

I hang up without another word, my mind moving too fast to worry about being polite. Because the blast wasn't just intentional. It was premeditated. Judging by the date on the receipt, it was planned over a week in advance.

And the man lying dead in front of me? Whoever he is, I'm confident he wasn't the one to set it. But it's obvious someone wants me to believe that he was.

34

MAGGIE

Someone's on a mission, and bodies are piling up in this tiny town as a result. It's late afternoon by the time I leave Railroad Street. The tense breakfast I'd had with Kal this morning seems like a lifetime ago. In a way, I guess it was—just not mine.

The man's pale face, now zipped inside a black bag strapped to a gurney in the transport van in front of me, is seared into my brain. I can't stop wondering who he was.

Did he have anything to do with the explosion, or is he simply a fall guy meant to make me think the danger's passed? And if that's true, if someone killed him to frame him, how many more bodies will I have on my hands before this is done, because that's the only thing I'm sure of right now—that this is far from over.

I skim an incoming text from Kal. The pipe, which he'd come by to pick up, along with the rest of the evidence, is clean of prints. It's what I expected, but still, it hits like a stomach virus, fast and hard and leaving me feeling turned inside out.

It's another dead end.

Earlier, while I was waiting for the transport van to arrive, I called the Armory Attic to see if they have surveillance cameras. They don't.

And the purchase didn't stick out because, strangely enough, it wasn't unusual—they sell at least a half dozen two-hundred-foot fuses a month. I'm trying not to think too hard about that.

What I need is a fresh angle to approach this from, but my mind is tapped. It's been a long day. I'm exhausted, and frustrated, and, frankly, I feel like I'm beyond being a help to anyone in my current frame of mind.

I chew my lip as I reach the end of the road, debating. Refuse to feel guilty as I text Kal back to let him know I'm heading home early. Besides the other day, when I almost became a part of the explosion that caused this mess to begin with, I can't remember the last time I did that.

The relief I feel as I drive away from my responsibilities is immense. But as I turn onto my street and start considering what the rest of my afternoon and evening might look like, I regret the decision. I need a night off, but I'm not sure I'm capable of that on my own.

How am I going to keep myself from thinking about this case? From obsessing over it? Maybe if Steve was here, but—

Pulling into the driveway, my heart soars. In an instant, I'm grinning so widely that my cheeks hurt. I have the door open before the car's even in park, turn off the engine as an afterthought before launching myself out of the vehicle, up the front steps, and into the pair of open arms waiting for me.

"I've missed you, too." Linda laughs, staggering back a step under the weight of my embrace. "I'm not sure I've seen this side of you before. Let me have a look at you."

She holds me at arm's length, head tilting as she inspects me. The smile on her lips falters. My own tremble as I attempt to blink away the tears in my eyes.

"I'm just so glad you're here," I rush to say before she has too much time to think. I look behind her at the almost empty bottle of water, the Kindle on the bench beside the door that she'd been sitting on when I first saw her, the familiar straw hat she wears when she works in the sun. The porch hasn't been in the sun for hours. "When did you get here?"

"Around lunchtime."

"Lunchtime! Why didn't you call and let me know? I could have let you into the house at least."

"I knew you'd be working. And I was happy out here reading. Do you know how long it's been since I've had such a long stretch of uninterrupted book time? It was heaven."

"Oh, well then, don't let me interrupt. I'll go back to work," I joke.

"Don't you dare. Now that you're here, I have to pee. And I want to hear everything that's been going on in your life."

I turn away, busy myself unlocking the door so she can't see how unenthusiastic I am at the thought of that. Linda's my best friend. For the longest time, she was my only friend. I'd trust her with my life. But how can I trust her with the truth if I'm not even sure what that is anymore?

The dogs dance around gleefully as we come inside, celebrating Linda's arrival. I know I should be doing the same. Fixing a smile on my face, I point her toward the bathroom. As soon as the door clicks shut behind her, I draw several deep breaths, preparing myself, not just for the night ahead, but for the weekend as I recall the reason for Linda's visit.

She's not just here to catch up, she's here for my bachelorette party. Which is tomorrow. And though I've had my reservations since the start, I can't imagine what it's going to be like now.

How can I rationalize having a party when a murderer is on the loose in my town? Is it wrong of me to celebrate my impending wedding when I'm having doubts about going through with it?

I swallow hard as the thought hits. My face turns to stone, freezing my fake smile in place as Linda returns, linking her arm through mine and pulling me over to the couch.

As we sit, she bends her knee up onto the cushion, facing me. I let my hand land heavily on my thigh, knowing the dogs will think it's an invitation for my lap. They spring up, and I hide my face in their fur.

"So, where's the groom at, anyway?" Linda asks.

My voice is muffled as I say, "Visiting his family."

"How do you get along with them?"

"Fine. They're great."

"That's lucky. I never got along with Marcus's family. Every time his mother looked at me I could tell she thought I was trying to steal her baby away and she hated me for it." Linda laughs before adding, "Bet she's wishing I'd kept him now."

Linda's marriage had been short, her divorce messy. I peek at her over the tops of the dogs, making sure she's okay. Her grin is still in place. Still genuine.

"Did you have any doubts?" I ask. "Before you got married?"

"Not a single one."

Something inside my stomach lurches, pushing a lump up into my throat.

"Of course, that's probably because I'd been drinking and was caught up in the whole Vegas thing. 'Cause as soon as I sobered up... Let's just say I had a bad case of buyer's remorse."

"But you guys had dated for a while before you got married."

"Yeah, but when it started it was because I was lonely and it was convenient. I didn't go into the relationship believing it was actually going to lead to something serious."

My breath hitches, chest tightening as I realize that I could say the same thing about me and Steve.

"Oh, Maggie." Linda puts her hands between the pups and gently pushes them to the side so she can see me. "Please don't let what I've said upset you. A lot of relationships start like that. And I'm sure a ton of them lead to long happy marriages."

I sniff and wipe my nose. Blink back tears and smile sadly. "It's not that. It's just, I was so sure this was what I wanted..."

"But now you're not?"

I shrug. She takes my hand in hers and gives it a squeeze.

"That's completely normal."

"Are you sure?"

"Yes. It's a big decision. Huge. It's only natural to want to make sure you're making the right one."

"How do you know you are?"

"I'm not sure that you can. That's where the whole love part comes in. Taking a leap of faith like that isn't easy, but if you love the person, then it's worth taking the risk. Do you love Steve?"

"Yes," I say without a moment's thought or hesitation. "I do."

"Then you have to believe in the commitment you're making to each other. Try to relax and enjoy it."

"But—"

"Nope. No buts. You've made it this far. Did you ever think that would happen?"

"No."

"Neither did I."

I mock gasp, widening my eyes at her like I'm shocked. She laughs as she pulls me to her in a hug. I stare at the long black braid hanging down her back as she whispers in my ear, "I know you have a habit of overthinking things, but not this. Trust me, everything will be fine."

I know I should believe her. I wish that I could. But the little voice in my head, the one connected directly to my gut, is warning me not to. Because Linda might know me, and I might know Steve, but I'm not sure if any of us truly knows the truth. Then again, thinking about Ruby Anderson, I can't help wondering if anyone ever does.

35

STEVE

I'm missing something important, and I feel like the consequences could be dire. I drove by two McAllister and Sons stores today. One looked like a facade from a movie set, a purposely weathered false-front general store straight out of an old Western planted right in the middle of a modern street between a Starbucks and a Verizon. The other was a long stand-alone building with a chained-in garden section to the side.

Neither was a match for the image I have in my mind, but here's the thing—I didn't remember passing the business until I was under hypnosis. So what exactly is this idea I have of what the store looks like, and where did it come from? Did I retain what I saw while I was under? Or am I imagining things?

Like the way Dr. Curry treated me yesterday after my session. Am I just being sensitive, or had the doctor really given me the brush-off?

What's the truth?

There are another four McAllister and Sons on my list, but I don't see the point in checking them out if I'm not sure if what I recall is real. It had seemed a good plan at the time, but now that I'm out here, all I can think of is the disappointment I saw in Maggie's eyes last night.

I shouldn't have left her. Or maybe I shouldn't have gone to check on her in the first place. I had thought it would make me feel better, but if anything, it's made me feel worse. I'm not sure what I'm doing anymore.

Not for the first time, I wonder if Maggie wouldn't be better off without me.

Even the people I pay to be around me can't get away fast enough. Or is there something that happened while I was under hypnosis that caused Dr. Curry's odd behavior? I have to find out.

So even though I know I shouldn't, I find myself making a detour to her office. Do my best to ignore the voice in my head telling me I'm making a mistake as I stride across the parking lot. Assure myself it's all just a big misunderstanding as I slip into her waiting room.

A patient must have just gone in before I got there, because I've been waiting almost an hour, nervously scrolling on my phone, by the time her door finally opens. I can't help noticing the appointment card grasped in the thin man's hand as he passes me on his way out.

The pleasant smile on Dr. Curry's face vanishes as I rise to my feet. She cranes her neck after the man who just left, but he's already gone. We're alone.

"Mr. Winters." She swallows hard and gives me a strange look. Her return to formality, abandoning the first-name basis she'd been so quick to establish with me, increases my anxiety. "Did we have an appointment?"

I clear my throat. "No. I realized I'd forgotten to make one before I left yesterday."

She retreats a step toward her office. I ignore the hint, rushing to say, "I just had a quick question. About yesterday's session."

When she doesn't respond, I take that as an invitation to proceed. "The store I remembered passing while I was under? McAllister and Sons? I think I remember what it looks like, but I'm not sure if I'm imagining it."

"It's not abnormal to retain memories of what you recall while under hypnosis. That's one of the reasons why it can be such a useful tool."

Suddenly, her eyes widen, as if what she's just said has triggered a memory of her own. Her nostrils flare, breath causing her chest to rise and fall heavily as her gaze darts around the room. She looks spooked.

"D... do you remember what you said when you were under?" she stutters.

"No. Nothing."

Her hand grasps for the office door as she takes another step backward. Her fingers tighten around the edge, curling into a fist.

"Wait. Please. Just one more thing."

"And then you'll leave?"

"Yes."

She nods stiffly for me to continue.

"You said I remembered the store and that the oak was surrounded by a wheat field, but it's just..."

"Yes?"

"I was under for an hour. Are you sure I didn't say anything else?"

She gives a slow blink. Glances over her shoulder into the room behind her, as if preparing to make a quick retreat. "Would you like my advice, Mr. Winters?"

I gulp as I nod, not quite sure if I really do.

Dr. Curry doesn't meet my eyes as she says, "Regression therapy isn't for everyone. Sometimes, it can cause more harm than good. Some things are best left buried, and in my opinion, this is one of them. Go home. Forget the past. There's nothing to gain from reliving that night."

"But what about—"

She shakes her head as she takes the final step back into her office, closing the door between us. I gape at the pristine white surface, feeling overwhelmed with disbelief. She's a professional. Her job is to help people. How could her recommendation be to forget what happened?

Forcing myself to turn around, I leave the waiting room, steps echoing hollowly as I tread down the hallway toward the exit. Crossing the lot back to my car, I can't help but feel disappointed. She'd seemed so confident that first appointment. I really thought she could help.

I can't believe I couldn't remember anything other than—

My feet lock into place. I slowly look down, lifting my palms so I can see them. They look clean. Now. But in that flash of memory I just had?

I spin around, staring in horror at the building behind me, thinking about the blood I've had on my hands. What if I told her too much? What if I spilled the whole truth about me and Wesley?

36

MAGGIE

Dusk has fallen, the fading day casting long shadows across the living room as Linda and I continue to catch up, talking animatedly about old times and acquaintances, a bottle of wine on the table before us. It's the first time that I've felt like myself in a long while. I try to pinpoint how long as I look at the wood-paneled walls of the luxury cabin around us, the nice furniture, the framed artwork, but can't.

I think of my house across the street nestled in the woods, the mismatched but comfortable sofa and love seat, the scuffed-up coffee table where I used to rest my feet after a long shift, walls painted a soft white with just the slightest, most soothing tinge of blue, and I realize for the first time that I'm not sure this place feels like home.

This is Steve's house. Everything in it was chosen by him. And while there's something magical about watching the sun rise over the mountains in the morning, the first rays of light causing the lake to glint and spark like it's catching fire, I miss watching out my back door the way the fog would drift from the woods, sometimes bringing with it a visitor, a deer, a moose, a raccoon. I reach to top off our glasses and discover the bottle is empty.

I've just opened my mouth to volunteer to grab another when there's a knock at the front of the house. Linda gives me a questioning look, and I shrug. Usually no one comes out here, yet there's no denying that this past week there's been a surge of visitors. Wondering about my sudden popularity, I stand and follow the dogs to the front. Run my palm over the firearm holstered to my side, then open the door.

A surge of guilt rushes through me as I find Dr. Ricky on the other side. I'd forgotten I'd asked her to come early, yet here she is, large as life, though the diminutive woman is barely visibly behind the parcels she's carrying.

"Dr. Ricky," I greet her warmly, deciding not to mention the body I just sent her way though I'm admittedly disappointed that I won't be able to count on her to rush an ID for me. "You made it. Here, let me take some of that from you."

I grab the top bag, finding it surprisingly hot. The aroma it emits makes my mouth water and my stomach rumble.

"I hope you like Mexican food," she says, brushing by me into the house. "I remembered that options were limited up here, so I brought dinner. And these." She lifts the box she's struggling with a bit, causing the bottles within to clank. "Where should I put them?"

Linda hurries over and takes it from her. "I'll bring it to the kitchen."

"Are you the forensic anthropologist?" she asks as we trail behind Linda.

Linda turns her head. Her lips twitch at the doctor's bluntness. "I am. Also known as Linda."

"I'm Dr. Erika Ricky. If you ask my coworkers, I'm also known as a headache or a pain in the—"

I cough, choking on a laugh.

"It's a pleasure to meet you," Linda says, setting the box down on the counter.

"We'll see if you still feel that way by the end of the weekend. Some people find me unpleasant. Plus, I brought this." She brandishes an oversized folder that had been pinned under her arm. "Work."

I've barely been listening to their exchange, too busy struggling with the knot holding the to-go containers hostage. "Did you really bring Mexican food?" I ask.

"Uh-huh. I didn't know what you'd like, so I got a bit of everything."

"I think I love you."

She looks at me and smirks. "I bet you say that to all girls who wield a scalpel."

Linda laughs. "Erika, I think you and I are going to get along just fine. Now I want to see my present."

I'm reminded of how lucky I am to have a friend like Linda as she holds out her hand for the folder, no questions asked, not even a raised eyebrow aimed in my direction. The doctor lays it in her palm. Sliding a file out, Linda flips it open and skims the chart inside. Next, she pulls out an X-ray and holds it up to the light. Turns on the bulb over the kitchen sink for a better look.

"I've concluded that most of the injuries were caused by blunt force trauma, most likely from a violent attack. See the nightstick fractures?" Erika points to marks on the arm bones in an area that would suggest they'd been held up to ward off a hit. Ruby had probably raised them to protect her head and face.

"I concur," Linda says. "Do you two want to tell me what we're looking at, or do you want me to tell you the story I'm reading?"

"You, please," Erika says.

"See here, and here?" Linda points to some dark shading on the right ulna. "This tells me that the remodeling process, when the blast cells in the bone work to repair a break or fracture, was interrupted. You can see where the ulnar shaft has been disrupted, knitting together in a slightly off pattern. And the lumpy appearance to the bones? That all signifies where injuries healed."

She pulls another film from the file and holds it up. This one is of the skull.

"Probable Caucasoid female based on bone structure, the shape of the nasal aperture, orbital rims, and dentition. Multiple displaced teeth, dental fractures, and instances of root resorption, as well as healed breaks to the nasal bones, mandible, zygomatic arch, and orbital rim."

"In English?" I ask.

"The victim's teeth show multiple signs of damage. She also suffered numerous breaks to her nose, jaw, cheeks, and eye sockets," Linda says, giving us a grim look. "These injuries are all old and healed long ago. I'd prefer to have my hands on the actual bones before saying for certain, but I've seen this pattern of injury enough times to suspect that this woman suffered through years of domestic abuse."

I set down the container I'd just opened, giving Linda my full attention.

"How can you tell that the injuries didn't come from a single occurrence?"

"The remodeling interrupted by being broken again. And the fracture lines."

I lean closer, squinting at where she's pointing to on the X-ray.

"Say I was to hit someone in the head with a baseball bat, causing a break in the skull. Fracture lines would extend out from the injury. If I hit them again, causing another break, the fracture lines extending from the second injury wouldn't cross those extending from the first. They'd stop. But if I'm correct, and that's what I'm looking at here"—she points to the area beneath the right eye socket on the film—"and here"—this time

her finger aims at the outside of where the cheek would be—
"then the fracture lines extend over this break, and this one,
which means they occurred at different times."

Linda passes me the X-rays. I stare at them, wishing I could
read them as easily as she had. Knowing that even if I can't,
Linda is one of the top in her field. If she says Ruby had suffered
multiple beatings over the years, I can trust her expert opinion.

But what does this mean in terms of my case? Ruby
Anderson died earlier this week in an explosion that had been
intentionally set. Had she been an innocent victim, in the
wrong place at the wrong time? Had someone been covering
their tracks? Or had an abusive husband been finishing the job
he'd started two decades ago?

37

MAGGIE

Images of the dead float around my head, filmy eyes full of accusation, upset that I haven't caught their killer yet. The result is that I can't sleep. Can barely even close my eyes.

Ignoring the pang of guilt I feel for leaving my guests, I drive through the predawn fog, unsure whether the viselike squeeze at my temples is caused by a mild hangover or fatigue. Either way, I should still be in bed right now. And yet, despite the early hour, as I pull into the CCPD parking lot, I find that Kal is already here.

"Good morning," Kal says, looking up from the paperwork on his desk to greet me. It's not just my imagination that he winces slightly when he sees me. "Or not. Are you here to report the bus that hit you?"

I roll my eyes, letting him know I'm not amused. The action sends a sharp pain shooting through my skull. It dampens my mood and makes me get right to business.

"Ruby Anderson was a victim of domestic violence."

"You sure?"

I think about telling him how I'd had a slumber party with a forensic anthropologist and a medical examiner last night. Or how it's all starting to add up. The reason why Kit remembered Nathan Anderson, who had probably acted scary and intimidating, but not Ruby.

Or Rachel's bruised face and how she'd been so skittish—she's probably repeating the cycle, stuck in an abusive relationship of her own. The way her young son had hit her supports the theory that he's witnessed violence in the home. Even the way Missy Anderson had been so private about the reason she was divorcing Ronny when Sue had asked has a new meaning now, when seen from this perspective.

But instead of going into details, I just say, "I'm sure." I glance down at the paperwork on his desk. "I don't suppose anything's come in on that overdose from yesterday?"

"Nothing yet."

"Then how about we start the day by paying Ruby's husband another visit?"

A smile spreads slowly across Kal's face as he stands. But it doesn't reach his dimples. And there's nothing friendly about it.

Most of the time, despite his size, my lieutenant reminds me of a puppy. But there are occasions where I'm aware of how dangerous the six-foot-three man could be. How dangerous any human could be, really. All that separates the good from the bad is their actions.

As I lock up and follow Kal to the cruiser, I can't help thinking about what drives those actions. What does a man who beats his wife get out of it?

It surely doesn't get him love, or even respect. Obedience? Maybe, but if so, only in a surface sort of way, when the fear of the repercussions— I buckle my seatbelt, realizing I've just answered my question.

What they want is control. And they get it by ruling through fear.

I stare out the window, the thick canopy of trees vanishing as we round a curve, a guardrail now all that separates us from the steep craggy drop below. Mountains stretch off into the distance, a jagged smile flashed by a cruel earth. What would I have done if I were in Ruby Anderson's shoes? Though I tell myself the answer to that is easy, it's not.

Because statistically, the most dangerous time for a woman in an abusive relationship is when she leaves. You see it on the news all too often: A woman killed by her abuser after she did the hard part and left. Got a restraining order. Started to rebuild her life from the ashes.

Struck down because she bore the brunt of a coward's rage. If he couldn't have her, no one could. Add in children, and it must seem like an impossible situation.

It's too late for Ruby, but not for her daughter. As Kal turns off the main road onto the narrow path lined with NO TRES-PASSING signs that leads to the Anderson house, I vow to do everything within my power to help Rachel.

By the time we reach the clearing, my resolve is set. I stare at the tiny house before me, imagining the horrors that went on behind those walls, the darkness contained under the roof.

"You okay?" Kal asks.

I give him a curt nod. "Let's do this."

"Don't forget about the shotgun he mentioned last time."

I thumb the snap on my holster as I exit the vehicle, give Kal a smile over the hood that's a match for the one he wore earlier.

He eyes me warily. "Should I be worried?"

"No. But Nathan Anderson should."

I stride through the front gate, over the littered walk, up to the door. Bang on it like I'm trying to send my fist through the wood, a constant knocking meant to anger the man within, wanting to kick the hornet's nest a bit to see what happens. But nothing does.

I look over at the truck parked in the same spot it was two days ago, just visible through the early morning light filtering through the clearing. "Mr. Anderson, we know you're in there. Open up."

I crane my head, listening hard. Press my ear against the door, then shake my head in response to Kal's questioning look.

"I'll go check around back," he offers.

The sound of Kal's steps as he crunches through the leaves fades as he rounds the corner, leaving me in silence. Not even the birds dare to chirp.

It's possible someone picked Nathan up, gave him a ride somewhere. And yet, I don't quite feel alone. My skin prickles, the fine hairs on the back of my neck rising to attention. I look around the clearing, scanning the shadows, wondering if I'm being watched.

"No one's getting through that way," Kal says, breaking the spell I'd fallen under as he reemerges around the side of the house, shaking his head. "It's too overgrown."

I shake off my lingering creeps and glare at the door, feeling irritated. Wishing I had a reason to kick it in, imaging how satisfying it would feel to drag a terrified Nathan Anderson kicking and screaming from inside. I want that feeling, want to inflict on him the same fear he inflicted on his wife.

So when I say, "Then we'll come back," it's not just a promise. It's a threat.

38

MAGGIE

Spree killers commit more than one murder in multiple locations without a cooling-off period. It's possible that's what I have on my hands. If that's true, more lives could be lost because of my inability to catch them, and that makes me very, very angry.

I scowl at the report on my computer, hoping that maybe if I look at it hard enough, I'll be able to see all of the information it doesn't contain about my John Doe. Starting with his name.

There had been no prints on file for the man, so he remains unidentified. But that's not the only mystery. Though high levels of methamphetamine had been detected in his initial blood work, there was no histological evidence of regular drug use, no injury to his lung tissue to suggest he had smoked, despite the pipe in his hand. And despite the discovery of an injection site, the surrounding tissue had barely responded—there was no redness, no bruising, not even swelling.

And yet, the medical examiner who conducted the autopsy wasn't surprised. Because this guy hadn't just shot up. He'd also ingested a large quantity of the drug—so much that, based on the fresh damage to the gastrointestinal track, the pathologist suspects that alone was a fatal dose. And the first one.

Which would have made the meth that was later injected into his bloodstream unnecessary. And unlikely to have been administered by the man himself.

An official cause of death can't be determined until the full tox screen is back, but it seems likely that the mode of death will be ruled an overdose. But what about the manner?

Because I don't think this was an accident.

Even though the army-navy store said the fuse that was on the receipt I found in his pocket was a common item, and I know it's possible that he bought it for a use other than the explosion that killed Ruby and her son, I can't help feeling like there's a connection between the two cases.

As crazy as it seems, I think that someone is trying to frame this man. And I think that whoever it is fed him the meth, then injected him after he was already dead or nearly so. Which would make the manner of death homicide.

Discovering John Doe's identity could break this case. But how am I going to do that when his fingerprints aren't in the system, and no one has reported him missing?

"I've got an address."

I spook upright in my seat, cast a guilty look at Kal hovering in my open doorway.

"For Rene?"

Minimizing my inbox, Rene Anderson's extensive police record fills the screen, telling a story I've read too many times. Petty crimes escalating to serious ones. Stints in juvie replaced by stretches in jail. The young woman's only twenty-two, yet it appears as if she's spent more of the last decade incarcerated than not.

And the most recent charges? They're all for possession of methamphetamine. The same charge that Marie Bouchard, the tenant who rented the trailer, had been arrested multiple times for. The same drug responsible for John Doe's overdose.

There's a theme here.

"A real one?" I ask.

Because every address Rene had given over the last several years had been false. Nobody had ever followed up or even noticed. Each parole officer she'd been assigned had just revoked her release and issued a warrant for her arrest when she failed to show up for her meetings. No one had ever even taken the time to look for her.

I think of the parallels between Ruby and her daughters, three women who must have felt like the world had turned its back on them, leaving them to the wolves.

"Yep. Seems like Rene tried filing for federal assistance a few months ago. She'd have to give a real one if she wanted to receive the checks."

It's all I need to hear. I stand, heading toward the door.

"Where is it?"

"Railroad Street."

We exchange a glance. It's one more link connecting John Doe to this case.

"Number three?" I ask, locking the door.

Kal nods. Another connection. It's the same building Doe's body had been outside of. The one that houses the most desperate residents of this tiny town.

Building three is what you'd term a drug den, if more of the residents could afford drugs. Dim, claustrophobic hallways that reek of bodily fluids lead to tiny rooms with peeling paint and floors worn thin and shiny by countless feet, the air humid from too many bodies trying to shelter in too small a space in an effort to pool enough money for their next hit.

We walk the few short blocks there, our destination quickly appearing ahead, the street as abandoned as I'd found it yesterday. Passing a dirty baby doll missing an arm lying abandoned on the sidewalk, one thickly lashed eye stuck open, showing only the white, we enter the building through front doors hanging askew on broken hinges.

The stench as we step inside hits like a one-two punch, a blow to the face, then the gut. A lone lightbulb works, flickering as we pass beneath it. Several of the doors have holes in them, punched or kicked in a drugged rage. Others crack open after we pass, eyes making the skin on the back of my neck crawl. I step over a bent spoon in the middle of the bare cement hall floor and come to a stop. We've reached our destination.

Kal gives me a grim glance, then uses his elbow to knock. The door to 12C opens almost immediately, like the resident was waiting for us, though the expression on her face quickly lets me know we weren't who she was expecting. She stares at us with wide hungry eyes that appear much too large for her drawn face. Her mouth knots, accentuating sunken cheeks, one with a small birthmark that looks like a tulip.

"Rene Anderson?" I ask.

"Um, no."

"Does Ms. Anderson live here?"

The woman in front of us shrugs. "Sometimes."

"Is she here now?"

"No."

"Any idea when she'll be back?"

Another shrug.

"What's your name?"

Her oversized eyes flash warily, the whites tinged yellow. After a lengthy pause, she says, "Mary."

"Mary what?"

"Just Mary. You know, like Madonna?"

She musters a quick smile. Despite the rotten teeth, you can see what a nice one it must have been, once.

Taking a business card from my pocket, I hold it out to her. She looks at it like it might bite. "If you see Rene, could you please ask her to give me a call? Or come down to the station? It's only a few blocks away."

"What do you want with her?"

Suspecting our chances of getting in touch with Rene will be better if she doesn't think we're going to arrest her for one of her outstanding warrants, I say, "I'm afraid we have some news about a relative of hers who recently passed."

"There an inheritance?" the woman asks.

"I believe there is," I lie.

She reaches out to take the card from me, her earlier fear forgotten. "I'll tell her. If I see her."

I hold on to the paper with my contact information on it for a moment, long enough to examine the dark stain on the edge of her sleeve, before releasing it.

"Are you hurt?" I ask.

She gives me a questioning look.

I gesture to her arm, now hanging by her side, my business card crumpled in her fist. "You've got blood on you."

She looks down, staring at the stain as if seeing it for the first time. Her jaw works for a moment before she says, "That's old."

"You sure?"

"Yeah, it's fine. Like I said, if I see Rene, I'll tell her you're looking for her."

I debate asking her if she knows anything about the man who overdosed yesterday. The one who'd died somewhere else, then been left at the curb like a bag of trash. The one who was possibly murdered.

But I decide against it. It will only further scare her off, and I can't risk that on the off chance that she'll actually relay my message to Rene. So instead I simply thank her and turn to leave.

"Which one was it?" she asks.

Kal and I stop, already several feet down the hall. Spinning around, I study her expression closely as I ask, "Which one was what?"

"The one who left her something? I only ask 'cause she don't think any of them cared about her. I think it would make her feel good to know that one of them did."

I give her a rueful smile. "I'm afraid I can't disclose who passed until I speak with Rene herself." She doesn't acknowledge my words, simply stares, her hungry eyes latched on to me like an all-you-can-eat buffet.

It takes all my willpower to turn my back and continue down the hall. Kal and I exit the building in silence, walking side by side down the street back to the police department. It isn't until we're inside the station, behind the closed door that we talk.

"Do you think it was strange that she asked which one of Rene's family members left her something and not which one died?" I ask.

"What do you mean?"

I shrug. "I don't know. The way she asked, it's almost like she knew more than one was dead."

"She was probably just fixated on the money," Kal says.

"You're probably right."

"Think she knows where Rene is?"

"If she does, I don't think she's going to tell us."

"I agree. Which means we've hit a wall, haven't we?"

"I'm afraid so."

"Good. Then there's nothing to keep you from going home. You've got a party to get ready for."

I give him my nastiest glare, but it does nothing to shift the grin on his face. I must be losing my touch. "That was a dirty trick."

His grin grows wider. It's infectious. I have to fight to keep my scowl in place.

"Go home, Maggie. I've got everything covered here."

I open my mouth to argue but know it's useless. If I don't show up, it's not like they don't know where to find me. There's nothing I can do to fight it.

39

MAGGIE

I feel like something bad is following me. Is it death from all my recent encounters? Despair clinging to my skin from Railroad Street? Or just reality?

Pulling into the driveway, I sit and stare at the cabin for a minute. The metal roof gleams in the early evening sunlight. Likewise, the golden honey tone of the log beams gives off a friendly glow. Everything about the place is welcoming.

Despite that, and the fact that I've come to know those walls and everything within them so well over the last few years, without Steve here, it doesn't feel like a home. At least, not my home.

I walk up the stairs and onto the front porch feeling slightly out of place, like I'm an unwelcome visitor. Tell myself I'm being ridiculous as I reach for the door. It opens before I can touch it.

Linda and Erika rush out to greet me, the dogs dancing at our feet. Their words come out in an excited jumble, grins wide, and as they finish each other's sentences with carefree laughs, it's clear that they've become fast friends. A small thread of jealousy stitches through me.

They make it look so easy—bonding, having fun, being happy—all things that I have such a difficult time with. It makes it hard to deny that there might be something wrong with me. That I'm not normal. I'm not sure I'd even know how to start trying to be. Not running away would probably be the best first step, but I'm feeling bombarded and overwhelmed and like I need to escape.

Before I get a chance to plan one, the sound of another car pulling into the driveway interrupts. I turn as the door slams, watch with a mix of anxiety and relief as CeCe jogs up to join us, the salon owner's blonde hair defying both gravity and physics as it remains perfectly in place.

"Hi there!" CeCe's bubbly personality seems a perfect match to the mood at hand, leaving me the odd man out. "I'm CeCe. Thought I'd stop by and help our girl get ready for her big night out."

I groan silently as she pats the oversized tote bag bulging at the seams that pulls down her left side. The thing probably weighs as much as she does.

"CeCe, this is Linda," I say, inching behind my old friend, hoping that once the stylist sees Linda's long thick braid that I'll be able to use her as a decoy and be off the hook. "And this is—"

"Dr. Erika Ricky." The medical examiner steps forward, introducing herself. "Are there going to be makeovers?"

CeCe's red lips spread in a wide grin. "Would you like there to be?"

"I wouldn't be opposed."

"Well, then, girl, let's get you inside and seated and I'll get to work. We all know Maggie here is gonna need a drink or two before she'll hold still for me. Linda, think you can help me out with that?"

Linda grins, taking the bottle CeCe pulls from her bag and turning toward me. Something in my expression must betray the way I'm feeling.

"Poor Maggie! You just walked through the door and we're jumping all over you. We should give you a moment to catch your breath."

I give a grateful smile, and though everyone in the room returns it, I feel bad to have dampened their enthusiasm. I take a seat on the couch, wrapping my arms around the dogs who jump up to join me and give myself a mini peptalk: *This is supposed to be enjoyable. There's more to life than just work. You can do this.*

I watch as Linda leaves the room to get glasses, as CeCe walks a circle around Dr. Ricky, one finger pressed against her lips.

"You got contacts with you, honey?"

Erika nods. "Shall I go put them in?"

"Please."

And then it's just me and CeCe. She sits on the couch beside me and throws her arm up around my shoulder, pulling me into a side hug. Laughs as the pups join in, giving her kisses. "You relax and try to have fun tonight, sweetie, you deserve it. But if any of it gets too much for you, even me, just say the word, all right?"

I nod, closing my eyes as I draw a deep breath, realizing that I'm making this more complicated than it needs to be. These women are my friends. They accept me as I am. All they expect from me is to be myself. I don't know why I have such a hard time believing that.

She gives another squeeze before letting me go as Linda returns, lining up a row of tumblers on the table. CeCe pulls a chair from the dining room, assessing the light before she decides on a spot close to the window. Dr. Ricky enters the room and heads straight for the chair, eyeing the beauty products that CeCe's pulling from her bag.

"So," I say, giving Linda a smile as she passes me a drink. "What was it you and Erika wanted to tell me?"

The two women look at each other. Dr. Ricky nods at Linda. Linda turns her attention to me. Her mouth opens then closes, a hesitant look spreading across her face. She darts a quick glance at CeCe.

Though her back is turned, she somehow knows and says, "Don't mind me, you girls can talk freely. A good beautician is like a priest. You don't repeat anything you hear in confidence."

Linda nods, pacing across the room with a finger pinned between her teeth. Pulls it out as she turns back toward me. "Okay, so, we probably shouldn't have done this, at least not without asking you first, but we were sitting here this morning after you left, having a cup of coffee, and, well, you know how awkward it can be trying to have a conversation with someone you just met."

I'm a little taken aback, because Linda's never seemed to have that problem, and Dr. Ricky has never seemed the type to care. It makes me feel a little less abnormal, reminds me that these are my people. If anyone understands me, they do. My muscles loosen, allowing me to relax against the back of the couch.

"Anyway, we were sitting here trying to make polite conversation, and we couldn't help but notice the file that was on the table."

My eyes drop to the polished slab of live-edge pine before me, but it's empty.

"So we opened it."

"It was for a hit-and-run case that happened approximately six years ago," Dr. Ricky jumps in. "The investigation was atrocious. But the autopsy was adequate."

"Michelle Sanders," I say

"Yes," Dr. Ricky confirms. "We figured you must have brought the file home because you were looking into the case, so we figured we'd help."

Something flutters inside my stomach. I look between the

two women, suddenly understanding the cause of their excitement. Feel myself become infected by it as I realize what they're going to say, because there's nothing quite like succeeding in the pursuit of justice. Obviously you're not righting any wrongs—once someone's been victimized, there's no way to take that back—but finding the person who caused the harm and making them pay is the next best thing.

But I'd read through Michelle Sanders' case several times myself. There hadn't been enough there to find her killer. Had there?

"CeCe, did you know her?" I ask, buying my pulse a moment to return to normal.

"I did. She was the sweetest thing. Would have given you the sweater off her back if she thought you needed it—you wouldn't even have to ask. It was heartbreaking, what happened."

I nod as she speaks, her words confirming what I've started to suspect. "What'd you find?" I ask.

CeCe stops what she's doing, lifting her hands from Erika's face as the doctor says, "There was an anomaly on the posterior tissue of the left thigh. The pattern of bruising was inconsistent with what you'd expect to see."

"She wasn't hit by a car?"

"She was, but there was something distinguishing on the front bumper."

Linda adds, "Whatever caused the anomaly to the soft tissue transferred to the bone as well due to the force of the impact. That's not something you tend to see when a victim is hit from behind. The musculature of the hamstring in healthy adults is thick, dense."

"Sit down. You're making me dizzy," I say, gesturing for Linda to stop pacing. She comes over and sits on the edge of the table in front of me. Our knees touch. I can feel the vibrations coming off her, the energy thrumming beneath her skin that comes from sharing something she's passionate about. And there you have it—the social equalizer of introverts. The thing that managed to turn Linda and Erika from a pair of relative strangers into friends.

"While the victim's transverse fractures are to be expected, there's some unexpected damage to the shaft of the femur around the break. I'm not surprised that the pathologist who performed the autopsy missed it. They're trained to read X-rays, but not bones, per se, and with the displacement of the long bone, well, it would be easy to overlook."

CeCe's eyes catch mine as she digs around in a makeup bag. Though her expression is blank, I can't help but wonder if we shouldn't be doing this, discussing one of her friends in such clinical detail. But before I can suggest that we postpone the conversation, Dr. Ricky jumps in.

"Given Linda's findings in conjunction with the soft tissue damage I observed, we feel confident that we've narrowed down the size and shape of the object that was present on the front bumper of the vehicle that hit the victim. We've both taken measurements of every facet of the abnormal bruising and the impression on the bone and our individual results concur."

"We think it was a winch hook," Linda says. "Specifically, one attached to a winch with a configuration similar to this one here made by Mile Marker."

She passes me her phone, open to a page displaying a compact but heavy-duty device mounted to the front bumper of a truck. Even CeCe stops what she's doing to look.

"Taking into account the victim's height, the thickness of the soles of the shoes she was wearing, and the location of the bone and tissue damage, the bumper of the vehicle that hit her was at least thirty-one inches high. Which means it was a very big, heavy truck, which should help to significantly reduce the pool of vehicles that could have been used in the hit and run."

"So if we find a vehicle that checks all those boxes, then we have a suspect," I fill in. "And if we can somehow prove it was in town at the time of the accident, enough circumstantial evidence based on the probable rarity of that exact combination to get a warrant to search the vehicle."

"Exactly."

I long to immediately start narrowing down exactly what vehicles would fit the bumper height parameters so I can run a search for the ones registered in the area. But one look at the excited faces around me and I know I can't do it tonight. That's not what they're here for.

I tell myself it's okay to set my burden down for a short while and give my arms a rest. So that's what I'm going to do. I'm sure all my anxieties and insecurities will still be there in the morning, but tonight is for me. I just hope this doesn't turn into another thing that I regret.

I don't like not knowing what to expect. There's an inherent danger in being unprepared. That's exactly why I don't like surprises. And yet, that's the entire point of tonight, and somehow, that's supposed to be a good thing.

I'd been hoping to get to the Loose Moose early so I could claim one of the bar's corners, sit in the shadows with my back to the wall as far away from prying eyes as possible. So I could already be in place before the crowd—inevitable given that it's one of only three restaurants in town and a Friday night—arrived.

But nothing's gone as planned. Steve's sister, Izzy, was supposed to meet us at the house by five o'clock. When she hadn't shown by five-thirty, I texted her to make sure she was okay. Fifteen minutes later, I got a reply that she had a flat tire and wasn't going to be able to make it.

Given the late start, by the time we arrive, the bar is packed. What's worse is that the tables the rest of the party have pushed together while they were waiting for us to arrive are in the very middle of the room.

If that wasn't enough to draw attention—what wasn't

already drawn by the chief of police appearing in the doorway—the shrill wolf whistle and cry of "There she is" Margot gives when we walk through the door sure is. My companions and I freeze on the threshold as every pair of eyes in the place turns to us.

As if I didn't feel conspicuous enough already with a face full of makeup and my hair waved like some kind of beauty queen. And the civilian clothes don't help, my jeans and the uncomfortably fitted t-shirt CeCe insisted I wear, black with IT'S NOT A PARTY UNTIL THE COP SHOWS UP on the front and CHIEF BRIDE-TO-BE on the back, both in hot pink glitter print, a far cry from the androgenous uniform everyone's used to seeing me in.

My chest tightens as anxiety wraps around me like a snake, constricting. My legs tell me I should run. My brain tells me to listen.

"A police chief, a physical anthropologist, and a medical examiner walk into a bar," Erika mutters under her breath. "Any idea what the punch line to that joke is?"

"That they turn around and walk right back out?" I ask hopefully.

"Nope. Not going to happen."

CeCe places her small hand in the middle of my back and prods me forward with surprising strength. Suddenly I suspect the real reason she showed up earlier. It wasn't to give me a makeover for the party. It was to make sure I actually showed up for it.

"Come on, girls. Heads up, shoulders back, move forward," she commands.

"Are you ex-military?" Erika asks in that deadpan tone of hers where you don't know if she's joking or if it's an actual question.

"Nope. But if Maggie here tries going AWOL, I *will* chase her down."

Something tells me not to give the salon owner an opportunity to follow up on the threat. So I force a smile and move forward, doing my best to make eye contact as we pass through the crowd to our table.

Margot gives me a huge grin as she points for me to take a seat in the chair at the end decorated with pink bunting. Greta, the town librarian, reaches over as soon as I sit and gives my arm a fond pat. Sue sits at the far side, the farthest she can get from me, refusing to look up from her phone.

"We were starting to worry that you weren't coming," Margot says.

"We were waiting for Izzy, but it turns out she isn't going to make it."

Margot's face creases in a frown. Her head shakes from side to side.

"What?"

"Nothing."

I pin her with my best cop look.

"Just something Joe said. It's nothing to worry about."

But I can't help but worry. Lately, it seems to have become one of the things that I do best. I watch as she retreats to the other end of the table, settling into the seat beside Sue.

"So, what's the bride drinking tonight?" Linda asks.

"Unsweet iced tea."

"Boo."

The noise doesn't just come from our table, but from several nearby ones as well, letting me know that I'll have to be careful what I say tonight. The novelty of me being here has others listening in, paying attention too closely.

"Margarita," I concede.

"And a shot," someone yells from behind me. The suggestion is seconded, until a chorus of, "Shot, shot, shot..." starts.

I hold a hand up, smiling as I look around, hoping to end the chant. If anything, it only makes it worse. Beth, the bartender, hurries from behind the counter, carrying a glass with a wedge of lime on a tray.

"What is it?" I ask her in a low voice.

"Tequila," she announces to the room.

The noise in the bar grows louder. I need it to stop. Against my better judgment, I pick up the glass and toss back the liquid inside, swallowing in one quick gulp. It seems like the whole room cheers, but as I'd hoped, the situation has defused and most of the patrons grow bored after the display, returning to their own conversations.

Beth bends down, speaking softly into my ear, "I've already had so many people come up and buy you a drink, I figure all you ladies can drink free all night and still have plenty enough left over to get a couple of elephants drunk."

I can't help responding, "And yet these are the same people who adamantly oppose having three dollars a year added to their taxes so I can afford to hire a third officer."

"Maybe after tonight, that will change." She shrugs then tells the group she'll have our next round of drinks over in a jiffy.

I wonder if she's right. Showing my human side might go a far way in terms of public relations with the residents of Coyote Cove. The pressure is on. But not just about that.

I look at Sue, trying to catch her eye. Though she's smiling and laughing with the other women, it's like she's actively avoiding me. Does she think I suspect her of doing something wrong?

I should. But no matter what the evidence suggests, I just can't. As foolish as it seems, being here, in the same room with her, I can't deny that I trust her.

But I need her to tell me the truth about what happened the day Ruby Anderson disappeared, along with what part she had to play in it. As if sensing this, she gets up from the table and heads toward the bathroom. I stand, intending to follow, but as I do, I knock into someone.

"Sorry," I say, automatically putting my hand out to steady the man I bumped. His gaze is glassy and out of focus.

"Hey, Chief."

"Hi." I give him a smile that I hope doesn't betray that I don't know who he is. But I do vaguely recognize him. I just can't place from where.

"Listen, I've been wanting to tell you, you're doing a bang-up job on the arson investigation out on Old Mill Road."

And then it clicks.

I freeze the expression on my face, keeping it neutral as the memory plays through my mind like a film reel. The long drive alone to meet Fire Inspector Larson at the scene of the explosion. A truck appearing in the distance. The driver staring at me as he slowly drove past.

This is the man who was behind the wheel. The other vehicle—the *only* other vehicle—that had been on Old Mill Road. What had he been doing out there? More importantly, where did he hear that the explosion had been arson?

"Do you have any suspects yet?"

I sharpen my stare, but he doesn't meet my eyes. Maybe it's just my natural inclination to be suspicious, but it sounds like he's fishing for answers. "No, I'm still working on that. You have any ideas?"

He chuckles, wobbles on his feet, earning himself a dirty look as he catches himself on the back of another patron's chair. "Nope. Wish I could help you there." He glances around as if suddenly shocked to see where he is. Straightening his back, he gives me a nod, still not meeting my gaze, "Well, I'll let you get back to it. Hope y'all have a good night."

I watch as he stumbles across the bar and ducks into the hall that houses the bathrooms. I tap CeCe on the shoulder and gesture before he disappears. "You know who that is?" I ask

"Dave Fischer. Why?"

I shake my head. "Just curious."

Drumming my fingers against my glass, I try to place why the name sounds so familiar. It hits me just as Sue slips back into her chair. I missed my opportunity to speak with her in private. And a man who I suspect is somehow related to Missy Anderson, maiden name Fischer, was just questioning me about the explosion.

41

STEVE

I feel queasy as I trudge down the hall to my mother's apartment. Part of it's guilt from the quick text I'd sent Maggie earlier. I should have called. Should have *been* calling. But I haven't.

When we first got together, it felt like magic. It was so much more than just the spark we had between us or the excitement of a new relationship. It was the way she made me feel. The way a part of her seemed to need me. Even though she was the cop with a gun and far tougher than I could ever hope to be, I could still be a hero. Her hero.

And yeah, I know I'm being a bit delusional about that, probably even a lot, but there's no denying that there'd been something sad lingering beneath the surface of her smile. A dark cloud that fell over her eyes when she thought you weren't looking. I tried so hard to make those shadows go away. And they had. For a long time, I managed to keep the demons that haunted her at bay.

But now I worry that I *am* the demon.

Unlocking the door, I slip inside, leaving the lights off as I head straight for the kitchen. I scan the counters for the tequila my sister had been drinking the other night, hoping she left it behind, but there's nothing there.

I do, however, find a dusty bottle of scotch in one of the upper cabinets, peeking out from behind a bag of flour. I pour myself three fingers, then add another healthy splash before replacing the cap and returning it to its hiding spot. Taking a long sip, I focus on the burning sensation as it travels down my throat, into my empty stomach.

Pulling out my phone, I stare longingly at the image on my home screen, a picture of Maggie cuddling the dogs. This is why I have to discover the truth, as painful as it might be.

And yet, there's a small part of me that yearns to give in and give up.

Izzy stumbles into the room, stopping when she notices me sitting in the dark. She flicks on the lights and rubs her eyes like she doesn't believe what she sees. When she drops her hands and blinks at me, her gaze is glassy and bloodshot.

"What are you doing here?" she asks me.

"What are you? I thought you were on your way to Maggie's bachelorette party."

"Guess there was a change of plans."

"Izzy, they're waiting for you."

"Relax. I told her I got a flat tire."

"You lied?"

She shrugs like it's no big deal. "Who's going to tell her the truth? You?"

The anger I feel at my sister right now matches the burning from the scotch. "Go home, Izzy. Take a cab."

"I am home."

"I mean your place."

"Like I said." She spreads her hands out, gesturing around her. "I live here now."

"Since when?"

"Since earlier today." She takes the seat across from me and grabs my glass. Gives it a sniff before tossing down the contents. "Got any more?"

I debate a moment before shaking my head. She doesn't look like she needs another drink tonight. "What happened to your apartment?" I ask.

"Apparently, it's only mine as long as I pay rent. Who knew?"

"You lost it?" When she doesn't respond, I ask quietly, "Did you just forget?"

"No. I ran out of money."

"But what about your job?"

My sister had taken a big pay cut when she left her psychology practice to work with troubled youth at a halfway home, but she loved the kids and the difference she felt she was making in their lives. There's no way she would have given it up. Which means...

"They canned me."

"Why?"

She gives me a look that breaks my heart, a look like she hates me. Like she blames me. And why shouldn't she? What she's going through right now, whatever this is that has her spiraling? It's my fault.

"Izzy, I'm sorry."

"You should be." I'm taken aback by the vehemence in her voice. "I was happy, Steve. Really happy. For the first time in forever, my life was going well. And now?"

She makes a noise, using her hands to illustrate how it had all blown up. Sits there across the table, glaring at me.

I hang my head, unable to look at her. "You shouldn't have... done what you did," I say. "You shouldn't have saved me. God knows that most days I wish you hadn't. It would be better for everyone if I had been the one to die out there."

There's a long moment of silence, and then, "You don't mean that."

"It's true."

"But Maggie—"

"She would have survived it. She'd probably be better off. And you would be, too. What's happening to you... I know it's my fault. And I know there's no way I can make this up to you, make it right. If I could go back in time—"

"Stop saying that."

"Saying what?"

"That you wish you were dead."

"That's not what I'm saying."

"Yeah, it is. Stop it."

"But—"

"No. You're not the one with blood on their hands, so just cut it out."

The memory returns so hard I'm knocked breathless. I look down, staring at my palms. They're clean now, but I when I close my eyes, I can see the blood staining them, can feel the tackiness drawing my skin tight as it dries.

"Besides, I'm not screwed up because of what I did. I'd do it again in a heartbeat. You're my brother, of course I would. What's done my head in is..."

She trails off, staring into space.

"Is what?" I prod, trying my best to pay attention to what my sister's saying and not the sensation of digging my hands into the dirt, rubbing the soil between them until the stickiness is gone.

She doesn't react, pretending not to have heard me. After a long minute, she shifts her eyes to mine. "Is that I'm glad I did it. And I'm worried that a part of me liked it. Now, when some jerk cuts me off in traffic... I think about following them. About teaching them a lesson. I have daydreams about violence, about *being* violent. And it scares me."

"You're not a violent person, Iz."

But am I? I wonder.

"Are you sure?"

"I'm absolutely positive."

Am I? Because there was a time I would have said the same about myself. Now, I'm not so sure.

"Then how do you explain what I'm feeling?" she asks.

"Trauma? PTSD? Maybe you should talk to someone." I lick my lips nervously, knowing I need to do the same. That this flashback I'm having must be something I recalled while under hypnosis. But what else had I remembered?

She gives me a funny look.

"What?"

"Are you crazy?" she asks.

"Why? You'd have doctor-patient confidentiality," I insist.

"You say that like it's a sure thing."

"Well, isn't it?"

Izzy shakes her head. Something inside me winds so tight it feels like it might snap.

"It's not?" I gulp.

"I mean, technically, yeah, but there are too many loopholes to risk it. All the doctor would have to do is claim that I was a risk to others and they could break confidentiality to report what I'd done to the police. Even if they just thought I was a risk to myself, they could take steps to have me hospitalized. And once they had me on a nice cocktail of meds, who knows what I'd say—probably enough to further incriminate myself."

I wipe at the sweat gathering along my hairline. You wouldn't have to be medicated to say things that might get you in trouble. I'm pretty sure that hypnosis would do as well.

Had I told Dr. Curry about the blood on my hands? Is that why she'd acted so scared of me? Or had there been something else? Something even worse?

42

MAGGIE

I keep a smile pinned to my face, playing the part of the happy bride-to-be. Laughing when I'm supposed to, thanking the seemingly endless string of people who stop by to offer their congratulations. And in a way, something about it is strangely comforting.

It feels like this one simple act of having a bachelorette party at the local bar has done more to make me accepted by the people I serve as chief of police than all the sacrifices I've made, injuries I've incurred, and crimes I've solved during my five and a half years on the job.

If only it weren't an act, and I really was relaxed and enjoying myself. Instead, I feel like a string pulled to just within its breaking point. Just one more tiny tug of pressure, and I'll snap.

My face hurts, the muscles tense. I'm so preoccupied with not revealing that I'm having a miserable time that I can't think straight. Though I've paced myself, keeping to one drink an hour after that initial shot, my brain feels fuzzy, my tongue thick and dehydrated. I need a break, just a few minutes free from the smiley act to collect myself. Excusing myself to get some water, I head to the bar.

Squeezing into a tiny gap at the counter, I catch Beth's eye. I feel a tinge of guilt as she stops what she's doing and rushes over. "What can I get you, Chief?"

"Just some water, please."

Her expression is unreadable as she fills a pint glass at the tap and hands it to me, but I can feel the disappointment radiating off her. I tell myself I'm imagining things as I take the cup. As soon as she turns around, I hold it to my forehead, using it to cool off before taking a long sip.

"You doing okay, Red?"

Any bit of tension that I'd managed to release is back in triplicate in an instant. This is the absolute last thing I needed tonight. I force myself to turn toward the voice and find Fire Investigator Larson on the stool beside me.

"What are you doing here?" I ask.

"Getting a drink. The real question is, what are *you* doing here?"

"What do you mean?" I rub at the blush on my cheeks, can suddenly feel the eyeshadow heavy on my lids.

"Don't get me wrong, you look amazing, but it's not you. None of this is you."

"You don't know me."

"But I think I just might. We have more in common than you think."

"I doubt that." I busy myself draining my glass so I can make my escape.

He lowers his voice, leans in closer so I can hear him. His body radiates heat. "If you were my fiancée, you wouldn't be here right now."

I give him my best "you've got to be kidding me" look and huff a laugh. "What? You wouldn't *let* me be in a bar without you?"

"I don't mean here, here. I mean here mentally. In the head-space you're in."

The response knocks me breathless. I stare at him, unable to respond. Swallow hard as I work to refill my lungs.

"You need to take it easy on yourself. You can't save the whole world, you know."

I want to tell him that I can try, but the response dies on my lips because I realize how foolish it is. I can't save the world. I can't even save myself. But shouldn't I try to do my best anyway?

"My guess is, you've held yourself to such an impossible standard for so long, got yourself so tied up in knots, you don't even know how to have fun anymore."

Suddenly, it's important for me to prove him wrong, if only about this one thing.

"I can have fun."

His expression tells me he doesn't believe it. I try to think of how to have fun, be fun, but I don't even know what that is to me anymore. He's right. But not for long.

"Here you go," Beth says, placing a tumbler of amber liquid neat in front of Larson. I grab it before he can and toss it back, tell her through the burn to put it on my tab, and walk back across the crowded bar to my party.

The only way I can think of to enjoy myself is to not be me for a while. But there's one thing I need to do first.

Reaching our table, I walk to the far side and tap Sue on the shoulder. Gesture for her to follow me before heading for the darkened hallway that leads to the restrooms. I meet the smiling faces I pass with a grin of my own, fueled by the heat in my chest from Larson's whiskey.

But as soon as I reach the bathroom, I let it fall. Holding my hair to keep it from touching the floor, I bend over, checking beneath the stalls. I'm straightening just as Sue enters. Brushing by her, I lock the door. This is it. One way or another, this ends here.

43

MAGGIE

Sue flinches, startled by the sound of the bolt turning. Frightened by the prospect of being trapped in here with me, judging by the way her eyes flash, searching the room frantically for a point of escape. But there's none. That's the point.

"What's going on?" I ask her.

"What do you mean?"

"Sue."

I give her a pleading look, but she refuses to meet my gaze.

"How much do you know?" she asks.

"How much do you?" I counter. "You heard me talking to Dr. Ricky in the car on the way back from Missy Anderson's, when we took Ronny's missing person report. You know that he and Ruby were victims of the explosion."

She sucks in a sharp breath and for the first time looks at me. "So it's been confirmed? I'd been hoping you were wrong, but I guess—" She shakes her head, wrapping her arms tight around herself.

"What happened back then, Sue? The day Ruby went missing? I've read Parker's report. I know it's not true."

The woman before me sighs heavily as she leans against the

bathroom counter, using it to prop her up. It strikes me that this is one of only a handful of times that I've seen her wear something other than pajama pants. I don't like it. It makes it seem like there are two Sues, one entirely different from the woman I know.

"Ruby Anderson was the first friend I made when I moved to Coyote Cove. She was, well, she was a lot like you, actually. She was smart and tough. But she had this soft side, too. You could tell that once you were in her circle, she'd do anything for you. But there was something guarded about her."

Sue's eyes get a faraway look, like she's gazing into the past.

"What happened—it's not what we had planned."

I silently file this away, waiting for her to continue.

"Her husband, Nathan, had been beating her for years. Almost their whole marriage. We—me and our friend, Michelle —had been telling her that she should leave him from the very second that we found out, but she always argued that it wasn't that bad. That it wasn't worth destroying her family over a few bruises."

There's a haunted look in her eyes as she says, "Then, one day, I get a call from her. *I'm ready*. It's all she said, those two words, but I knew what they meant. He was the janitor at the school back then, so I drove by, made sure his car was in the lot, then went out to their place."

Her hands tremble as they clench the edge of the counter. Her voice is soft as she says, "It was bad. Really bad."

Clearing her throat, she speaks louder, with an edge. "I insisted she see a doctor, get her arm set by a professional. She was terrified Nathan would get in trouble and that would make it worse, but nothing happened. Ruby had to have surgery— they had to use a pin to hold the bone in her arm together he'd broken it so badly. Everyone knew he was responsible, but no one even looked at him funny. And once he'd found that out? It was all downhill from there."

"Did you tell Chief Parker? Did he try to help?"

Sue snorts.

"You do remember that I used to work for that pig, don't you? By that time, I'd worked for him long enough to know that he fully supported what he called 'a man's right to discipline his wife.' Besides, he and Nathan were buddies. He wasn't going to do anything to stop him. No, we knew we were on our own."

Pushing away from the counter, she starts pacing across the tiny room. "We started planning her escape that very day, but we knew it would take a while to put anything into action. She'd need money for her fresh start, and to take care of the kids. We had to make sure that Nathan couldn't find them once they were gone. But then... we ran out of time."

I want to reach out to her, take her by the hand, but I'm afraid that if I do, she'll stop talking. So I shove my fists in my pockets and wait.

"I don't know if he found out what we were planning, why he took it so far that day, but... he almost killed her. And Ruby... she knew she wouldn't survive next time. We all knew it. So once Michelle and I got her into the car, we just drove. Used one of the back roads to take her over the border into Canada, checked her into a hospital as a Jane Doe. Told them we'd found her along the side of the road. And then we left her."

Tears stream down her face as she turns to face me. "She begged us not to do it. Just the thought of leaving her kids behind was breaking her heart, but there was no other choice. Everyone had to think she was dead. So we came back and gave Chief Parker a story about going kayaking, said she'd flipped and drowned. I'm not sure if he ever believed me or not, but luckily he was too lazy to ask any questions."

"Why didn't you just tell me this from the start?" I ask, thinking of all the time and angst we could have saved.

"Because I wasn't sure you'd believe me."

"Sue—"

"—And I was so ashamed. Ruby insisted that Nathan had never hit any of the kids before, and I did my best to keep an eye on them and make sure that stayed true, but still. I feel like I failed them. All of them."

"You did what you had to do to save your friend."

"And look what happened anyway. That bastard finally killed her."

"You really think it was him?" I ask.

"Don't you?"

"Honestly? I'm not sure. It makes the most sense. I mean, he must have known the kayaking thing was a cover story. Must have suspected that she was still alive somewhere. But it's not the only possibility."

I think of Dave Fischer questioning me, of him knowing the explosion was arson. Of Ruby's oldest son, soon to be the ex-husband of a woman whose maiden name is also Fischer, being caught in the blast. Maybe I was wrong. Maybe Ronny wasn't leaving just as I reached the trailer. Maybe he had just gotten there.

Had someone been waiting for his arrival to trigger the explosion? Have I focused on the wrong victim? Were Ruby and Marie Bouchard just collateral damage?

And then there's my John Doe, his body found outside the building with our only known address for Ruby's daughter Rene, a receipt for two hundred feet of fuse in his pocket. Dead from an overdose of meth though he hadn't borne any signs of being a user.

No arrest record, no prints on file, no ID. Someone had left him there, a pipe in his hand, for me to find. Until I know who he is, I can't rule out his involvement in this.

"There are a lot of loose threads left to unravel in this case," I admit. "I'm not even sure yet if Ruby was the intended victim."

The look on her face—it's sheer relief mixed with absolute

sorrow. Without thinking I reach out for her. There's a moment when she just looks at me, and I hold my breath, not knowing if she's going to trust me to comfort her or not. And then she's in my arms, sobbing against me.

"I'm sorry. I've ruined your party." Her words are muffled against my chest.

"Don't be ridiculous. Besides, you haven't at all. In fact, I'm going to go out there, and you know what I'm going to do?"

She shakes her head against me.

"I'm going to celebrate."

Sue pulls away and gives me one of the looks I've come to know so well.

"I am," I insist. "Because I'm that confident that we're going to find out who *was* responsible for Ruby's death. You, me, and Kal."

"I know you wouldn't say it unless you believed it was true."

"I wouldn't," I agree.

Sue studies me as if she's trying to make up her mind, and for a moment, I think she's going to call my bluff. The standoff is broken by the noise of someone trying the handle on the locked door. She shakes her head, the doubt on her face turning into a smile.

"Go on, then. I'll be out in a minute after I clean up."

"Sue, I understand if you want to go home."

"And miss seeing what it looks like when Maggie Riley actually lets loose and celebrates? Not on your life. I'll join you in just a sec. Just try not to get too crazy until I get there."

I'm laughing as I unlock the door and slip past the patron rushing inside, which is me practicing being someone else, because I hate making promises I'm not sure I can keep. But that's exactly what I just did.

Would I have done it if I were in a better frame of mind? If I wasn't so desperate not to lose another loved one from my life?

As I head back to the party, I catch myself searching the

counter where Larson had been sitting, checking to see if he's still there. Once I realize what I'm doing, I look away quickly, before I can make certain that he's not. What do I care if he's gone? If anything, I should feel relieved. Which is why it's so odd that I find myself feeling disappointed instead.

44

MAGGIE

My cheeks ache from smiling, my belly from laughing, and my thighs from hours spent dancing by the time we decide to call it a night. The crowd has thinned since we arrived, making it easier to see the individual faces watching us with curiosity. And for once, it's easy to give them a smile.

I focus on walking straight, trying not to think about what I'm going to feel like in the morning as we make our way through the bar. Pause to do a quick head count to make sure we're all together.

CeCe bounces off me, checking her phone as we walk toward the exit. "Oops. Sorry, hun." She covers her mouth with a manicured hand as she hiccups. "I was just making sure our rides were on their way. I have some girls from the shop coming to drive us home."

"Oh, good." Margot throws an arm around her neck, knocking them both off balance. "I thought I was going to have to sleep it off in my car."

"I walked," Gretchen says. The tall librarian stumbles, spreads her arms out wide for balance. "It was easier, earlier."

"Well, don't none of you worry, the girls will make sure we all get home safely," CeCe assures them.

I pause, my hand on the door. "I think Kal was planning on doing that."

CeCe grins. "I wish I'd have known. That's one man I wouldn't mind being alone in a car after dark with."

"Yes," Gretchen says. "Your lieutenant, he's very, how do you say it? Light on the eyes?"

"It's *easy*," Margot corrects. "And you're both just lucky that I'm in a relationship or neither of you would stand a chance."

We burst through the door laughing, the cool night air a balm to my overheated skin.

"This was fun," I say. "Thank you. We should do this more often."

"We should make it a regular thing," Sue suggests.

Gretchen nods. "Like a book club."

"One where the focus is more on the booze than the boo—" CeCe falters midsentence, her expression stiffening as she squints into the darkened lot, where something's snagged her attention.

The rest of the women fall silent, realizing something's wrong. I feel instinctively for my gun on my hip, only to find that it's not there. I put my hand on her arm, stopping her as she takes a step closer to whatever's caught her eye.

"What is it?" I ask, straining to see through the shadows.

"There."

I try following where she's pointing, but her arm is wavering, or my vision is. I cast a desperate glance over my shoulder, searching behind me. Spot Kal parked in a corner, no doubt trying to be politely unobtrusive until we're ready to leave. I gesture for him to come join us, to hurry as CeCe breaks free and stalks forward.

"That truck."

Over half the vehicles here are trucks. I have no idea which one she's talking about or why it's caught her interest. Or what I'll do if this situation turns dangerous.

This. This right here is why I don't let loose.

I don't like it when my senses are dulled, my reactions slow. I don't like being unarmed or unprepared. And I can't stand feeling vulnerable. I check Kal's progress, then make a judgment call, breaking into an unsteady trot to catch up with CeCe.

"CeCe, wait up. Stop for a moment."

She turns to face me looking spooked. Points again. This time I'm close enough to see that her finger is aimed at the metal winch hook retracted into the front bumper of a black Chevy truck. "Is that like the one you're looking for?"

My pulse quickens as I realize what she's talking about. I scan the pickups surrounding us. Most of them have hooks visible, but none of them look quite like the one that's caught CeCe's eye. The one that looks just like the picture Linda had showed me earlier.

"Do you know whose vehicle this is?"

"No clue," she says as Kal joins us, the rest of the group at his heels.

"What's going on?" Sue asks.

Ignoring her, I turn to Kal and point at the truck. "Can you see the VIN through the windshield?"

He cranes his head to look, then nods.

"Good. Get pictures of that and the plates, then run them. We need to know who this truck belongs to."

"I feel like I've missed something." Margot says it like a joke, but her voice is tense, strained. I follow her gaze to where Linda has dropped to her knees in the dirt by the front bumper and realize I'm not the only one who's sobered up fast.

It's possible that this is the truck that hit Michelle Sanders, that the person who killed her is inside the bar behind us right now. But there's no telling how long that will hold true. And if they come out and find us inspecting their truck, chances are that they won't be happy. I need to minimize risks.

"CeCe, can you make sure everyone's on their way home safely with a designated driver?"

"Of course." She fixes a wide smile on her face as she turns to the others. "Come on, ladies."

I hear Margot asking questions, but I ignore them, checking only that she's allowing herself to be herded back toward the entrance of the Loose Moose.

"Kal, you got the numbers?"

"Yeah."

"Give them to Sue then go get in your car. When the driver comes out, I want you ready to follow. Dr. Ricky?"

Erika's standing behind Linda, taking pictures of the tow hook with her cell phone while Linda holds a credit card up beside it for size reference. Understanding the urgency in my tone, she says, "Just a few more close-ups."

"Sue?" I ask.

She doesn't glance up from the screen as she pecks at her phone. "On it. But are you going to tell me why?"

"That truck might be the one that hit Michelle Sanders."

Her eyes lift to mine for one brief second. Her jaw tenses. Her gaze hardens. She swallows hard, then goes back to the task at hand without saying a word.

Linda hands her phone to Erika, who uses the device to take a second set of close-ups of the tow hook. Rubbing her fingertip in the dirt, she makes a stain on her jeans to mark the height of the bumper. Then both women back away from the vehicle taking midrange pictures, then farther still for some overview shots. When they're done, I gesture for them to head to the car we came in.

"Come on," I say to Sue, intending to follow.

She ignores me, raising her phone up high in an attempt to get a stronger signal.

"Sue." I put a hand on her arm just as the door to the Loose Moose opens, the sound of laughter spilling out into the night. My heart races as I pull her into the shadows. We watch from around the side of an old GMC as a trio of men exits the building, voices loud as they come toward us across the lot.

"I'm parked over here," she whispers. Her palm is hot as she wraps it around my elbow, using it to guide me toward her vehicle. We stay low as we creep closer to the men, backtracking to the Pinto. I hold my breath as she unlocks the car.

Sue reaches in and quickly extinguishes the interior light as we climb inside, closing the doors all but a crack. We sink in our seats as the men approach. My chest tightens, breath catching as one of them stops in front of us, sure we've been spotted, but he bends to tie a shoelace before continuing on.

"Fred Wallace," Sue whispers from the seat beside me.

"Huh?"

"The truck. It belongs to Fred Wallace."

"Does the name mean anything to you?" I ask.

Two of the men get into a truck several vehicles away from us. The engine roars to life. I slip a little farther down in the seat as the headlights cut through the night. As we watch, the third man climbs up into the cab of the black Chevy with the tow hook.

"No."

"Send the address to Kal."

Moments later my lieutenant passes by, following the truck from the lot. Catching his eye, I give him a nod.

Almost six years. That's how long Michelle Sanders' case has been unsolved while whoever killed her walked free. And if this turns out to be the lead that cracks it open, it will be because of an oversight—because I left the file out on a table when I had guests over.

This right here is why Larson was wrong. Because no

matter how hard you try and how much you give, it's never enough.

But that might also be why he's right, too.

"Now what?" Sue asks, interrupting my thoughts.

"Now we go home."

"Maggie."

We stare at each other through the darkened car. I think I'm going to have to explain to her that there's nothing more we can do for now. That Kal will find out where the man ends up for the night.

That we have to check the bumper height against the injury, compare the photographs with the bruising that was present in Michelle's autopsy photos and with the impression that was made on her bone, see if we can somehow prove that the truck was in Coyote Cove the night the accident occurred to see if we have grounds to get a warrant. And then even after that, there's no guarantee that there will be any evidence left to prove that the truck was the vehicle that hit her friend.

But instead, she says, simply, "Thank you."

I nod. "You want to come back to my place?"

"I think I'm ready to call it a night. But if you're free tomorrow?"

"Of course. Head on over whenever you're ready."

Standing in the parking lot, watching her drive away, I wonder how many times I might have seen that truck before. How many times I may have unwittingly stood next to a killer. How many times I was one of the lucky ones, the women who stayed safe, while so many others have fallen prey.

45
STEVE

Danger lurks around every corner. Not just dark parking lots, shadowed alleys, and strangers, but friends, neighbors, loved ones, coworkers, classmates, and acquaintances. How had Wesley convinced Georgia to get in the car that night?

And what percentage of women reported missing across the world have met a fate similar to hers—a body hidden in a shallow grave under a tree? How many families out there are looking for their loved ones in the wrong places—among the living? Is it just hope? Or is it the belief that killing someone isn't something you're supposed to be able to get away with?

But it had been so easy, hadn't it? Too easy.

Steam rises from the scalding water flowing from the tap. Sweat beads to the surface of my skin. And though my flesh feels like it's melting, I plunge my hands back under the stream with a fresh glob of soap between them, washing and scrubbing until they're almost as red as the blood that stained them in my memory.

Because it was a memory, wasn't it?

As much as I want to deny it, to believe that it's just something I imagined, a symptom of my guilt, I know in the heart beating double-time inside my chest that it's not. It's too real. Not just the sight of it, but the feel of it. The smell of it, the sharp copper scent so strong that I can practically taste it.

But what does it mean?

I turn off the water, blot my painfully tender hands dry, then study my reflection in the mirror. I don't look any different than I had before that flash of memory rose to the surface in my brain. Maybe the circles under my eyes are a little darker, my face a little paler from the sleepless night I'd had, but there's nothing about the eyes looking back at me that tells me what I need to know.

What had I done to get that blood on me?

My head throbs. My body feels heavy. I long to close my eyes, but every time I do I'm plagued by that image of my bloody hands. There has to be an explanation.

Maybe I fought with Wesley that night. Or maybe I cut myself.

Stumbling down the hall I enter the kitchen, pour myself a cup of coffee, and slump into a chair at the table. Dr. Curry had said it was normal to retain what you'd recalled under hypnosis, but she hadn't said it would come in bits and pieces. I need to know what else is lurking in my subconscious.

I reach for my phone, desperate to have the woman explain what's happening to me. Remember that it's Saturday morning. I'm not sure I can survive the entire weekend like this, crushed under the weight of self-doubt and crippling suspicions.

Maybe I should try to find her home address, though that's probably the quickest way to guarantee that she reports what I've done. But what have I done? The not knowing is killing me.

"Good morning, darling."

I straighten in my seat as my mother drops a kiss on my head. The smile she wears slips, replaced by a frown as she catches sight of my face.

"Are you feeling all right?"

"I'm fine."

"Are you sure? The clinic on the corner has weekend hours. Maybe we should try and make you an appointment."

"I'm sure," I say, blocking her hand as she tries to feel my forehead.

She makes a growling noise. "Well, at least let me make you something to eat, then."

"I'm not hungry."

"Nonsense."

She opens a bag of bread and fills the toaster. Grabs a stack of plates out of the cabinet. Removes the butter dish from the refrigerator.

"Pass me that knife, would you?"

She holds her hand out, waiting for me to fill it.

A match strikes in my memory. It catches, sparking into a blaze as Dr. Curry's voice plays in my mind.

"What's he doing right now?"

"Holding out his hand."

"For?"

"The knife. The one he gave me to use."

I stand so abruptly that I knock my chair over.

"Stephen, what happened?" my mother asks.

But Dr. Curry's questions rings louder.

"For what? Did Wesley tell you what to do with it?"

"No. I just knew."

"What did you do, Steve? What did you do?"

"I don't know," I whisper.

"Maybe you should go lie down, honey. Try to get some rest."

I nod woodenly at my mother before retreating from the room. Straining to recall the rest of the memory as I trudge down the hallway. I can't. But now, when I look down at my hands, I don't just see blood—there's a pocketknife in my palm as well.

All these years I thought Wesley was to blame for what happened. I thought that I was innocent. But what if I blocked out what happened that night not because of what I didn't do, but because of what I *did*?

The instant I wake up, last night comes flooding back to me. Running into Fire Investigator Larson at the bar. The iffy promise I made to Sue that I'd discover the truth about what happened to Ruby Anderson. The truck in the parking lot of the Loose Moose with a winch hook that could potentially match the injuries on Michelle Sanders' body. Dancing to a song that had been one of my favorites as a teenager, the same way I would have danced to it back then.

I groan as I roll out of bed, only partly because of the dehydration headache throbbing behind my eyes. Had I made a fool of myself last night? Had the whole town watched?

Shuffling to the kitchen in search of liquid, I find Linda and Erika already awake and hovering over a laptop on the island, the dogs settled at their feet. Linda takes one look at me and passes me a glass of water. Dr. Ricky gives me a big smile, her eyes sparkling as I drain the cup.

"Good morning. I enjoyed your bachelorette party very much. Did you?"

"Maybe a bit too much."

"I agree, it was very exciting. I'm aware that not all of them involve investigating a cold case, so I feel very fortunate that yours did."

Pouring myself a cup of coffee, I take the seat beside her and look at the laptop.

"Uh-uh." She covers my cup with her hand. "Not on an empty stomach. Too acidic. Eat this first." She nudges a plate in front of me.

"What is it?"

"Avocado toast."

I take a bite as I scan the images on the screen, a side-by-side comparison of the bruising on Michelle Sanders' body as photographed during her autopsy, and a picture of the winch hook taken last night.

"The measurements match," Linda says, anticipating my question. "If that truck was in town that night, there's enough circumstantial evidence that I doubt there'll be any issue getting a judge to issue a warrant to process the vehicle. I don't know if there will be any blood evidence or other trace left after all these years, but we can try."

A knock at the door interrupts before she can say more. I go to set down my avocado toast, but there's only a corner left. I pop it in my mouth and, brushing the crumbs off my fingertips, follow the dogs to the front of the house to find Sue waiting on the front porch.

"Morning," she says, brushing by me to come inside. "Here." She pushes a book into my arms before squatting to give the pups a cuddle.

I look down at the hard navy cover, the word *Photographs* embossed in fancy gold script.

"What's this?"

She ignores me, still cooing to the dogs.

"Sue?"

After a final round of pats, she holds her arm out to me so I can help pull her up. She groans as she stands, mumbles a comment about the joys of getting older. Flexes her knees. Catches sight of me and frowns.

"Geesh. How long did you keep the party going last night?"

"Until Kal was back at his apartment safe and sound."

She nods in approval and heads toward the kitchen, leaving me standing by the door with the photo album. I glance after her, knowing I should follow. Then again, she wouldn't have left me alone with this if she hadn't wanted me to look.

I detour to the living room and settle on the couch. Lay the book across my thighs. It feels heavier than it appears. I suspect it's from the weight of the secrets inside.

Flipping it open, I find myself staring at a much younger Sue. Her face is unlined, her hair a rich chestnut without a hint of gray, the glasses she's worn since I've known her nowhere in sight. She sits cross-legged in front of a fireplace with a young child on her lap, flanked on either side by women holding babies.

I study the photograph, trying to absorb all the details. The way Sue's been caught mid-speech, mouth open. How the blonde to her left has her head thrown back, eyes squeezed shut in laughter. The way the redhead to her right smiles shyly, the hint of a bruise yellowing the skin around her eye.

My skin prickles as I realize what I'm looking at. I glance toward the kitchen, then flip the page. A cluster of toddlers sits on the grass among a collection of Easter eggs, the women behind them wearing bunny ears and silly grins. Then the same toddlers in cutesy Halloween costumes, the mothers each wearing a superhero t-shirt. A baby with its head poking out of a wrapped box, a bow stuck to its bald head.

The children grow older. More of them appear. Dozens of holidays and celebrations frozen in time fill the album. I stop at a shot that catches my eye, studying it.

This time the women are outside, standing behind a picnic table lined with children. A cake sits half sliced in the center.

The blonde blows a noisemaker while Sue appears to be clapping. The redhead wears a tense expression, a frown accentuating her scabbed lip as she looks somewhere off camera.

In the next picture, the redhead appears smaller, as if she's been shrinking. Her shoulders are raised to either side of her ears, and though she smiles for the camera, you can tell it isn't real. A man I recognize as a much younger, slimmer Nathan Anderson stands beside her. In the back right corner of the photograph, I spot Sue and the blonde looking deep in conversation though they both have their eyes cut in the couple's direction.

Page after page, photo after photo shows Ruby's evolution from the pretty young woman captured in the first photograph to the woman she becomes in the last, a frail looking creature with wide troubled eyes. A scar severs one eyebrow into halves. Thick streaks of gray stain her hair prematurely.

She sits with her arm in a sling, balancing a little girl on her lap. Though she doesn't seem aware that her picture is being taken, the child glares at the camera. There's a small birthmark on her cheek in the shape of a tulip. I've seen that birthmark before.

Keeping my hand pinned inside the album, marking the page, I hurry to my feet and into the kitchen. "Who's this?" I ask, pointing to the little girl in the picture.

Sue looks at the photo. "Who, Rene? That's Ruby's youngest. Why?"

I don't answer, instead pulling out my cell and dialing Kal. I imagine him sitting at his desk at the CCPD right now, bored out of his mind during his Saturday shift. Well, things are about to get more interesting. He answers on the first ring.

"We need to go back to Railroad Street. We were right about Mary lying to us about Rene. She *is* Rene."

"She—seriously?"

"Yeah."

"So her question about which one it was that left her something? The one you thought meant she knew more than one of the family members was dead?"

"Yeah."

He curses. "We had her."

"We'll get her again. I'll meet you at the department in twenty."

Ending the call, I hurry to catch a quick shower, only to find the way blocked by Sue.

"That girl's been through a lot, Maggie. She's had a rough time of it."

"I know, I've seen her arrest record."

Sue sighs heavily like I'm missing the point. "If she lied to you, it was probably because she was scared."

I muster a small smile. Soften my voice as I say, "I understand that. But I still have to question her, Sue."

"Promise you'll be gentle with her?"

I snap my mouth shut, swallowing my response, because I'll agree to no such thing. I need to find out what Rene knows. The young woman's already lied to me once. I can't risk her wasting more of my time by allowing her to do it again. Luckily, I'm saved from having to explain that as my phone rings.

"Chief Riley."

"Hey, Chief. My name's Doug Byrd. My buddy Lou asked me to call you about the trailer I rented out for him out on Old Mill Road. The one that blew up?"

"Yes, Mr. Byrd, thank you for calling."

I hurry down the hall to my bedroom. There's no time for a shower now, or even to change my clothes.

"No problem. What is it that I can help you with?" he asks.

Shoving my wallet in my back pocket, I pin the phone between my shoulder and ear and wrap my duty belt around my waist, drawing it tight until my firearm is snug against my side. Grab my badge and clip it on.

"I was hoping you could tell me a bit more about Marie Bouchard."

"You mean Mary?"

A tingle races down my spine.

"I'm sorry. I thought the tenant's name was Marie."

"It's spelled that way, only she put a little accent mark on it when she wrote it out. Told me the pronunciation was French."

I stare at the keys in my hand, trying to wrap my head around what he's just said. "Are you telling me that the name of the woman who rented the trailer sounds like 'Mary,' not 'Marie'?"

"Yep."

"I'm sorry, Mr. Byrd. I'm afraid I'm going to have to call you back. Is this a good number to reach you at?"

"It's the only one I've got."

The throbbing behind my eyes starts again as I hang up, this time stronger than before. It's what I've been looking for this whole time—the connection between the Andersons and the third victim of the blast. And Ruby's youngest daughter appears to be that link.

It seems obvious now that it's staring me in the face. The young women were the same age and they both had a criminal history that centered around drug charges, specifically methamphetamine. The difference is, only one of them ended up dead. And my gut is telling me that Rene knows the answer why. I need to find her now more than ever.

47

MAGGIE

My pulse thunders in my ears, my senses hypervigilant, searching for danger as I step from the light of day. The apartment building on Railroad Street is no less depressing than the last time we were here. Our footsteps echo down the narrow hallway, the tempo irregular as we step around a discarded syringe, a rotting banana peel, a puddle of something that makes the toast in my stomach climb up the back of my throat.

We come to a stop in front of 12C, the door behind which we found the woman claiming to be Mary on our previous visit. Kal steps to the side, back against the wall, staying out of sight of anyone peering through the peephole in the door like we'd discussed, hoping the sight of me alone out of uniform will help our chances of having the door opened. Drawing a deep breath, I raise my hand and knock.

I hear scurrying inside the apartment, the sound conjuring the image of rats skittering across a paper-strewn room. There's a low murmur of voices from within. But no one answers.

"Hello?" I ask, keeping my voice as light and casual as I can. "I'm looking for Rene Anderson. I was told the other day that I might find her here. I have news about her inheritance."

It sounds like an argument is being held in whispers. Finally, after an interminable moment, the door inches open. A yellowed bloodshot eye appears. It bounces around warily, scanning the hallway around me.

"You've got money?"

"Is Rene in there?"

"How much are we talking about?" The door opens a little wider, revealing a man with jaundiced skin, cheeks sunken deep in his narrow face. His head's been shaved haphazardly, spots taken down to the skull, the rest with a thin buzz cut left covering it. He licks scaly lips, revealing broken, rotten teeth. "You got it on you right now?"

Flinging the door open, he jumps out into the hall, using his momentum to pin me to the far wall with his fingers curled around my throat. The back of my head throbs with the impact, but before the stars flashing in my vision have a chance to clear, I grab his wrist, hold it steady as I jam the heel of my other hand as hard as I can into the underside of his elbow joint, making his arm buckle. As soon as his grasp is released, Kal has him pinned against the filthy floor, handcuffs making a satisfying snap as they click into place.

I rub a hand across the back of my scalp as I catch my breath. My body trembles with adrenaline.

"You okay?" Kal asks.

"Fine," I say. I swallow down my jangling nerves and shake my arms out before drawing my pistol. Pressing my back against the wall, I peer around the side of the doorframe into the apartment beyond.

"Coyote Cove Police Department. Hands up."

A woman stares at me, frozen, a pipe clenched in her fist.

"I said hands up! Against the wall."

Kal finishes patting down the man who attacked me and pulls him to his feet, dragging him into the room. He covers me as I pull on a glove and take the pipe from the woman, setting it on the cardboard box being used as a table before guiding her to a pockmarked wall.

"Is anyone else here?" I ask her.

"No."

"You have anything on you that can stick me, poke me, or hurt me?"

She mutters a negative.

"I'm going to pat you down real quick to make sure."

When I'm done, I turn her around.

"Stay put."

I leave her under Kal's watchful eye as I quickly check the rest of the barren apartment to be sure, then return to the living room.

"What's your name?"

I can barely hear her answer as she mutters, "Amy."

"Amy what?"

There's a long pause while she thinks up a fake surname. "Smith."

"What can you tell me about Rene Anderson?"

She simply stares in reply to the question, but the man glares at me and says, "She owes me."

"For what?" When he doesn't answer, I take a step closer. "What did you do for her?"

"I didn't do anything."

"Then why does she owe you?"

He looks between me and Kal, suddenly seeming to realize his mistake. "I fronted her a hit, is all. She said she had some cash coming her way, that she was good for it."

"When was the last time you saw her?"

"She was here when I got here."

"When was that?"

His look tells me his addiction has reached the point where time is judged by his next fix, not hours or days or weeks. He could have been here when I first spoke to Rene, when she told me her name was Mariè. Or she could have just left.

"You know where I can find her?"

The woman shifts nervously as he shrugs.

"How about you?"

Her eyes dart from me to the floor. She shakes her head from side to side.

"You on parole? Probation?" When she looks away from me, I add, "You want to go back?"

Amy keeps her gaze on her feet, but swallows hard. I glance at the box where a small baggie lies beside the pipe I'd taken from her. It's not a lot split two ways. It's not a lot, period. I shoot Kal a look. He nods almost imperceptibly.

"You tell me what you know, and I'll forget about this."

It's only half truthful, because I'll be requesting that the state police raid this building, but for now, I'm willing to forget about bringing charges against the woman in exchange for the information I sorely need.

Her dark gaze flits to me, then darts away. She picks at a scab on her arm. Her face twitches. Finally, she breaks her silence.

"All I know is, she said her family lived around here some-where. And that they had some business to discuss."

"Did she say what?"

She shakes her head.

"She tell you where she was going?"

"No."

"What about Mariè Bouchard? You know her?"

She lifts one shoulder and lets it drop. "She and Rene were friends. Maybe more."

"What do you mean by that?"

"They met in the pen," she says by way of explanation.

"Nah, that ain't the way it is," the man in handcuffs interrupts. "Mariè was seeing some guy. Think his name was Wally or something like that."

I feel a surge of adrenaline as I turn to face him, recalling the name Sue had said last night, the owner of the black truck that might have hit Michelle Sanders—Fred Wallace.

"Could it have been Wallace?"

"Yeah, that sounds right."

What are the odds that one of the victims of the explosion, the blast that also killed Ruby Anderson and her son, just happened to be dating the man who may be responsible for killing Michelle, one of the two women who helped Ruby escape her abusive marriage, in a hit and run?

"What can you tell me about him?"

"Nothing. Never met him. Just heard Mariè mention him a couple times, is all. He could have just been some john she got money from."

"How long ago did she first mention him?"

"Do I look like her mother? I told you everything I know."

I turn back to the woman, something she'd said before we got interrupted niggling at my brain. "What did you mean that Mariè and Rene 'were' friends? They aren't anymore?"

She shrugs. "Haven't seen Mariè in a while. Figured maybe she'd had enough."

"Of what?"

Tears gather in her eyes as she gestures around. "This."

"Is there anything else you can tell me about either of them?"

"That's all I know."

"You have anything to add?" I ask her companion.

The question is met with a surly look. Pulling my cell from my pocket, I bring up one of the pictures I'd taken of John Doe, a close-up of his face, and hold it out to him.

"Have you ever seen this man before?"

He frowns at the screen, then looks at me like I'm asking a joke. "Nope."

"You sure?"

"He ain't a regular around here, if that's what you're asking."

"What about you?"

I turn the screen so Amy can see. She shakes her head, covering her mouth with a hand.

"Is he dead?"

When I nod, she goes green.

"Okay, we're done here."

Palming the pipe and baggie, I pull my nitrile glove off around them, trapping them inside.

"Hey—"

The look I give cuts off any complaints. Kal pulls the man up and walks him toward the door. The man plants his feet and turns his handcuffed wrists toward us.

"Aren't you gonna take them off?"

"Why would I do that?" Kal answers. "You're coming with me."

"Aw, come on, man. You lied."

"No, I didn't."

"You said—"

"I didn't say anything. She did. To your friend here. You assaulted a law enforcement officer. Did you really think you were going to get away with that?"

"Her? But she's not wearing a uniform. How was I supposed to know?"

"You're not helping your case any."

The man shuts up, shooting a poisonous-looking glare at my lieutenant. He lets his legs go limp, refusing to walk until Kal grabs him by the beltloop to help him along. Kal waits until he has him secured in the back of the cruiser with the door closed before asking, "What do you make of all that?"

"Hard to say, considering the source. I'm interested in finding out if Wally really is Fred Wallace. It would be a little too convenient if the same man who might have killed Michelle Sanders was dating the woman who died with Ruby Anderson in the explosion."

"You think he had something to do with it?"

I shrug. "No clue yet. But I think the key lies with finding Rene. Seems like another visit with Nathan Anderson is in order."

Kal casts a doubtful glance at the back of his car. "You want me to turn him loose?"

"Definitely not."

"Are you going to wait to go out there until I get back?" He sighs heavily at my expression. "I didn't think so. Chief, that's not a stop you should be making on your own."

"I know." I pull on my lip, thinking. "I'll tell you what. Why don't we both drive out there? If our buddy has any complaints about the detour, just tell him to save it for his lawyer."

It's not a perfect plan, but it will have to do. We need to find Rene Anderson, and we need to do it quickly.

The young woman knows more than what she'd let on, not to mention that her friend and two members of her family have been killed, putting her at the center of this case, which is a dangerous place to be. It's where the crosshairs are.

48

STEVE

There's a deep sense of dread growing in the pit of my stomach, a stone made of lead and fear. I can't shake the feeling that I'm unprepared. But I'm still not sure for what.

Which is why, even though I know I shouldn't be here right now, I feel like I have no other choice. I'm desperate.

My gaze travels over the faded navy blue quilt that covers the bed, a stain on the top left that I know was made by grease from a slice of pizza. The movie posters on the wall, Kiefer Sutherland's face on *The Lost Boys* scratched by the zipper on a jacket carelessly flung toward the dresser beneath, the crinkle in the *M* of *Mortal Kombat* the only evidence of the hole hidden behind it, put there by an errant baseball. The jumble of worn sneakers tumbling out of the overstuffed closet.

It's like a time capsule in here. Everywhere I look memories threaten to breach the wall I've worked so hard to erect, the one I've got my emotions hidden behind. I know I need to hurry up and get this over with. But I have no idea where to start.

I busy myself folding an empty cardboard box into shape. Flinch at the sound as I run a strip of tape along the bottom seam. It's too quiet in here. The sound of the past too loud.

Setting the box down, I ease the door open and peer down the hall to where Mrs. Banks is nestled on the couch under a thick blanket, napping. It's painful seeing this version of her, the one ravaged by time and grief and who knows what else. There's no telling what Wesley's put her through over the years. What it feels like to spend your days knowing that your son has taken a life.

I back away, closing myself in the room again. Try not to think about how my own mother would feel if she knew what I'd been involved in. But what is it that I'd really done?

I'm still waiting for my fragmented memories to coalesce and reveal the whole story of what happened that night—and how big a part I played. Because I can feel that knife in my sticky blood-smeared palm. I have to keep searching for answers.

Every fiber in my body is telling me that there's something here. I just have to be smart enough to find it.

My eyes land on the dresser. I pull the top drawer free and dump it on the bed. Check the bottom, then lean down to inspect behind it. Start unrolling each pair of socks that were inside, patting them down before rerolling them and placing them in the box. It might seem excessive, but I'm not taking any chances of missing what I'm here to find.

As I go through the compartments, checking each item, every pocket, my thoughts drift to Maggie. I think of that first day I'd heard her laugh, watching between the trees as she emerged from her driveway, the dogs frisking down the road ahead of her, making her jog to keep up. How I'd thought to myself that I'd do anything to be the one to cause her to make that sound.

I haven't done a very good job of it lately. And though this whole crusade I've been on has been about ensuring that changes, now I'm not so sure it will.

Because I'd had blood on my hands. A knife in my fist. And

I said something when I recalled those memories that left the hypnotherapist terrified.

Had I hurt Georgia? As impossible as it seems to believe about myself, I'd been drugged. Who knows what I did under Wesley's guidance? I can't remember what happened, and until I do, I can't be around Maggie.

And that's what this is all really about, isn't it? The trust I've lost in myself. The fear of what lurks in that shadowy part of my psyche that I can't see.

I fold another box and move on to the closet. Search every jacket for tears in the lining. Every shoe for a secret hidden in the toe.

I'd known Maggie for almost six months before I worked up the nerve to kiss her. It was my first winter in Coyote Cove. It was one of those days where the sun never bothers to appear, the sky the color of dull steel, the wind subzero and treacherous. Snow had fallen thick and heavy during the night, smothering the landscape more than blanketing it.

The plow trucks had been running nonstop to keep the roads clear, leaving a three-foot ridge of dirty slush that had frozen solid along the sides of the street—including the openings of the driveways. Bundling up, I'd stepped out onto my porch to survey the damage, when I could hear the telltale clink of metal against ice.

I'd hurried into a pair of boots and grabbed my shovel, then waded through the sea of white, climbed over the small mountain range of ice, and crunched across the salted road.

Maggie's eyes met mine over the barrier that kept her vehicle trapped, her face flushed red, hair stuck to the sweat on her face, and she said, "I don't want to be here anymore."

I felt a zing of panic at the thought of losing her, even though I was painfully aware that she wasn't mine. And she never would be if she left. I knew I needed to get her talking, to find out what I could do to make her change her mind.

"Where would you go?" I asked.

"Home."

"Do you miss your family?" She didn't answer. Sensing it was a sensitive subject, I offered, "I miss mine."

"Then why are you here?"

"I'm not quite sure. I came up on vacation and something about the place just felt... I don't know. Like it would be a good place to start over, I guess."

"Yeah."

The sounds of our heavy breathing and the clangs of our shovels as we chipped at the ice filled the air.

"They need you up here, you know," I said.

She snorted. "They hate me. They'd be glad to see me go."

"All the more reason to stay, then," I said, grinning. "To stick it to them."

Her lips twitched into a small smile, the first she'd offered that day. We continued working in silence, and though it might have made more sense for us to work at opposite ends of the barrier, we stayed together, mirroring each other's movements on opposing sides of the ridge.

When there was just a small hump left, one she could easily drive over, I stopped working, leaning on my shovel as I looked at her. "Are you lonely?" I asked. The question had been circling in my head, begging to be set free.

Maggie frowned. "No. I have the dogs. And work."

"There's more to life than work."

She shrugged, not looking at me as she said, "It's what I've got."

"But that's not all."

"It's enough," she insisted.

"Is it?"

Her frown deepened like she might argue with me. I reached out, putting my hand on her shovel, stilling her movements. She looked at me in surprise, eyes glistening.

Letting both shovels drop, I pulled off my gloves and cupped my hands around her cold cheeks. Held her gaze, watching closely, giving her time to object as I slowly moved forward until our lips touched.

The kiss that followed was long. Hungry. Needy.

When it was over, she backed away like she was embarrassed. Muttered an apology about having to get to work as she hurried back to the house. As I watched her leave, I knew it would be a battle to get past the barriers she had put up. But I also knew that if I succeeded, it would be the most worthwhile reward I'd ever earned.

I vowed that very second to never give up. I can't back down now. Not even if it's me who's the one who's scared and broken this time.

I seal the box containing Wesley's bedding and the contents of his nightstand. Check the mattress and boxspring then lean them against the wall. Break down the metal bedframe. Stand back and survey the room.

It looks bare, the furniture pushed along one wall, a stack of boxes piled against another. I'd been so sure that I'd uncover something useful. So convinced that I'd once known Wesley well enough that I'd be able to predict this one tiny thing.

For the first twenty-two years of my life, he was my closest friend and confidant. And though I'd never grieved the end of our friendship, I now find myself overcome with heartache and despair. I still don't have a clue what I did that night. What if I never remember?

Tears sting my eyes, tighten my throat as I turn to the last vestiges of Wesley Banks that still exist. Removing the tacks from the wall, I roll up the poster closest to me and add it to the stack. Turn back for the next one. And freeze.

My muscles spasm, tensing as I lean closer for a better look. My hand shakes as I reach for the two small rectangles sitting on the cross brace between studs visible through the hole in the wall. The sharp edges of Maggie's business card dig into my palm as I stare at it in disbelief.

How had Wesley gotten it? And what was he doing with a picture of Maggie from when she was younger?

Only, as I examine the other item I'd found, the student ID in my hand, I realize that it's not my fiancée in the photograph—it's Georgia Pierce.

The resemblance is uncanny.

This isn't the Georgia from my memory. When I think of her, I see the way she'd appeared in the MISSING posters her family had distributed. But she doesn't look anything like that in this picture. Instead of curly hair, it's straight. And it isn't brown. It's auburn with reddish highlights.

I sit down hard, striking my tailbone painfully against the floor as my muscles go weak, my entire body trembling violently. Is it just a coincidence that Maggie looks so much like this woman from my past? Or is that the very reason why I've pursued her?

49

MAGGIE

The drive out to Nathan Anderson's house seems to take twice as long as our last two visits. Maybe that's because I'm in the car alone this time, with nothing but my thoughts to keep me company. Or maybe it's because of the anticipation of what I hope to discover when I get there—ideally, Rene Anderson.

I swallow down a fist-sized lump of nerves as I make the turn off the main road onto the narrow drive. I don't need the NO TRESPASSING signs posted every thirty feet to remind me of what Kal and I are heading into. Mr. Anderson did a good enough job of that himself the last time we spoke. He won't be happy to see us.

Glancing in my rearview, I check that Kal's still behind me as I pull up in front of the house. I scan the yard as I get out of the car, hoping to see a person or another vehicle, but nothing appears to have changed since our last visit. I hear the brief flash of an annoyed voice, and then Kal's car door shuts, cutting off his prisoner mid-complaint.

He flashes me a grim look and a nod, closing the distance between us, then we stride up to the front door side by side. Leaf litter crunches under our feet. A single filament of spiderweb catches me in the face. I wipe at my cheek, ignoring the creepy-crawly sensation it triggers as Kal knocks on the door.

Everything is silent. Not a sound can be heard coming from the house. Nor from the eternal dusk of the woods around us.

"Mr. Anderson," I call. "It's Chief Riley. We need to talk."

Still nothing.

"The truck doesn't look like it's moved since last time," Kal says.

He gestures toward it with his head and I nod, watching for a moment as he approaches the vehicle before I step off the stoop and walk over to the window to the right of the door. Cupping my hands around my face, I peer inside.

I find myself looking through a thick layer of grime into the kitchen. The lights are off. Dirty dishes litter the sink and counter. A stack of trash bags lies piled in a heap against a wall. Not exactly the way you'd leave your house if you were going out of town. Then again, I suspect Nathan Anderson isn't exactly the type known for his housekeeping.

The sound of Kal's steps grows louder as he returns from inspecting Anderson's vehicle. "I don't think that truck has moved since we were last here. Not even sure it works, to be honest, judging by the layer of pine needles on it."

A muscle in my jaw spasms. I don't like this. Something feels off.

Kal peers past me into the house. "Lights are off. You think he's gone? Or in there hiding, hoping we'll go away?"

I shake my head, not sure what I think yet. "Let's keep checking."

The skeletal limbs of a dead bush snag at my pants as I squeeze past to the next window.

"Lights are off in here, too," I call, peering through a gap between a pair of curtains into a bedroom that's in a similar state of chaos as the kitchen.

"Same here," Kal says. Then, "Maggie."

There's something about his tone that tells me everything I need to know. I fight my way back through the brush and around to the front of the house, where Kal is still staring through the window to the left of the door. He points. "Look there. By the bottom of the couch."

I follow his outstretched finger and see a dark stain on the carpet. Something about it is off, the play of shadows in the room giving it too much depth, making it appear 3D. And then I realize—it's not the shadows. The ripple in the stain? It's a hand.

Kal's at the door by the time I make the connection. He pulls his firearm from his holster. I do the same, check to make sure he's ready, then bang on the window.

"Mr. Anderson? Coyote Cove Police Department."

Nothing inside the room moves. I hurry to join Kal on the front stoop, pull my shirttail out and use it to test the knob. It's locked. I shake my head. Stand back and yell, "We're coming in."

Kal gives the door a solid kick and it crashes open, slamming into the wall behind it. I cover him as he steps into the room, checking to the right. We switch and I check to the left.

A cursory glance at the body on the floor as we pass by lets us know it isn't going anywhere, so we clear the rest of the house. Once we've made certain that there's no one else inside, we return to the living room, where Nathan Anderson's corpse lies in a pool of drying blood behind the couch. The handle of a kitchen knife protrudes from his chest.

"Want me to call it in?" Kal asks.

"Please," I say, studying our surroundings.

I need to find out everything I can before the staties get here, but it isn't going to be easy with all the mess. There's no telling how much evidence lies concealed among the clutter.

But there's still plenty I can learn without disrupting the crime scene.

Squatting beside the dead man, I take a closer look. A horde of flies buzzes busily around the body. Judging from the rice-sized maggots squirming around the wound and body orifices, and the stippling on the flesh, this isn't something that just happened. Nathan Anderson has been dead at least twenty-four hours. Which means the man had already been murdered when we were here yesterday, and our knocks went unanswered.

Cursing, I swat at a fly trying to land on my face and continue my examination of the body. Nathan Anderson was a big man, yet the only injury I can see is the stab wound—the man's hands and arms appear undamaged. He hadn't fought during the attack. Had the killer incapacitated him in some way before burying a knife up to the hilt in his chest? Had they caught him by surprise? Or had the man not realized he was in danger?

He hadn't seemed like the friendly type. Given the many NO TRESPASSING signs posted on the property, it's unlikely that he would have invited a stranger inside. Which means he knew whoever did this.

Half of his family, his wife and son, were killed earlier this week. It would be foolish to think that his murder isn't connected to theirs. Which means the man's daughters, if they're still alive, might be in trouble. I need to find Rene and Rachel Anderson before it's too late.

50

MAGGIE

I can feel time running out, the ticking of each passing second matching the rapid drumming of my pulse as I pull into the pitted drive, once again parking between the battered minivan and ancient station wagon. I can't help noticing that the house looks even more dismal than it had the last time I was here. Is what I've learned about the Anderson family shading my perspective? Or is it the cloud cast by all the bad news I've delivered to them lately?

And now I have more. I knock at the door, staring down at a handful of plastic toys half buried in the dirt by the front step.

My skin prickles, feeling like I'm being watched as I wait. I know that someone is here, can feel the floorboards beneath my feet bend and flex as they walk around the manufactured home. A door snaps shut somewhere inside. I knock again.

Just as I'm getting ready to knock a third time, Rachel Anderson's face appears before me. Though the bruise on her cheek has faded, a fresh welt makes the right side of her mouth look puffy and swollen. Her eyes flit around nervously, looking everywhere but at me.

"What do you want?"

"I need to speak with you. It's urgent."

"I've got nothing to say."

"I'm afraid you may be in danger. Can you come outside for a moment so we can talk?"

She shakes her head and tries to shut the door.

"Rachel." I grab the edge, preventing her from closing it. I glance behind her, keep my voice low so her children won't overhear as I say, "I've just come from your father's house. I'm very sorry, but he's dead. He's been murdered."

She draws a sharp breath, eyes growing wide as she searches my face for answers.

"Please, may I come in? Just for a moment."

A muscle in her jaw twitches as she steps back. I seize the opportunity and enter before she has a chance to change her mind. Glance around as I trail behind her, the house curiously still as she leads the way to the kitchen.

"Where are your kids?" I ask.

"They're sleeping."

"Is there anyone else home?"

"No."

She leans against the counter, gripping the edge to either side of her as she tracks my movements warily. She looks like a feral animal getting ready to bolt. And why shouldn't she? Over the last week, I've told her that three members of her family are dead. I've just implied that she could be next. I can only imagine what the poor woman must be thinking.

"Your father was stabbed, Rachel."

Her eyes drift to the half-empty knife block on the counter.

"I'm not sure what happened yet, but considering the explosion earlier this week that killed your mom and brother, and now this, your family seems to be at the center of whatever's going on. I'd like to arrange to have you placed into protective custody."

"It's a little bit late for that, don't you think?"

"Not for you or your children. Rachel, let me help you."

Tears well in her eyes as she shakes her head.

"Can you at least help me find your sister? I'm afraid that she may be in trouble, too."

"Rene *is* trouble."

"What do you mean?"

"You should go."

"Rachel, please. If you know what's happening—"

"No."

She shakes her head, not wanting to listen to anything I have to say. Not that I blame her. I can't even begin to imagine what her life has been like, the number of people who should have kept her safe who let her down instead.

"I know that you've been failed before—"

She huffs a bitter laugh.

"You and your sister."

Her grip on the countertop tightens.

"I'd like to get you both the help you need. If you know where Rene is—"

"I don't."

But her eyes jerked hard to the side with the lie. Her chest heaves with each breath. She looks terrified.

"Rachel, if your sister's done something—"

"I said no." She pushes away from the counter and points toward the door. "There's nothing I can tell you. You need to go."

"Will you at least take my number? Just in case you change your mind and need to reach me?"

She ignores my offer, turns and leaves the room without even glancing at the business card I'm holding out. I place it on the counter before following her, feeling desperate.

"If you know who's doing this to your family..." But she's not listening. I need to change tack, do something to get her attention. "Does the name Fred Wallace mean anything to you?"

She pauses halfway through opening the door. "Who's that?"

"He owns the truck that we suspect was involved in the hit-and-run death of Michelle Sanders. She was one of the women who— There's so much to tell you. I really wish you'd just give me a few more moments of your time."

When she opens the door wider in response, I say, "Your mom didn't want to leave you, Rachel. She had planned to bring you and your siblings with her when she left your father. But the abuse was escalating, and her friends—Michelle Sanders and Sue Bailey—were afraid they wouldn't get a chance if they waited any longer. They helped your mom escape before it was too late."

A thump sounds from the back of the house. She shoots a desperate glance over her shoulder. "My kids are awake. You can't be here anymore."

"Wait, just one more thing. Please. Do you know who this man is? I think he has something to do with what's going on."

She doesn't look at the picture on my phone, slamming the door shut in my face instead. I stare at it, replaying what just happened. I'd offered to put Rachel and her children in protective custody, but she hadn't been interested. Yet there's no denying that she was scared. Especially when I mentioned her sister.

What was it she had said? *Rene is trouble?*

I think about the young woman with the criminal record who'd lied to me yesterday. The one who'd had a stain on her sleeve that looked suspiciously like blood. About Nathan Anderson, lying stabbed to death on the living room floor in his home. What if the person annihilating the members of this family isn't an outsider, but one of their own?

51

MAGGIE

My thoughts are racing as fast as my car as I speed toward town. Twenty years ago, Sue and Michelle Sanders helped Ruby Anderson escape an abusive marriage by faking her death. And then... nothing.

Besides the youngest daughter's trouble with the law, all was quiet for over a decade until Michelle Sanders was the victim of a hit and run. An accident that may have been caused by a man who was possibly involved with one of the victims of the explosion.

I shake my head, erasing that line of thought like a scribble on an Etch A Sketch. There are too many maybes there, not to mention that Michelle's death occurred six years ago. That's an awfully long cooling-off period if it had anything to do with the mess on my hands now.

I've had five dead bodies in my town in under a week, three of them Andersons. A fourth who was friends with one of them. Who knows what connection John Doe will have? Or Wesley Banks.

Whatever's going on, it's clear that the family is at the center of it, and that it all has to do with the mother's return.

Ruby stayed away for two decades. What made her come back to Coyote Cove after all these years? The answer to that question is the piece I need to solve this puzzle.

I have to learn more about her family, but how?

Rachel isn't talking. Rene is missing. Everyone else is dead. I've almost made my way back to the department when it hits me.

Turning down a side street, I park at the curb in front of the two-story house with yellow siding and faded blue trim. Jog up the walk and ring the bell. When the door opens, Missy Anderson looks confused to find me standing on her front porch.

"Chief Riley. Is this about Ronny?"

"I need to know about the Anderson family. All of them."

Her head turns from side to side. "I can't help you there. I never really spent much time with any of them besides Ronny. They just weren't that close."

"Did Ronny hit you?"

"What?"

"Listen, I know that it's not really any of my business, but lives are at stake and I'm trying to figure something out. Were you getting divorced because he was abusive?"

"Ronny? No. There's no way, I mean, not after what he saw his mother go through. I know some kids grow up watching that and that's what they learn to do, but not Ronny. We were just too different, got married too young."

"What else did he tell you about his family?"

"Not much. Just that his dad used to beat his mom until she died."

"Did he ever suspect she was still alive?"

Her mouth drops open. "What?"

"His mother was still alive until this week. She was one of the three victims who died in the explosion out on Old Mill

Road. I'm very sorry to have to tell you this, but Ronny was, too."

Missy staggers back a step, mouth still open as she stares at me with wide eyes. She blinks rapidly as they start filling with tears. Shaking her head, she says, "No."

The woman trembling before me now is much different than the one I met the first time, the one who joked about the ex always being a suspect. Pending divorce or not, she's genuinely distraught.

"I'm afraid so. That's why it's so important for me to find out as much as I can about them. Especially whether or not Ronny knew his mom was still alive this whole time."

She draws a long, shaky breath. "If he knew, he never said anything to me. But he did tell me once that he thought his dad had killed her and the whole kayak thing was a cover-up."

It's a viable theory, but Nathan Anderson hadn't killed his wife back then. But had he been the one to kill her now? If that's true, then who put that knife in his chest? Or is that why it was put there?

"Do you know if Ronny's dad ever hit him or his sisters after their mother was gone?"

Her face scrunches up. My phone buzzes in my pocket, but I silence it, waiting for what she's about to tell me. Her voice is soft as she says, "I'm pretty sure he never hit Ronny or Rachel, but..."

"But what, Missy? It could be important."

"But they both left that house the first chance they got. Rene was the one who, I mean, I don't know if she got hit or not, like I said, I didn't know her, but she was just so... messed up."

"What about Rachel?" I ask.

My phone buzzes again. I slip it out and take a quick peek at the screen, but I don't recognize the number. I send the call to voicemail, hoping whoever it is will leave a message.

"Well, yeah, they're all a little damaged."

"Do you know if she's repeating the cycle?"

Missy stares at the ground between her feet. "I mean, I've heard rumors."

"That her relationship is abusive?"

Missy nods. "Yeah. I asked Ronny about it once, but he didn't want to talk about it."

"Do you know if anybody has ever tried to get her help?"

"I know that one of his mother's friends checked up on her occasionally. All three of them, actually. But none of them really wanted the attention. And Rene, I mean, from what I heard, she did her best to chase her off. And to get her to leave Rachel alone, too."

"Really? Any idea why that was?"

"No clue. The few times we were all together, Rene seemed kind of... I'm not sure how to put it. Possessive of Rachel, maybe?"

"How so?" I ask, thinking about Mariè Bouchard, Rene's friend. Had Rene been possessive over her, too?

"She just seemed really focused on keeping Rachel away from everyone else, like she was trying to keep her to herself. Almost like she was guarding her."

"And this was normal for them?"

Missy shrugs. "I really don't know them well enough to say, but..."

"But what?"

"I was ahead of them in school, I never even talked to one of them until Ronny and I got together, but even back then, well, the only way to describe their relationship was weird. They were just always together. And Rachel, I mean, she was so pretty then, before life chewed her up. Boys would practically fall over themselves just to stand next to her, but Rene?"

Her eyes bug out as she shakes her head.

"I heard about this one time—I was already out of school, this was after I graduated, but you know how gossip spreads around here. Anyway, Rene caught Rachel kissing some guy at a track meet and she just went off on him. Like physically. Got herself suspended and everything. It's no wonder Rachel moved out and left her behind as soon as she could. She'd probably still be single if Rene had her way. Rene might have been the younger one, but she definitely seemed like the one in control."

I can't help but wonder if Rene's control had been limited only because of all the time she'd spent behind bars these last few years.

"Now that I'm thinking about it, Ronny mentioned something once about Rene bullying Rachel into giving her a spare key to her house. How he had tried to convince her how foolish it was to let an addict have access to her home and to get the key back, but I don't think she ever did."

"So Ronny knew about Rene's drug problem?"

"Oh, yeah. Not to be mean, but it's pretty obvious. She's got that desperate junkie look going on, like she'd knife you in an alley to steal your wallet just so she could get her next fix."

This seems like an awful lot of information for someone who claimed to know nothing only a few minutes ago. I can't help wondering if it's all true—or if maybe she might be trying to shift my attention away from someone else.

"I feel kinda bad. It must seem like I don't have anything nice to say about Ronny's sisters, but like I said, I don't really know them. We hardly ever spent any time with them, and thinking back, like, I remember telling Ronny stories about me and my family from when I was growing up, but he didn't really have many stories to tell. I'm starting to think maybe he didn't have any good memories about them."

"Can I ask you a personal question?"

Her eyebrows arch, letting me know that all the questions I've been asking have been personal. But she humors me anyway.

"I guess."

"Who's Dave Fischer?"

She flinches like I've slapped her. "Why?"

I stare at her, holding her gaze. "Who is he, Missy?"

"One of my brothers," she says, almost timidly.

"Did he get along with Ronny?"

"I mean, they weren't friends, but they didn't not get along, either. Why? What's this all about? You don't think he had anything to do with what happened to Ronny, do you?"

"Do you think it's a possibility?"

"No. Absolutely not. I don't even know where you'd get a crazy idea like that."

"It might have something to do with an odd conversation I had with him the other day. Any idea why he'd be so interested in the explosion that killed your husband? Specifically, how he'd know it was arson?"

The muscles in her face relax as if suddenly it all makes sense. "He was a firefighter back before they pulled funding for the local department and made it volunteer only. He was supposed to move to Lincoln with the rest of his crew, only his home is here, you know? He works for one of the logging camps now, but I know he misses it."

I study her for a long moment. She has to know it would be easy enough for me to confirm if what she's just told me is the truth or not. My gut's saying that it is.

"Is there anything else you think I should know?"

Missy shakes her head sadly. She swallows hard, then says, "Just that if someone hurt Ronny on purpose, I really hope you find them and make them pay. He really was a good guy. Just because we weren't in love anymore doesn't mean... I hadn't expected to miss him so much. He deserved better, you know?"

"One last thing," I say, pulling up the picture of John Doe on my phone. "Do you know who this man is?"

She looks at the screen, recoils when she realizes the man in the picture is dead. But she doesn't look away. Recognition slowly dawns across her face.

Her eyes are wide, terrified when they meet mine. "I'm pretty sure that's Raymond."

"You mean Rachel's—?"

Missy nods. "What happened to him?"

"That's what I'm trying to find out."

She retreats into her house as I thank her then hurry back to my car, mind racing as the pieces of this case fall together in a chain reaction like dominoes. I've got to tell Kal what's happening.

I clear Raymond's picture from my screen, a list of notifications taking its place, a reminder that someone had been trying to get ahold of me while I was speaking with Missy. Clicking on the voicemail that's been left, I start the car and press play.

When I hear the panicked voice on the message, fear seizes me by the throat. It tightens its grasp as I continue to listen. By the time the call is done, I can barely breathe. Grabbing the cherry from the glove box, I slap the police light on the top of the rental car and peel away from the curb, praying that I'm not too late.

52

MAGGIE

My hands wrap around the steering wheel in a white-knuckled grip—the kind you might use on a knife if you were trying to stab someone. I do my best to push that thought from my mind, instead scanning the yards to either side of me, making sure no kids or animals are near the road as I travel much too fast through the residential area. Pairing my phone with the rental's Bluetooth, I press the call button and set it in the middle console.

The rings sound distant and canned through the car speakers. Each buzz seems to mock me, taunting my imagination with all the reasons it's going unanswered. My heart pounds against the walls of my chest as I reach a stop sign, unsure which way to go.

But I have to keep moving, have to feel like I'm doing something. Turning left, toward home, I end the call and place another. This one blessedly gets answered after only two rings.

"Hello?"

I blow through the stoplight at the edge of town. The tires screech as I take a turn too sharply.

"Maggie? What's that noise?"

"Linda! Is Sue still there with you?"

"No. She left a couple of hours ago."

"Did she say where she was going?"

"Home, I think. What's going on?"

I don't answer, bracing as I pull a U-turn in the middle of the road. The phone slings out of the cup holder where I'd set it, falling somewhere out of sight in the passenger seat footwell.

This is all my fault. I'm the one who said Sue's name back at Rachel's house. I'm the one who put her on the killer's radar. If anything happens to her...

The screen on the dashboard shows that my call to Linda has disconnected. I don't dare stop the car. And there's no way I can search for the phone while I'm driving.

"Call Kal," I yell, hoping that the voice command feature on my cell works. Tears gather in my eyes as the sound of ringing echoes around me. I don't give Kal a chance to speak when he picks up.

"Have the state police arrived yet?" I ask.

"I'm still waiting on them, why?"

"Call over to Lincoln, we need backup. Send them to 1890 Route 3. Tell them we have a 10-2000." My stomach threatens to empty as I recite the address of the home I'd just so recently left—Rachel Anderson's house. My voice hitches as I say, "Have them send an ambulance, too."

Kal repeats the address I've just rambled off to him. "Got it. You want me to head over there?"

"No, I need you with me."

"Where?"

"At 1414 Cherry Blossom Lane."

There's a long moment of silence. Worried that I've entered one of the many dead zones where reception fails to work in this mountain valley and that the call has dropped, I chance lifting my eyes from the road long enough for a quick glimpse at the screen on the dash. We're still connected.

Kal's voice is uncharacteristically quiet as he says, "That's Sue's place."

"It is," I confirm.

"Should I request any additional services to meet us there?"

I know what he's so delicately asking—if he should have an ambulance go to Sue's as well.

The asphalt in front of me blurs. I hurry to blink the tears away. My voice threatens to fail me—and so does my heart—as I whisper, "Yes."

53

STEVE

Fear wraps its icy fingers around me as I stare at the battered gray walls of the building before me, struggling to breathe deeply enough to fill my lungs. Feel sick as I contemplate going inside. But it's something I have to do.

I open the car door reluctantly. Force my foot from the vehicle onto the blacktop of the parking lot. Tear my fingers off the steering wheel as I step outside.

Though I'd thought this moment would feel victorious, it doesn't. This isn't something I should be dreading, and yet, there's no denying that I do.

Because this is it—no more excuses.

I've found the McAllister and Sons from my memory, the one Wesley and I passed on our way home after burying Georgia Pierce. The answers I've been seeking for so long are finally within my grasp—and I'm terrified. What if the truth isn't something I can live with?

Blood on my hands, a knife in my grip, and a dead girl buried under a tree. My wedding to a police officer only two weeks away. A ghost who shares my fiancée's face. The weight of it is almost too much to bear.

A bell rings as I push open the door. A voice greets me, its owner emerging a moment later from between a pair of red curtains that separates the sales floor from the back. The older man draws to a stop when he catches sight of me, obviously not expecting a stranger.

But it takes him only a second to recover himself, to decide that the man before him isn't a danger, just a day-tripper stopping for a snack, or maybe directions. Certainly no one to be scared of.

Is he right? Or is he wrong?

"Hi there. How can I help you?" he asks, giving me a friendly smile.

I look around desperately, realizing that I should have thought of what I was going to say before coming inside. My eyes land on rack of gardening tools near the back wall.

"I was hoping to buy a shovel."

"What kind were you looking for?"

"Um."

His smile grows a little wider at my confusion. "Why don't you tell me what you want to use it for, and I'll help you find the right one."

"Digging," I say, before I can think about it.

"For what purpose?"

I glance over my shoulder, back toward the door, debating how strange it would seem if I turned tail and ran away.

"Are you planting? Making a trench? Or you got a body you need to bury?" He winks, not seeming to notice my growing discomfort as he gestures for me to follow him to the back of the store with a wide grin. "You okay, son?" he asks when I don't follow.

"Fine," I say, pushing a pleasant look onto my face. There's no way this man won't remember me after I leave. I imagine him telling his wife about the awkward customer who came into the shop today. His friends. The cops.

I ask myself what Wesley would do in a situation like this. When the answer pops into my mind, I wish it hadn't. I tear my gaze from a pair of gardening shears, feeling ill. Force my feet to carry me to the back of the store.

"How about this one?" he asks, pulling a shovel with a pointed blade from the rack. "Good all-purpose digger, right here. Why don't you try it on for size, see how it feels?"

He holds it out to me. I hesitate a moment, then take it in my sweaty palms, fingers curling tight around the smooth metal shaft. I take a step back as I test its weight. Nod my approval.

"Let's go ring you up, then. Or was there something else you needed?"

"No, that's it." I glance around the empty store. "Actually."

He stops on his way up to the front, turns to face me. I crane my head, peering around the end of the aisle, checking to make sure that we're indeed alone. His polite smile falters as I take a step closer to him.

"Yes?"

I clear my throat and lean forward. Keeping my voice low, I say, "Wheat."

"Wheat?"

His eyes squint as he scratches his head.

"Wheat," I say again, this time louder, with more confidence. "Are there any wheat fields around here"

"Why?"

The truth is on my lips. I wonder what he'd do if I spoke it. Instead, I say, "I'm an amateur photographer. I was hoping to grab some shots while I was out this way, but I haven't seen any yet. Just lots of corn."

"You must have come from the east, then," he says.

"I did."

"You go any other direction, and you'll find it. As much wheat as your heart desires."

"Great, thank you."

A wave of relief washes over me. My muscles relax. I look around, this time actually taking in my surroundings, for the first time noticing the row of glass containers filled with candy lined up along the counter. The plastic collection box for 4-H that sits beside the register. The corkboard on the wall, covered with handwritten ads, pictures of livestock, a MISSING poster for a young woman, her eyes staring accusingly at me from the page.

My heart spasms, clenched inside an invisible fist as a jolt of panic strikes through me. The old man gives me a funny look, suspicion clearly visible on his face as he reaches to take my credit card. I tighten my grip, refusing to release it.

"You know what. I think I'm going to pay cash."

"You sure?"

He's still holding on. His eyes flick to the piece of plastic between us. I shift my thumb to cover my name.

"I'm sure."

"I don't mind. We don't add on a surcharge for credit, the way some stores do."

"I'm sure," I repeat, sweat sprouting along my hairline and down my back as I wrench the card free from his grasp.

Knowing I've blown it, that I've just gone from a bumbling city slicker to someone dubious, I grab a handful of bills from my wallet, set them down on the counter, and hurry for the door, the shovel's handle growing slick in my clenched fist.

"Sir, your change," he calls after me.

Remembering the box on the counter, I say, "4-H donation," as the door closes behind me.

Hurrying to my car, I toss the shovel across the cabin to the passenger side and get behind the wheel. Peel out, hoping I was quick enough that he didn't have time to make it to the door to see my plates. My pulse threatens to burst my veins as I drive away, knowing that this is far from over.

54

MAGGIE

A montage of my friendship with Sue plays in my mind as I turn onto her tree-lined street, praying I'm not too late. I force myself to slow, worrying about drawing too much attention. The element of surprise is the only thing I have going for me right now.

While most of the residential areas in Coyote Cove have a distinctive look—obviously New England, Cape Cod shingled farmhouses and quintessential log cabins on one end of the spectrum, run-down trailers, sagging shacks, and Section Eight slums on the other—Sue's neighborhood is one of the few that you could imagine fitting anywhere in America.

The well-maintained homes belie the harsh winters that wreak havoc on the valley, with fresh coats of paint, tidy yards lush with flowerbeds, and neatly trimmed lawns. There are no trash heaps or stacks of salvaged materials here. No signs warning off trespassers or drug paraphernalia littering the streets. There aren't even abandoned toys or bikes left out. Everything here is in the place where it belongs.

Well, almost everything.

It's not lost on me how much Sue's Pinto must stick out in a place like this. It speaks of her stubbornness that she hasn't caved in and bought a nicer, newer vehicle. But it also speaks of her sense of loyalty.

I turn off my flashing light and park at the curb in front of a house several properties down. Unsnapping the latch on my holster, I creep forward, cutting across a neighbor's lawn as I approach the cluster of trees that separates their yard from Sue's. Peering through the dense foliage, I spot her car in the driveway. And parked right behind it is an ancient station wagon, the same one that had been in Rachel's yard on both of my previous visits.

Fighting the urge to rush forward, I force myself to stay where I am, taking a moment to assess the scene. Both vehicles appear vacant. There's no movement anywhere. The only sound is the faint ticking of the station wagon's engine as it cools.

Feeling a surge of hope that I haven't arrived too far behind its driver, I take a cautious step forward, then another, weaving through the trees as silently as possible. Pulling my firearm as I exit the wood line, I stay low as I hurry across the yard, exposed, approaching the second vehicle. Pressing my shoulder against one of the faux-woodgrain panels, I stretch until I can see inside.

The interior is a mess, a jumble of discarded food wrappers and trash. The torn headliner hangs down in billowy folds. A dried puddle of what looks like vomit stains the back seat. And the worn dirty beige cover on the steering wheel is stained with rust-covered smears. Blood. My heart trembles inside my chest as I turn toward the house. I need to get Sue out of there, fast.

I jog across the clearing, ducking below Sue's living room window. Steel myself, then raise my eyes above the sill. Empty.

Of course it is. Because if Sue had a guest, someone who she felt comfortable with, who she thought she knew, like one of

Ruby's daughters, she wouldn't seat them on her couch. She'd insist on mothering them. She'd bring them to her kitchen.

A sharp pain lances through my gut as I picture the knife imbedded in Nathan Anderson's chest. I can't let the same happen to Sue.

I pause for a minute, debating. Should I ring the doorbell and try to interrupt whatever's happening inside? Or would that accelerate whatever plan the killer has in mind? I can't risk making her desperate.

Right now, the only advantage I have is that they don't know I'm here. I need to keep that edge until I have a chance to gauge the situation.

I set off around the side of the house. Rounding the corner, I'm still several yards away from the kitchen window and I can already hear the murmur of an angry voice carrying through the walls. My throat tightens as I hurry closer.

Squatting beneath the window, I risk a peek. Duck lower so I won't be seen.

Sue has her back turned to me. Her hands are raised in a placating gesture as the young woman paces back and forth in front of her, face screwed up in a mask of rage.

"Do you know what it's like, to never have had anyone in your life put you first?"

She reaches the end of the room and pivots, stalking back the other direction.

"I mean, aren't kids supposed to be the ones who get protected? Isn't that the way it's supposed to be? It's not like they asked to be born. To experience whatever screwed-up situation life puts them in. I certainly didn't."

"Sweetie—"

"Don't!"

My chest seizes as she jabs a giant kitchen knife in Sue's direction, her narrowed eyes full of fury. Sue takes a step backward, closer to the window.

I long desperately to shatter it and break inside, but I can't risk it. Not when there's so little distance between them, and so much between us. She could stab Sue before I could aim and get a shot off.

But I have to do something.

Memories of over a half decade of friendship storm through my head. The good times and bad. The laughs and teasing. The scoldings and reprimands.

I wasn't the only one on the receiving end of lectures all these years. Sue may be older and wiser, but she doesn't always seem it. She does some foolish things. And chief among them, the one I've given her the hardest time about, has been her insistence on keeping a spare key in such an obvious place as under the flowerpot by her front door.

Forcing myself from the window, I take several small careful steps away as silently as possible before propelling myself toward the planter. It looks like it hasn't been moved in ages. Roots from the plant inside rip away from the ground as I lift the side carefully, not trusting my grip.

I stare at the dirt beneath it in disbelief. No key. Using both hands, I pick up the entire container, hugging it against myself with one arm while running a hand along the underside, but still nothing.

Wouldn't you know it. She finally listened to me.

Setting the pot down, I scan the doorstep. Pull up the mat. Run my hand along the trim above the door, all the while feeling the seconds ticking away like sand through an hourglass. Time is running out. I'm going to have to break through the window after all and hope for the best.

As I'm turning away, a rock beside the front stoop catches my eye. She wouldn't have. Why change one obvious hiding spot for another?

My relief is overwhelming as I lift the edge of the smooth stone and find the key. Brushing the dirt off, I let myself inside without a moment's hesitation, opening the door just enough to slip through, easing it shut behind me.

The sound of a muffled voice carries down the hall. As I stalk toward it, making my way to the kitchen, I can't help glancing at the framed pictures hung on the wall as I pass them —Sue's children, her grandchildren, a family portrait that includes her late husband, the man grinning widely beneath a bushy mustache, his eyes gleaming merrily as he looks at his wife instead of the camera.

It speaks of a far different life than the one Ruby Anderson and her family led. One with happy memories. One without abuse.

But that doesn't make this rampage right. Plenty of people have bad childhoods and don't grow up to go on murder sprees.

As the doorway to the kitchen appears ahead, the murmuring becomes clear. Though the speaker is calm, the words drip with venom.

"You chose to protect her. You decided to take her away, to somewhere safe, and left me behind. Who were you to make that decision?"

"I didn't have a choice." Sue's voice sounds weary, weak. "He would have killed her if I hadn't gotten her away."

"Good!"

I flinch as the word is shouted.

"Did you ever once stop to think that maybe that's the way it should have been? What should have happened?"

"You don't mean that."

The animalistic snarl that answers makes my skin crawl. My pulse thrums fast and hard as my heart thrashes frantically inside my chest.

"Oh, but I do. Because if he had killed her, then I would have been the one to get out. Not her. But I didn't, and it's all your fault, all because you decided to play God."

"Sweetie, I tried to help you all I could. I checked on you all the time. I asked you if you were all right there, if he was hurting you. You always told me you were fine. Please, believe me, if I had known otherwise—"

"You would have what? Faked my death, too?"

"If that what it took, yes."

"Here's the thing about not getting to have a real childhood. When you don't get to play like a normal kid, you never learn how to pretend. I spent years trying to imagine what my life would have been like if my mom were alive, but I never could. All I could see was my reality."

Her voice drops an octave, each word spoken slowly, carefully as she says, "So when I saw her walking down that street in Lewiston a few weeks ago, I knew it wasn't my imagination. I knew it was really her. And I knew I had to make her pay for what she did. But do you know what the saddest part was?"

I'm close enough now that I can see into the kitchen. Sue's trembling, making herself as small as possible as she cowers away from the butcher's knife pointed at her. I press myself as hard as I can against the far wall, trying to remain out of sight. Dry the palm of my gun hand on my pants, adjust my grip, and inch closer.

"The saddest part is that I wasn't even sure if she'd come see me. I bet that your daughter's never had to worry about that, has she? That you'd come if she told you she needed you?"

She thrusts the knife closer to Sue, the blade almost touching Sue's chin, then jerks it away, waving it through the air as she talks.

"Or maybe the saddest part is that I actually cared if she would. I mean, why should I? Especially after the way she just turned her back and left me behind. I should have just finished this whole mess that day, after I followed her home. But what can I say? I was curious to see if she'd actually bother to give me five minutes of her time."

Sue's eyes rise in stops and starts until they find her captor's face. They quickly dart away from what they see there, flit briefly toward the doorway. I can tell by the way her body stiffens, the way her quaking stills, that she's seen me. She shifts her weight in my direction.

"Of course, I knew the way it was going to end. Had it all planned out. I wasn't sure if I'd have the nerve to go ahead with it, but you know what? After meeting her? It was easy. Wanna know why?"

The knife points toward Sue again until she asks, "Why?"

"I decided to do a little experiment. Have a decoy there, see if she could tell the difference between her baby and a stranger. And my *mother* didn't even realize what was going on. She didn't even recognize her own daughter, just hugged and fussed over someone she'd never met before. Can you believe that?"

"It's been a long time—"

"Don't you make excuses for her! A mother should know."

Sue flinches as a glass slams into the wall. She cringes as it shatters, tiny slivers showering down through the air like rain.

"She should have known better than to think some desperate sleaze who'd been pathetic enough to get ghosted by the murdering old guy she'd been hooking up with was her daughter."

My mind reels. Had Fred Wallace confessed to Mariè about killing Michelle Sanders? Or was it someone else? An image of the photograph I'd found at the crime scene flashes behind my eyes. Is it possible that Mariè's boyfriend wasn't called Wally, but Wesley?

"And that backstabbing loser just lapped up the attention from *my* mother."

I don't have time to think about it as she takes a step closer to Sue.

"They were so wrapped up in each other that they didn't notice when I pulled my sister to the back bedroom. I could hear them just chattering away as we climbed out the window.

My mother never even suspected her new BFF wasn't her daughter until Ronny showed up."

Her voice breaks as she says, "But then he told our mother that Mariè wasn't her daughter. And Mariè told her who was. And I could hear the shock in her voice. I get that my sister and I aren't much to look at, but we've had hard lives, and that's her fault. Hers, and my father's, and yours. And now there's just one of you left to apologize."

Sue looks up, surprised.

"I am so very sorry," she says sincerely, as if her words are enough to make this nightmare end. "So sorry, honey. If I could do it all over again, I would. I know I failed you then, but please. Let me help you now."

The joyless laughter that fills the room makes my blood run cold, goosebumps rising to the surface of my skin. Time has run out. I need to make my move before she makes hers.

I raise my gun in front of my chest, the barrel pointed at the ceiling. Draw a deep breath. Sue glances at me just as I round the threshold into the kitchen, dropping my arms into shooter's position. Her eyes widen in fear even though she doesn't notice Rachel Anderson lunge at her with the knife.

"Freeze."

"Maggie, no!"

Sue jumps in front of me, pushing at my gun arm, not seeing that glinting metal blade coming at her. I cede to her momentum and add my own, pivoting with the motion until I've changed direction, wrapping my body around Sue and getting between her and the attack.

Searing heat burns deep into my flesh. I gasp at the shock of it, legs going weak beneath me. I hear Sue screaming my name, Rachel cursing as the young mother tries to withdraw the knife and can't, the steel lodged in my bone, glass breaking and Kal's voice thundering commands through the window.

On second thought, maybe that was the way I should have made my entrance after all.

"Sue, it's okay," I tell her, mustering a smile, though I can't quite remember what has her so upset, and her expression tells me she doesn't believe me.

"My shirt feels wet."

I glance down and notice that I'm standing in the middle of a red puddle. The room starts to swirl, making my surroundings blur together into a kaleidoscope of colors. I feel dizzy and a bit sick. I look for Sue to tell her but can't find her. She must have left the fun house. I don't blame her. This isn't fun at all.

And I'm caught in something. I struggle to escape as it tugs at me. I want to get out of here, not allow myself to be pulled further in.

Then out of the haze, a face appears.

"It's gonna be okay, Red."

I stare at Fire Investigator Larson, wondering what he's doing here. Find myself sidetracked questioning where here is.

Then I'm weightless. I feel his arms around me and realize that he's carrying me. I know I should tell him this still doesn't mean I'm going to have that talk with him he's been after, but I'm too tired. So I close my eyes and lean my head against his chest. Listen to the sound of his heart and wonder why it sounds so different from the faint pulse of my own.

55

STEVE

My heart thrashes wildly against the walls of my chest. My fists tighten around the steering wheel. I feel the urge to both laugh and cry, yet can't manage to do either.

I stare out the windshield, afraid that if I blink it will disappear. But it doesn't. It's really happening. This is it. I've worked so hard to find this tree, and now here it is. I knew it the instant I saw it, it's gnarled, sweeping boughs just like I've remembered all these years.

As soon as I caught sight of it, I pulled over onto the edge of the country road, a cloud of dust kicking up as my tires hit the dirt shoulder. A red double-crib barn, suddenly familiar from my vague memory of that long ago night, hovers in the distance. The scene is disturbingly picturesque.

It looks like a photograph you'd find in a calendar hanging on the wall in an old general store that still sells Coke in a bottle. The quaint kind of place where you can't imagine anything bad ever happening. Oh, to be naïve enough to believe such a place exists.

Because I know firsthand that bad things can happen. Have happened. Even in a place like this.

Maybe that's why, as hard as I've searched for this tree, longed for this moment I was scared would never come, now that it's here, I can't seem to make myself get out of the car. All I can do is stare at the oak, the centerpiece among a sea of wheat, and think about that night.

I close my eyes and the sun vanishes, replaced by the moon as I travel back in time. My limbs strangely heavy as I struggle out of the vehicle that long ago night. My head spinning. My mouth so uncomfortably dry that I could barely choke out a whisper as I stared at the body lying in the middle of the road.

"What happened?"

"It was an accident," Wesley says, curiously calm given the situation. "She came out of nowhere."

I look around at our surroundings, shocked to discover that we're in the middle of nowhere. Where could the girl have possibly come from?

"We need to go get help."

"It's too late for that."

"We need to call the police."

"Do we?" He turns toward me, his eyes black under the night sky. "Are you sure about that?"

"Of course!"

Adrenaline surges through my veins, seeming to replace the blood. I feel twitchy. A cold sweat seeps from my pores, giving me a chill.

"Is it really worth losing your future over?"

"What do you mean?"

"It was your car."

My mouth drops as I stare at my best friend. "I wasn't driving."

"Are you sure they'll believe that? I mean, you've obviously had too much to drink."

I don't remember drinking that much, just a couple of beers. Then again, I don't remember leaving the party. Or the drive out here. Or anything until the thump that jostled me from my slumber in the back seat.

"She's dead, Steve. Nothing's going to change that."

"What are you suggesting?"

"Do you still have your snow shovel in the trunk?"

I suck in a sharp breath at the crispness of the memory. Feel myself being drawn back into the past as more from that night comes flooding back to me.

Hurt at the betrayal as my best friend made it clear he'd deny being the driver responsible for what happened if I went to the police. Fear of the consequences I'd face if the authorities believed Wesley's word over mine. Defeat as I agreed to his plan. Shame as I took her ankles, her spilled blood warm on my palms as I helped carry her across the field. Shock as her hair fell to the side when we set her down, exposing a face I recognized.

One that looked even more similar to Maggie's than it had appeared on the student ID.

I lean my head against the steering wheel, tears welling in my eyes. My breath comes too fast and shallow. I wish the memory hadn't surfaced, because now I can't unsee it.

The high cheekbones. The full lips. The auburn hair softly framing a face eerily close to Maggie's.

My chest squeezes so tight it feels like I'm going to burst. How have I never made this connection before?

Seeing Georgia laugh at Wesley earlier, while we were still at the party, is one of the few memories I'd managed to retain from that night. And yet, not once did I register the resemblance between the coed and my fiancée. If I could block that out, what else have I managed to forget?

Dr. Curry's voice echoes inside my head.

"What's he doing right now?"

"Holding out his hand."

"For?"

"The knife. The one he gave me to use."
"For what? Did Wesley tell you what to do with it?"
"No. I just knew."
Once again, I wonder what it was that I had known to do.

Outside, dusk falls, casting long shadows across the landscape. The kind of shadows that you could imagine coming to collect someone like me, to drag them off into the darkness. Maybe that would even be for the best.

Because despite staring at the tree for hours, waiting for the last few blanks from that night to fill in, I still haven't remembered why I had the knife—or what I did with it. Until I do, until I'm sure that it's not possible that I was drawn to Maggie so strongly out of some deep-seated desire to do it again, how am I ever going to trust myself around her?

56

MAGGIE

I'm so cold. I pull at the rough blanket, trying to raise it higher. Hiss as a sharp pain stabs through my back. My eyes flutter and I think I see Sue curled up, sleeping in a chair in the corner of the room. This is a strange dream.

The light in the room has shifted when I'm awoken by something squeezing my arm. An annoying beeping starts as it strengthens its grip, becoming uncomfortably tight. Somewhere in the distance, a voice sounds over an intercom. A doctor is being paged.

It comes back to me in a cloudy haze.

Sue, Rachel, the knife. I'm in a hospital, that much is clear, but why? Did I manage to stop Rachel? I don't think that I did.

Sue!

I struggle to sit up, gasping at the pain from the attempt. Sweat sprouts at my temples, my breath coming quick and shallow. The beeping beside me gets faster.

"It's okay, Maggie. Relax."

A cool hand strokes my brow. I allow myself to sink back against the thin mattress. Opening my eyes, I find Sue looking down at me, concern etched across her face.

"How are you feeling?" she asks.

"Like I got attacked by a moose and lost."

"I'll call the nurse and see if she can give you something for the pain."

"No." I grab her arm as she turns away. The stiffness in my muscles sets off a chain reaction, a series of spasms traveling until they tug at my injury. I draw deep breaths, trying to chase away the darkness encroaching around the edges of my vision.

Sue comes back, settling herself gently on the edge of the bed. "You should really try this thing. It's called not moving. I hear it's all the rage among women who get themselves stabbed saving a friend."

She's smiling, but the corners of her mouth twitch. Tears fill her eyes.

"That was really stupid of you, Maggie. You could have—" Her voice hitches. She clears her throat but is still too emotional to speak. Instead, she squeezes my hand harder than the blood pressure cuff when it was strangling my arm.

"But you're okay?"

She sniffs. "Thanks to you."

"And Rachel?"

"In jail, where she should be. Maggie, I'm sorry I—"

"You don't need to apologize, Sue."

"But I almost got you ki—"

I hold up a hand, stifling the groan that accompanies the gesture. "She was your friend's daughter. You didn't know."

"Except maybe I kind of did."

I stare at Sue, waiting for her to elaborate. She sighs heavily, worries at a pull in the overbleached hospital blanket as she says, "That girl was never quite right, even before Ruby left. She's always been a bully. Always acted like she owned her little sister, forced her to take the blame for anything she thought she'd get in trouble for. And what she did to her family..."

"Is Rene all right?"

It had been Rene who had called while I was speaking to Missy Anderson. Rene whose message had let me know that Sue was in danger. Even now, recalling the tortured sound of her voice while she told me that she had been in the house when I visited her sister, that Rachel had drugged her own children, that they had all been in the back in need of help while I was standing in the kitchen, suspecting Rene of murder—I shudder, wincing as my stitches pull.

It's a miracle that despite being beaten and tied to the radiator, Rene had managed to get loose to make the call. That I had made it to Sue's before it was too late.

"Physically? She was fine, just some bruises. Psychologically?"

Sue doesn't need to finish the thought. After what Rachel had already done, it's surprising that she had left her sister alive, though I suspect being the sole survivor of your family who isn't in prison for murdering the rest of them will take a toll of its own.

But hopefully there's some relief for her as well. Because Sue wasn't the only one who had known there was something off about Rachel Anderson. I suspect Rene had been trying to protect others from her for years.

"What do you mean *was*?" I ask.

"She's left."

"Do you know where?"

"No." She shakes her head and looks down at the floor. "I wish I did. That poor girl needs our help. And now there's no one to take the kids."

"That's right. Raymond, the John Doe, Kal needs to know—"

"He does, Maggie."

"So the kids?"

"They're in state custody at the moment. But you don't

need to worry about any of that. Just concentrate on getting better."

"But my dogs—"

"Linda's taking care of them."

"What about Steve?"

Sue's mouth tightens into a thin line. "I tried calling him, but he didn't answer. I didn't think this was something I should relay in a voicemail, so I left a message for him to call me back. I can try him again, though. I should."

"No, that's all right. He's..."

I can tell by Sue's expression that she placed the first call a while ago. And that there's probably been several others since. It's strange that he hasn't called her back, since he obviously hasn't been able to get ahold of me. Then I realize—he probably hasn't even tried.

He's obsessed with this mission of his, can't focus on anything besides achieving his goal. How many times have I done the same, putting our relationship on the back burner while I worked a case? Still... it sucks being on this side of it.

"He's probably out of cell range," I say.

Sue gives me a look that says she doesn't believe me, though she's kind enough to let it drop.

"How long have I been in here, anyway?"

"Three days."

I'm speechless. I take a closer look at Sue—the dark circles under her eyes, disheveled hair, rumpled clothes that I now notice have dark stains on them that look suspiciously like blood. My blood.

"Have you been here the whole time?"

"Of course I have."

"Sue."

"Maggie." She brushes a lock of hair back from my face. "You saved my life." She holds a single finger up to shush me before I can reply. "You did. You're bigger than me. Younger."

She arches an eyebrow as she says, "You might even be stronger, but if you ever try to say I admitted it I'll convince everyone that it's just something you imagined hearing while you were hallucinating. Yet despite all that..."

"Geesh. You're talking like I almost died or something."

"You were unconscious for most of three days."

"I was faking. I needed a vacation." I give her my best grin, but it doesn't feel very convincing. I swallow hard before asking, "How serious was it?"

"The knife nicked your axillary artery. If the paramedics hadn't already been on the scene, you probably would have bled out."

I swallow hard, remembering the puddle of blood at my feet, the fun house that wasn't fun, Fire Investigator Larson carrying me in his arms.

"Did I say anything?" I ask, suddenly embarrassed. "When I was hallucinating?"

"I don't know if you were hallucinating or not, to be honest. But the struggle you put up when the poor paramedics were trying to get you to lie on your belly on the stretcher... In the end, that fire investigator had to carry you out."

"That really happened?" A rush of blood heats my cheeks. "What was he doing there, anyway?"

Sue darts an annoyed glance at the closed door. "You can ask him yourself, if you want."

"He's here?"

"Despite my best efforts to make him go away? Yes. He's been here almost as much as I have."

"Why?"

The looks she gives me makes me blush all over again. "I'll tell him he can come in, but I'll be just outside. If he gives you any trouble—"

"It'll be fine, Sue. Why don't you go home and get some sleep?"

"I've had plenty of sleep."

"Then how about a change of clothes and a shower? I'll still be here when you get back. I promise."

She holds my gaze for a long moment before softly nodding her head. Folding me in a gentle hug, she whispers in my ear, "You better."

She presses a kiss against my cheek, and then she's gone. I watch the door after she leaves, but it remains closed. Larson must have left. I feel an odd stir of disappointment.

I've been by my myself for all of sixty seconds, and already being alone with my thoughts is almost unbearable. I find myself wishing that I hadn't told Sue to leave.

In an effort to distract myself, I try thinking about the first thing I'm going to do when I leave here. If I'm in the hospital, then that means I'm in Lincoln. There's a little Italian place Steve and I ate at once that was incredible. We always said we'd go back, but I never made it a priority to find the time.

And now... what if we never get the chance? We almost didn't. I'm reckless, and foolish, and yet, if I had the same choice to make, I'd do it again.

The door opens. I turn toward it with relief. I've never been a fan of being poked and prodded by medical professionals, but it seems a small price to pay if it will keep me out of my own head, if only for a bit.

But the person who enters isn't wearing scrubs, but rather a fatigued expression strained with worry. Fire Investigator Larson runs his eyes over me with an intensity that makes me want to squirm. He rubs a hand against the back of his neck as he hesitantly closes the distance between us, stopping at the foot of the bed.

"You okay?" he asks.

I feel suddenly self-conscious. I try to ignore the fact that I'm wearing a hospital gown, that I haven't had a shower in days, that I probably look so close to death that he has to ask to make sure that I am, indeed, actually alive.

"I am."

Larson sighs heavily and collapses into the chair that Sue so recently vacated. He sits with his head in his hands, elbows propped on his knees for what seems like a very long time. I use the opportunity to study him while he won't notice—the faint scars that crisscross the back of his large hands, the cords of his muscles beneath his skin, the way everything about him exudes strength, and yet, it's there.

It's hard to see. Most people probably miss it, but there's no denying—this man's been broken before. And though I'd be the first to insist that I'm stronger along the fault lines where the shattered pieces of myself have knit back together, I know it's a lie. There's an instability that's been left behind.

"You really scared me there, Red. When I heard on the radio that all emergency response personnel were needed, I knew it was you. I've never been so glad to have done EMT training in my life."

He sits up and I look away quickly. This time, he studies me while I pretend not to notice.

"I'm guessing this is the kind of thing a guy has to expect if he wants to be in your life?"

Pretending I didn't hear the question, I say, "I've been told I have you to thank for carrying me to the ambulance. So... thanks. I'm sorry if I bled on you."

He looks shocked for a fraction of an instant, then explodes with laughter. Shaking his head, he rolls his eyes as he stands and moves to leave. "Thank you."

"For what?"

"For making me believe you came out of this just fine." He pauses on the threshold, facing the hallway. Lowers his voice as he says, "Even if we both know the truth. I'll be here when you need me, Maggie Riley. Until then, take care of yourself."

I stare at the closed doorway for long after he's left, wondering what it would be like to play with fire.

57

STEVE

It's still early, the sun weak overhead in a sky the color of ice. Several birds rise up into the air, startled, as I once again pull over onto the verge. I've been coming here every day, hoping that something will trigger my memory, filling in the rest of the holes from the night Georgia Pierce died.

But it hasn't. Day after day, as I've watched late morning turn to afternoon, afternoon fade to evening, I realized what I have to do. And I can't put this off any longer—even if it wasn't a part of the original plan.

This is no longer about making amends. About alleviating some of the crippling guilt I carry. About being a better man for my fiancée. It's a matter of life... and possibly death.

I *have* to remember, no matter what it takes. If I did something to hurt Georgia, then I can never see Maggie again. I'll call the cops from the open grave and confess, wait for them to come take me away, anything to keep Maggie safe.

As I get out of the car, my phone buzzes in my pocket. I don't bother to answer it, don't even look at who the caller is as I round to the back of my vehicle and pop the hatch. I've been out of communication for days, ever since finding the tree, knowing that if I answered, I might lose my nerve. I can't allow that to happen.

I stare at the shovel in the back of my SUV and flash back to that night, looking down into the cluttered trunk of the little fourth-hand Honda I drove in college. Watching as my best friend shoved aside my emergency roadside kit, an old wool blanket from army surplus, a shopping bag containing something my mother had insisted that I take with me on my last visit that I'd never bothered to look at, to free the snow scoop.

The blade of the shovel I bought at the McAllister and Sons several miles away is much better suited for the job at hand than the battered aluminum rectangle I used to free my tires when the snow buried them between classes almost two decades ago.

That cheap metal tray couldn't handle much weight—it used to buckle when I scraped my tires free—but somehow, perhaps out of sheer desperation, it worked for us that night. I have to believe that this one will work for me now. Grabbing the spade, I set off across the field.

Stalks of wheat tug against me as I weave my way through, as if trying to hold me back. A cloud drifts over the sun, its large shadow heavy and ominous overhead. The tree hovers in front of me like a mirage, always seeming just out of reach.

Until finally, the crop thins. The heat leaches from my skin as I step beneath the oak's shade. Thick roots breach the soil under my feet. And as I run my palm over its trunk, my fingertips playing over the cross carved crudely into the rough bark, the missing piece of my memory crashes against me with the force of a runaway train

Wesley and I hadn't talked that night as we set about the grim task of burying the girl he'd hit with my car. What was there to say? No words would have been adequate.

We'd been friends so long, our entire lives, until that night—when he'd dug out his pocketknife and held it out to me, I'd known what he wanted me to do.

I'd been so young back then. So naïve. I'd had such high hopes for my future, right up until the very moment that I'd used that tiny piece of steel to carve a burial marker into the oak for a girl I'd never known—and never would.

That was almost half my lifetime ago. Am I any smarter now? Any wiser? I fear that I'm not.

But it doesn't matter that all I used the knife for was carving a cross into the tree, because I kept a horrible secret. Would have kept keeping it, if Wesley hadn't resurfaced to use it against me.

And while it's an overwhelming relief to know that I didn't pursue Maggie out of some sick desire, I'll never be able to rule out the chance that her resemblance to Georgia was part of the attraction. An opportunity to spend the rest of my life trying to make things right to the girl I couldn't save.

But maybe that's okay. An extra incentive to keep me motivated to always do my best for Maggie. And as I push the blade into the dirt beneath that tree, using my foot to drive it deep, that's exactly what I plan to do.

I'm only a foot down when I find a scrap of fabric. I stare at it for a long moment before reaching down hesitantly, giving it a tentative tug to free it from the soil. Carefully brushing the earth off it, I fold it and put it in my pocket.

Then I keep digging.

The metallic chink of the shovel as it scrapes against rocks and stones makes me cringe. Each time I expect it to be bone, but it never is. Sweat runs in grimy rivulets down my skin as I dig deeper and deeper still. I check the sun in the sky, see that it's fallen toward the western horizon. And still I dig.

I dig until the hole is much deeper than we could have possibly dug it that night. Then I spread out in every direction, excavating hollows beneath gnarled roots, still searching. The light had drained from the day, the cicadas have started their evening song, by the time I'm forced to admit—she's not here.

I collapse against the tree, staring at the upturned land around me, the cross that I branded into the trunk that night directly over my head. Pulling the piece of fabric from my pocket, I rub it between my fingers, convincing myself that it's real.

It wasn't a nightmare. She was here. But she's not anymore.

Wesley must have moved the body. Even in death he's managed to maintain his hold on me.

I tried so hard to find her, to set things as right as I could, return her to her family so they can give her the proper burial she deserves, but I was too late. Now she's gone. This scrap of fabric is all that's left.

The sound of my phone joins the gentle soundtrack of the night. I fish it out of my pocket on autopilot, answering before I can register what I'm doing.

"Hello?"

"Steve?"

"Yeah."

"Is everything all right?"

"I'm not sure. I don't think so, no."

"Where are you?"

"Still in Massachusetts. I located the tree. I'm under it right now. I... I know we had a plan, but I had to do it. I had to dig her up, make sure that she was found."

Maggie inhales sharply. I hurry to continue, unloading my burden on her even though it's not fair.

"She's not here, Maggie. She's gone."

"Are you sure you have the right tree?"

"One hundred percent."

"Then she must be there. Unless..." Her voice fades as she comes to the same conclusion that I've already reached.

There's a hiss of static over the line, what sounds like an intercom announcement on her end.

"Where are you?" I ask.

There's a long pause before she answers, "At the hospital."

"Are you okay?"

"Yeah, everything's fine, just passing through. Any idea when you'll be home?"

"Soon. I might need another day or two down here to wrap things up. Is that okay?"

"Take your time."

"You sure?"

"Yeah. Are you going to be all right?"

I huff a laugh. "I'm working on that."

"Seriously, Steve. You don't sound well."

"I'm trying, Maggie. I promise."

Looking down, I find that I'm still rubbing the fabric I'd found between my fingers. It seems in better condition than you'd expect after being buried for almost twenty years. I give it a closer look.

I don't remember exactly what Georgia had been wearing that night, but I thought it had been jeans and a t-shirt. This scrap in my hand doesn't appear to belong to either. The texture is coarser. Though now stained the color of cardboard—is it stained? Turning it over, I can just make out a faded symbol. I scratch at the dirt crusting the emblem with my thumb nail. Raise it up closer to my eyes, not believing what I'm seeing.

The logo on the fabric bears the letters CCPD.

This isn't from something that Georgia Pierce was wearing when we buried her that night—it's from a Coyote Cove Police Department uniform. Hadn't Maggie mentioned she was having problems finding one of hers?

My heart thumps against the walls of my chest, pumping fear into my veins with each pulse. "Did you ever find that uniform you were looking for?"

"No, why?"

"When did it go missing?"

"I'm not sure."

"Could it have been missing for months? Say, at least two?"

"Why? What's going on?"

I stare down at the piece of her uniform in my hands and gulp. I don't want to tell her, but I have to. She might not be safe.

"There was a piece of fabric in the dirt where—" I can't bring myself to say it, clearing my throat instead. "It's all I found when I was digging. And I'm pretty sure it's from your missing uniform."

There's a long moment of silence, and I can't help fearing this is it. The final straw. The thing that makes Maggie wash her hands of me.

"It could have been missing that long, yeah."

"But how would he have gotten it? Do you think he was in the house with the dogs?"

"No. I'm sure I left it in my Jeep."

It's little comfort. He'd still come too close. Who knows what his intentions were? What other surprises he arranged for me.

"Maggie."

"He's dead, Steve."

"But that picture you found—"

"He was in a relationship with the woman who lived in the trailer that exploded. Who's also dead. It's over."

"What if it isn't?"

"It is."

"What if you're in danger?"

"I'm not."

I draw deep breaths, doing my best to believe her.

"I'm sorry I dragged you into this."

"You didn't drag me into anything."

"You know what I mean."

"Steve?"

"Yeah?"

"Do what you need to do, then come home, okay?"

"Okay, yeah."

We say good night and I click to end the call. Looking down at the scrap of my fiancée's uniform grasped in one dirt-caked hand, my phone in the other, I think of all the things I should have said. More importantly, what I should have asked: *What aren't you telling me?*

Because Maggie doesn't just pass through a hospital. That hair of hers is like a red flag, and she doesn't hesitate to wave it in front of every angry bull she encounters. It's always been my contribution to our relationship to try and pull her back from the edge, to keep her safe. But how can I now, when I might be the one making her a target?

I'd sell my soul to get to spend the rest of my life making that woman happy. Though I'm starting to suspect that I lost that piece of myself long ago, I'm still going to try my best.

58

MAGGIE

I lower myself into the vehicle slowly, stiffly, clenching my teeth to keep from sounding my discomfort. This injury has been a big blow to my pride. Though it was my left shoulder that got stabbed, somehow, my entire body aches. It reminds me that I'm getting older.

Settling into the seat, I turn toward the driver. "You don't have to do this, you know. Steve will be back tonight. He can take me."

There's no denying that I'm anxious to get my Jeep back. Learning that it had been released by the state forensics lab and that the repairs were complete had been the highlight of the last few days.

"I know I don't have to. But I want to." Kal gives me a shy smile.

I find myself returning it, even though if Kal drives me, it means leaving the Cove without a cop. But maybe that's a good thing. It will give me a chance to practice my new resolution.

While I was trapped in the hospital, trying to convince the doctors I was well enough for them to release me, I promised myself that I'd try to relax my stranglehold over life, let unimportant things go and allow myself to be a bit more human.

So, yes. I do want to go pick up my Jeep right now. And I want Kal to be the one to take me.

"Thank you."

He waits until I've buckled my seatbelt, then puts the cruiser in gear and backs down the driveway.

"Believe it or not, I've missed you," he says.

"It's been only five days since you last saw me."

"Yeah, but you weren't looking so good that last time."

I avert my gaze, looking out the window. Watch as a chipmunk scurries along a tree trunk with enviable agility. Sensing my discomfort, he changes the subject.

"I was able to prove Fred Wallace was in town during the hit and run using his employment records. The warrant for access to his truck was approved while you were out."

I turn my full attention toward him.

"The staties sent a forensics team."

"And?"

"They had several swabs test positive for hemoglobin."

I know that just because they found evidence of blood, it doesn't mean that we have enough proof to charge Fred Wallace with Michelle Sanders' death. The initial test done in the field can't tell us if the blood belonged to a human, or an animal the driver might have hit. And even if the blood is human, there might not be enough, or the sample might be too degraded to test for DNA.

"Did they tell you when they think they'll have the results?" I ask.

Kal gives a one-shouldered shrug. Glances at me, a small smile playing about his lips.

"Doesn't really matter now."

"Why's that?"

"Because when Mr. Wallace was served with the warrant, he gave a full confession."

"Seriously?" My pulse quickens. The wound in my shoulder throbs along with it, but I ignore the pain.

"Seriously. Said he couldn't live with the guilt anymore. Of course, that doesn't mean he hasn't lawyered up, but still, it feels like a win, don't you think?"

I nod. "Did he say why he did it? Was it connected to Ruby's disappearance?"

"He claims he doesn't know anything about that. Said he was on his way home from the Loose Moose one night. Was messing with the radio, when he looked up, Michelle was in the street right in front of him. Said it was too late to react."

"That would explain the lack of skid marks at the scene. Did he say why he didn't stop and try to get her help?"

"Apparently his pal Chief Parker had told him he was out of warnings and that the next time he got caught driving under the influence he'd have to charge him."

Cursing to myself, I glare out the window. If the man had faced the consequences for his actions *every* time he'd been caught drunk driving, Michelle Sanders might still be alive. As far as I'm concerned, her blood is on Rufus Parker's hands. It strengthens my resolve to start looking through more of his past cases.

It doesn't matter how many reasons I give myself for why I should draw boundaries between my personal life and my job, this is why I don't: because in a town as small as Coyote Cove, where the police department is so tiny, the efforts—or lack thereof—of the person in charge can make such a huge difference. In some cases, to some families, that difference means everything.

Thinking about Kit, I ask, "Has anyone told her daughter yet?"

"No. I was waiting to hear what charges the DA was going

to bring against him first. And Sue thought that maybe you might want to do it."

I nod, even though I'm not sure about that yet.

We fall into a comfortable silence. I lay my head back against the seat, resting. The world beyond the window turns into a blur through my half-shut eyes.

"Maggie?"

"Yeah?"

"The reason I don't want my family coming to your wedding? It has nothing to do with you. You know that, right?"

"You don't have to explain—"

"I know. But I want to."

He stares out through the windshield with a grim expression. Stretches his neck to each side. When he speaks again, it's in a tone so low that I almost can't hear it.

"My family... they don't know where I am right now. Not exactly."

"What?" I ask, sure that I've heard wrong. They are, quite possibly, the last words that I could have imagined coming from his mouth.

"They know that I'm still in Maine." He glances at me quickly before returning his gaze to the road. "But that's it. It's safer that way. For them and for me."

His jaw clenches. The joint pops. I'm reminded of how many times I've wanted to ask about it but haven't. Am I about to learn the cause behind it now?

"My ex-fiancée, Melissa? She didn't dump me. That's not why we're no longer together."

I'm rushing to think of how to properly word my condolences when he takes me by surprise for the second time in as many minutes.

"She stalked me."

I ignore the tug against my stitches as I turn my entire body in my seat to face him. He continues staring out the windshield, unable to meet my gaze.

Ruby Anderson's case has been an eye-opening reminder of the perils of domestic violence. Of how desperate a victim can be made to feel, of how hard it can be to get out of an abusive relationship alive. So often we think of it as a problem that only women face, but the truth is, it goes both ways.

"It started when we were still together. She'd turn up wherever I was. At the store. Loitering across the street from the police department where I worked. Following me in her car. Not to say hi or visit, just watching me. Whenever I tried talking to her about it, she'd get irate. Accuse me of cheating on her, of being untrustworthy."

He clears his throat before saying, "I tried to convince her that she didn't have anything to worry about, but finally, I just got tired of it. It wasn't healthy. I figured the best thing I could do was end the relationship. But that only made it worse."

The vehicle has fallen so silent that I can hear the sound of every breath I take. Every swallow. A strange knocking beneath the hood that should probably get checked by a mechanic.

After a very long pause, Kal continues, "I'm a cop. I know the channels you're supposed to go through, all the legalities you're supposed to use to protect yourself. So that's exactly what I did."

"And what happened?"

He shrugs sadly, finally turning to look at me.

"I'm a cop," he repeats. "And a big guy. No one took me seriously that the woman half my size who I'd been engaged to was a danger. Not until..."

A muscle in his jaw tics, causing the joint to pop again.

"I was jumped one night after work on the way across the parking lot to my car. Went a few rounds with a baseball bat. The perp was dressed in all black. Their face wasn't caught by any of the surveillance cameras overlooking the lot."

"But it was her? Melissa?"

"Once she stopped, she told me I'd brought it on myself. That if I came back and apologized, behaved, and obeyed, we could be happy together again. Then she left me there on the asphalt, bleeding."

"Did they charge her?"

"They couldn't make it stick. There was no evidence. A friend gave her an alibi. It was her word against mine, and they said that with the concussion I'd received, a defense lawyer could make a good argument to get the case dismissed."

He flexes his fingers on the steering wheel, readjusting his grip.

"I took a leave of absence, hoping she'd lose interest, but she started harassing my family, following them thinking she'd catch me visiting."

"So you left?"

"So I left. Called you about the job opening from a new phone I'd purchased. Once you'd hired me for the position, I set my plan in motion. Bought a car she wouldn't recognize through one of those online dealers that deliver, had them leave it a few streets over. Asked a friend to tail her to make sure she was at home. Then I snuck out in the middle of the night, left my old life behind. Pulled over on the drive up here and called her. Told her she'd won. That my parents and sister didn't want anything to do with me anymore because of her, so I was gone for good."

"And it's worked?"

"It seems to have so far."

"But your family?"

He sighs heavily. "I'm not saying the plan was perfect. I've had to make a lot of sacrifices. But not," he says, pulling into the parking lot of the body shop where my Jeep is being held. He turns to face me. Manages a small smile. "Not the most important thing. Not my actual life."

"But your freedom, Kal. This isn't right. Let me help you. I'm sure we can find a way to get your ex off the streets, to make it safe for you to go back to your old life."

His smile grows a little bigger. "Are you trying to get rid of me?"

My mouth drops open. "No. Definitely not. I love having you here, but—"

"And believe it or not, I love being here."

My first response dies on my lips. Giving him side-eye, I ask, "You do?"

"Don't you?"

I think of the seemingly endless frigid winters when I spend months unable to get warm—or even comfortable. The mountains of snow that have to be moved. The dark, dreary days where I long to feel the heat of the Florida sun on my face.

There's nothing tying me to this place. I could leave anytime I want, start over new. And yet, here I am.

"Well, I wouldn't say I love it."

"But there's something about being in the valley," he says.

"It does grow on you," I admit. Grinning, I add, "Kind of like a fungus."

Kal laughs. "I suppose you're right. But what I'm getting at is, a part of me almost feels fortunate that this happened, since it's what brought me to Coyote Cove. And if you want to help me find a way to safely be in contact with my family more often, I'd really appreciate it. But this"—he gestures around—"is home now."

His expression turns serious as he adds, "And I've grown attached to having you in it, so I'd really appreciate it if you'd try not to get yourself killed."

I press my lips, still chapped from the harsh hospital air, together. "I'll work on that. I promise."

"Thank you."

Feeling kind of awkward and emotional, I point toward my

Jeep and grab the door handle, eager to make my escape. But first, "Kal?"

"Yeah?"

I glance over my very sore shoulder at him. "You and Sue? You're my people, you know that, right? You're my family."

"You've got Steve, too."

"Of course."

I give him a big smile, but the instant I turn away, it's gone.

59

MAGGIE

I'm in the kitchen trying to wash dishes one-handed, the dogs napping at my feet, when suddenly their heads perk up. Ears cock, noses twitch. In a flash they're up, bolting toward the front of the house. Drying my hands, I follow them to the door, but when I get there... I don't know.

I find myself hanging back a bit, nerves stirring deep in the pit of my stomach as I listen to the door being unlocked, watching as the bolt turns. A moment later, Steve appears. He doesn't look well—he's too pale, his sickly pallor accentuated by the dark circles under his eyes.

"Hey," I say, lifting a hand halfway in an almost wave like he's someone I recognize but don't know. Certainly not someone who I'm marrying in less than two weeks.

"Hey."

We stand there staring at each other for a moment, the dogs jumping up between us, celebrating Steve's homecoming enough for the both of us. Finally, I end the standoff.

"You hungry?"

"You cooked?" he asks, unable to hide his disbelief.

I get it. Admittedly, my cooking skills are limited, but the fact is I usually don't have time to spend in the kitchen. I work long hours, and when I finally get a chance to relax, that's what I want to do—not worry about burning whatever's on the stovetop or forgetting about whatever's in the oven. But I still haven't returned to work yet. The truth is that I'm bored and a little restless.

"Yeah, nothing fancy. Just tacos. Why don't you go sit on the couch and I'll bring you a plate?"

I hurry off to the kitchen, not waiting for him to answer. Why does this feel so awkward and weird? Is this normal? Shouldn't we be greeting each other with hugs and kisses? Instead, it feels like he's a stranger, like we need to get reacquainted with each other after just a short time apart.

I take my time as I put meat in a shell, followed by cheese, onion, and cilantro. I add a handful of tortilla chips, spoon some salsa and guacamole onto the plate. Glance around, searching for something else to do, another reason to delay, but there's nothing. I can't put it off any longer.

Heading to the living room, I find Steve standing beside the couch, looking lost. He seems relieved as I come to join him, finally taking a seat. In an instant the dogs are on him. Tempe jumps up onto the back of the frame and curls herself around his neck, using her forepaws to pin his shoulder as she threatens to remove his skin with the force of her tongue. Sully hops onto his lap and flops belly up, staring at him adorningly.

Our eyes lock and the ice between us melts. We smile at each other as I settle onto the cushion beside him. His hand snakes over to mine, holding it tight.

"You look tired," I say.

"I haven't been sleeping well. Too many covers when there's no one to steal them."

"Haha."

"Seriously, though. I missed you."

"I've missed you, too."

"I don't like being apart."

He holds Tempe steady as he leans toward me for a kiss. Wraps an arm around me. I brace myself, stifling a hiss when my stitches tug as he pulls me close.

"Maggie."

My mom used to say my name the same way when she knew I was hiding something.

"I'm fine."

"What happened?" he asks softly, as if he's afraid to hear the answer. And he probably is. I've lost count of the number of injuries I've received since we've been together. But none of them were as serious as this. "Why were you at the hospital when you called me a couple days ago?"

"I might have kind of... got stabbed."

Steve curses. Carefully withdraws his arm and faces me. "Where?"

"In the shoulder."

He shuts his eyes for a long moment. His voice is tense when he opens them, looking at me intently. "How serious was it?"

I look away and he curses again. Even though I know I should, I can't bring myself to tell him. Not about the nicked artery and the blood transfusions. Not about the three days when I was mostly unconscious. Not about the tip of the blade still lodged in the bone, in too dangerous a position for the doctors to remove, which means I'll have to watch closely for any signs of infection. It's bad enough that he'll see the bruising that covers almost half my back.

"That's why Sue was calling me, wasn't it?"

"Yes."

"Because you couldn't call me yourself." When I don't confirm the statement, he adds, "Don't you think this is something you should have told me when you did get ahold of me?"

"It didn't seem like the right time. You had just—" I don't

say that he'd just discovered that Wesley had moved the body. "I didn't want to put you under any additional stress."

"There's no amount of stress in this world that would keep me from wanting to know something like that. You get that, don't you? That's what I'm here for." He sighs heavily and shakes his head at me. "I love you, Maggie. That means I'm here for you, no matter what. It doesn't matter what else may be going on in my life. You have to stop pushing me away. It isn't fair."

"That goes both ways, you know," I say, suddenly angry. "You left, and it's like I just ceased to exist to you. And I get that you were having a hard time, but you could have talked to me, told me about it instead of avoiding me. It made me feel... unsure."

My heart spasms in my chest. I can't believe I just did that. I think I just told him that I've been having second thoughts about getting married.

I instantly feel horrible. He's been having such a hard time lately, has seemed so fragile, that it feels like kicking him while he's down. But at the same time... it's a huge relief to have this off my chest. I stare at him, waiting for his reaction.

For a long minute, it's like he didn't hear me. Then his breath quickens. His eyes lift from the floor, are wide by the time they find mine, the gaze pleading. His voice cracks as he says, "I'm so sorry. It kills me to know that I made you feel that way. It wasn't my intention, but you're right. I closed down out there, shut you out."

He slips off the couch onto the floor, kneels in front of me. Takes my hands in his. "I love you, Maggie. I want to spend the rest of my life with you. You're the absolute best part of my life. I need you to know that."

I press my lips together hard to keep them from trembling.

"You're the sun to my day. The stars to my night. The Hyde to my Jekyll." He grins wickedly.

I give him a dirty look, but join in, "You're the cheese to my enchilada."

"You're the conditioner to my shampoo."

"The sock to my foot."

"The detergent to my laundry."

"The gas to my Jeep."

"Say you'll marry me, Maggie Riley."

"Yes," I laugh. "I'll marry you."

Steve jumps to his feet, punching a fist in the air. Does a little happy dance, strutting around the living room. The dogs frisk about joyously, eager to get in on the action.

All the concerns that have been building up over the last week fade away, because this? This is the man I fell in love with. It's been a long time since he's made an appearance, but it's a relief to know that he still exists.

When he's done, he takes a seat again, careful not to jostle the couch. Gives me a long, lingering kiss. Withdraws just enough so the tip of his nose is touching mine. "You love me?"

"I do."

"Great. Hold on to that thought."

"Why?"

"Because my mom sent something for you—her wedding veil. She wants you to use it as your 'something borrowed.' And I may have accidentally agreed to it when I when I wasn't paying attention."

"That was sweet of her."

"I tried to get you out of it. I know frills aren't really your thing. And let's face it, it's really old. But she's convinced it won't actually turn to dust the moment it's exposed to the light."

"You didn't really tell her that, did you? You're a mean boy."

He shrugs. "She married my dad a *looong* time ago."

"Which makes the veil just a little bit older than you, and you aren't dust yet," I tease. "Where is it?"

"Still in the car."

"Is it unlocked?"

"Yeah, why?"

"Because I'm going to go get it."

"Honestly, Maggie, you don't have to wear it."

"I know. But I might want to. I want to see it." I don't mention that it may be the perfect solution for concealing the mess that my open-backed wedding dress will reveal.

"Want me to get it?"

"No, you stay here with the pups. They've missed you. I'll be back in a sec."

Though the sun has set, the sky seems brighter than it has in days as I exit the house. I take the porch stairs slowly, muscles still a bit tight and sore from being still so long during my hospital stay, but despite that, I feel more hopeful than I have in a long time.

Steve's back. My Steve. We're going to get married as planned in just under two weeks, and we're going to be happy. Together.

Dear reader,

First, an enormous and most sincere thank you for choosing to read *The Day She Died*, the fifth book in the Chief Maggie Riley series! I always enjoy my stay in Coyote Cove and hope that you enjoyed your time there as well! I can't wait for you to discover what comes next for Maggie and the rest of the gang!

If you'd like to keep up to date with my latest releases, you can sign up at the following link. Your email address will never be shared, and you can unsubscribe at any time.

www.bookouture.com/shannon-hollinger

If you enjoyed the story, I would be so very grateful if you'd leave a review and recommend the book to your fellow readers. Please know that your review really does have a huge impact! On future books, future plots, future character development... I love reading what you think! Your review is also incredibly important in helping other readers find my books for the first time, which is an amazing gift to give an author!

When ideas strike, sometimes they come whole. Other times there's a single inspiration around which the plot develops. In this case, I knew I wanted to make a big bang. Literally (or, at least, on the page). I had the first chapter. I just had to figure out how to make it part of a larger story. And then how to make that story interesting.

That's when I decided that one of the bodies recovered in the blast needed to have a history, in that she was already supposed to be dead. From there, I had to figure out what would make a woman leave her children behind.

What resulted was a motivation that stems from a very delicate subject.

I've done my best to handle it as sensitively as I can. My sincerest apologies to anyone who found otherwise.

If you or someone you know is a victim of domestic violence, there are many available resources to support you. Please know that you are not alone. Help is out there:

United States

National Domestic Violence Hotline
* Call 1-800-799-7233 or 1-800-787-3224 (TTY)
* Text "START" to 88788
* Chat online at www.thehotline.org
* Find resources at thehotline.org/get-help/domestic-violence-local-resources

Office of Family Violence Prevention and Services
* Find resources at www.acf.hhs.gov/ofvps/news/resources-survivors-domestic-violence

Victim Connect Resource Center
* Call or text 1-855-4-VICTIM (1-855-484-2846)
* Chat online at www.victimconnect.org
National Network to End Domestic Violence: Legal information for victims of abuse, including information about each state's laws.
* Email hotline |**www.womenslaw.org**

United Kingdom

My Support Space
* Find resources at mysupportspace.org.uk
National Domestic Abuse Helpline
* Call 0808 2000 247

Refuge
* Call 0808 2000 247
* Find resources at refuge.org.uk

Women's Aid
* Chat online at chat.womensaid.org.uk
* Find local support at www.womensaid.org.uk/
womens-aid-directory

I'm always eager to hear from readers, so please feel free to get in touch. You can find me on Facebook, Instagram, Goodreads, X, or my website.

Thank you so much for your support—it really is hugely appreciated!

Until next time,

Shannon Hollinger

facebook.com/thiswritersays

x.com/thiswritersays

instagram.com/thiswritersays

goodreads.com/shannonhollinger

ACKNOWLEDGMENTS

Thank you. Yes, you. Seriously. You, the reader, get my very first thanks of this book, as well as my undying gratitude. You are why we—authors, publishers, editors, and all the countless people toiling behind the scenes—do this. So again, thank you.

Thank you especially if you have left a review. Even just a few words can have a huge impact on a book's success, and you have no idea how much I appreciate you taking the time to let others know when you think one of mine is worth reading!

Thank you to everyone who's emailed, messaged, and tagged me in posts sharing their love for the Chief Maggie Riley books! Your support means the world to me!

A special thank you to super-readers Angela Frank, Heather Flaherty, and Heather Morrison for their amazing support! I'm so glad we've become friends!

Endless thanks to all the readers, reviewers, BookTokers, Bookstagrammers, book tweeters, bloggers, book clubs, and librarians out there who spend so much of their valuable time sharing book love and reviews!

Please don't underestimate how important you are! Knowing that there are people who enjoyed reading the book you've spent so much time, sweat, isolation, and occasionally tears on is a tremendous feeling, and your kind words get me through the days when I want to pull my hair out while obsessing over a plot twist, character arc, or sometimes even just a single sentence or word.

A huge thank you to my editor for this book, Nina Winters (no relation to Steve). This was our first time working together, and it was a fantastic experience. This book is so much better than what I first gave you, and I can't thank you enough for that!

Thank you to copy editor Ian Hodder for cleaning up my misplaced modifiers, dangling participles, compounds that need hyphens, and the other finer points of grammar I like to pretend don't exist, as well as for spotting opportunities to make the story stronger! And thank you to Deborah Blake for her eagle eyes on the proof!

Thank you to Lisa Brewster at the Brewster Project for another gorgeous cover!

Many sincere thank yous to the publishing team at Bookouture, especially those whose hands, talent, and skill have touched this book and helped make it into what it is today! Thank you to the wonderful publicity and social media team, who work tirelessly to get our books out there, and to my fellow Bookouture authors, who are unbelievably friendly and supportive across both genres and oceans!

To my mom, Stacy, who instilled in me my love of both reading and writing—thank you so much for all your encouragement, for being the shoulder I cry on in times of need, and the one I laugh hysterically with.

Thank you to my dad, who never got to see me live my dream but had faith that I'd one day make it happen.

Thank you to my grandmother, Marvis, for introducing me to the work of so many great authors over the years who have influenced my own writing, for always feeding my book addiction, for all your support, and for giving me the nerves of steel needed to stomach things dark and gritty!

Thank you to my husband, Ben, for pep talks and days of fun, for hiking, camping, and adventuring, and for being my partner in crime (while at the same time doing your best to keep me out of trouble). It's been a really tough year—thank you for holding my hand through it.

And to my sweet, sweet Sully. This was by far the hardest book I've ever written. Though we started it together, I was forced to finish without you. Thank you for being my guy. Miss you, baby bear.

Copyeditor
Ian Hodder

Proofreader
Deborah Blake

Marketing
Alex Crow
Melanie Price
Occy Carr
Cíara Rosney
Martyna Młynarska

Operations and distribution
Marina Valles
Stephanie Straub
Joe Morris

Production
Hannah Snetsinger
Mandy Kullar
Ria Clare
Nadia Michael

Publicity
Kim Nash
Noelle Holten
Jess Readett
Sarah Hardy

Rights and contracts
Peta Nightingale
Richard King
Saidah Graham